David Makes A Decision

Andrew Croughton

Pine Tree Press

2 Pine Tree Drive
Barnwood
Gloucester
GL4 3LJ

ISBN: 978-0-9526501-1-9

Preface

David Anderson is a widower of just a few months, with adult children. Eleanor Jenkins is a sixteen year old schoolgirl in the same church. The circumstances which bring them together reveal a maturity beyond Eleanor's years. Despite the age gap, a genuine friendship develops between them based on mutual interests and church service.

As their friendship continues, they both develop more than just a platonic interest in each other. Eventually, Eleanor's parents become aware of their friendship, and tell her in no uncertain terms that she must end it.

Now the problems start. Commandment number six states: "Honour your father and your mother." The Apostle Paul said that children should obey their parents. What does honour mean? Should the obedience be for ever? Even over matters of the heart? Should Eleanor obey or disobey her parents?

For David there is the issue of heart or head. His heart says one thing but his head tell him another. Should he end the friendship? Things need to be resolved, one way or another.

Chapters

Chapter 1

Airport Run

David was not pleased when the phone rang at 3.30 a.m. Although he had a bedside phone, the ringer was turned off, so it was the hall phone which woke him. He was tempted to ignore it, and let the answer machine deal with it, but then he thought it could be family. He picked it up groggily.

"Hello," he said slowly.

"David, it's Mark," the voice said. "Mark Rogers." Mark Rogers was the assistant pastor.

"Mark? Is there a problem?"

"Yes, I'm afraid there is. It's to do with the young people coming back to Heathrow this morning. It's Eleanor's dad's car. It won't start."

David's brain was still sluggish. Young people returning to Heathrow? Then he remembered. The group was referred to as 'young adults,' and they had been out in Romania helping at a church and an orphanage. Eleanor was among them. "His car won't start?" he said slowly.

"Yes, and he is supposed to be going to Heathrow to pick up our young people. He's just phoned me, but my car is in dock. I mean at the garage which means I can't go. The others have gone on without him."

"Oh! Yes, I'm with you now. Right, so you're stuck. Do you want me to go?"

"Would you? I'd be very grateful. By the time he gets Green Flag, it will be too late. The others have had to go on."

"Okay. So, I need directions. Let me get a pencil."

Twelve minutes later he was on the way. In that time he had written down the information on where to meet, dressed, made coffee – some to drink and some into a flask. The plan had been to arrive at the airport after the plane had landed, and shortly before the party would clear customs. It was a 'just-in-time' arrangement, and such arrangements did not allow for emergencies. However, Mark had already checked the latest flight details on the internet, and if David did not hang about – a euphemism for putting his foot down – Mark thought he would make it in time.

"Do they know about Eleanor's dad?" David asked.

"I texted someone saying either he would be late, or someone else would turn up." Mark said. The roads were clear, and David did 'put his foot down' although not without a twinge of conscience. He drove towards the dawn, and by the time he had reached Heathrow, it was getting light. He found a place to park in the short stay car-park and ran towards the arrivals hall, looking around for the drivers, and also for the signs which displayed the arrivals. He had been given the flight number, and saw that first. Then he recognised the other three drivers – all parents – and went across. They were obviously very relieved to see him, and were wondering what the latest situation was.

"Mr Jenkins couldn't get his car going so he phoned Mark, who then phoned me. Mark's car is out of commission at the moment," David informed them.

"Well, glad you made it in time," someone said.

"Only just. Look, they're coming through."

There were fifteen of them. A young married couple leading the party, then six boys and seven girls. They walked through, three with large haversacks, the others with cases, two of them quite large, and then waved as they spotted their reception. There were hugs all round, but David hung back. He wasn't directly involved with any of the youth activities, although of course, he did know their names. He also carefully avoided being close to Eleanor, or even looking at her directly. He was aware that his heart was beating faster. and he was relieved when Philip, the married leader, came across.

"Hi, David. So where's Ellie's dad?"

"Car problem. Mark phoned me this morning. I said you should walk home."

Philip grinned, and punched him lightly on the arm.

"Thanks for coming. I appreciate it." Then he turned to the others. "Okay folks, let's go."

"Yes, Moses," someone muttered.

"Hey," that person's parent said. "We could leave you here!"

"Or put her on the roof rack," Philip added.

Once outside and in the car park, the young people tended to get into groups, based on who was who's mother. Tom's mother was speaking to Tasha, and suggesting that Philip and Tasha should join her and Tom. Philip walked over to David, with Eleanor.

"Where's your car, David?"

"It's down the other end."

"Right, can you take Ellie, obviously, and … " he looked around. "Fee?" he called.

"She's with her dad," Eleanor said quietly.

"Oh yes. Um. Where's Sue?" But Sue was already in a car, as were most of the others. "Bother," Philip said.

"Don't worry, Philip, I'm sure David won't eat me," Eleanor said.

"Oh," Philip said. The word eat reminded him of something else. "Did you bring any breakfast for Ellie?"

"No, sorry. Should I have done?"

"Ellie's dad was supposed to. Oh dear. Would you like mine, Ellie? Apparently, Tom's mum has bought some for Tasha and me?"

"Thanks for the offer, Philip," Eleanor said sweetly. "But look, I think they are waiting for you."

"And I'll buy her breakfast on the way, Philip, all right?"

Philip hesitated, but someone then sounded a car horn, so he turned to walk to his lift. David picked up Eleanor's bag, and led the way along to his car. He unlocked and lifted his tailgate to put Eleanor's case into his boot as Eleanor slid in to her seat, with her cabin bag on her lap.

"Shall I put that behind you?"

"Yes, please, David," she said, this time with a smile. That smile. David thought that his heart would stop as he walked round to his side and slid into the driver's seat.

"Coffee," he said, reaching for his flask.

"Yes, please."

He half-filled the cup and handed it to her. She took it and began to sip it. "What about you?" she said suddenly, stopping.

"I'll have what you don't want," he replied.

"Here," she said immediately.

"No, drink some more, there's more in the flask."

"So why no breakfast? Didn't they serve breakfast?" David asked a few moments later.

"Breakfast was quite a bit extra. Anyway, I wasn't hungry then."

"What about now?"

"I'm okay, thanks"

"So if I stop for breakfast, you won't mind," David said, starting the car. The others had already gone.

"No, of course not."

"Eleanor!"

"What?"

David laughed. "You mean you could watch me eat a bacon butty, and not mind? What's got into you?"

Eleanor didn't answer.

"Well," David said more quietly.

"I didn't fix this," she said.

"Fix what?"

"Fix it so that I would be in your car."

David turned to her. "I didn't say you had, Eleanor."

"No, but you might be thinking it."

"I didn't. Whatever gave you that idea?" he said, turning briefly to look at her, but she didn't answer. "Okay, tell me about it, I mean, Romania," he added, partly to change the subject.

Eleanor paused. "David, you wouldn't believe how poor some of the people are. The gypsies, I mean. Oh, the capital city looked quite modern in places, but once outside." She shuddered, and David waited. Finally he spoke again.

"But you are glad you went?"

"Yes. I think we did some good, and it certainly did me some good."

"And do the others feel the same way?"

"I think so. We didn't talk much coming back partly because we were tired. I did manage a short nap on the plane."

"Do you want to sleep now?"

"I thought you wanted to hear about it."

"I do, but only if you feel up to it."

"Okay."

Eleanor began to tell David about the visit, with him asking the odd question here and there. There were occasional pauses, when David suddenly realised that the last pause was not in fact a pause – she had gone to sleep. David drove on in silence, and then left the motorway, but moderating his speed so as not to disturb her. However, it was the sideways force on a roundabout that woke her.

"Have I been asleep?" she said.

"Yes, princess," David replied.

"Princess?"

"Sleeping beauty," he said. "Go back to sleep."

"I don't feel a beauty at the moment," she said, closing her eyes again.

Within seconds, it seemed to David, she appeared to be fast asleep again.

"You are a beautiful person as well," he said very quietly, and after a few minutes. "Totally and thoroughly." He paused. "Oh, Eleanor, I have missed seeing you." He sighed.

"And I've missed you too, David," she said.

"Eleanor!" he gasped. "I thought you were asleep." She opened her eyes again, and smiled at him, making his heart lurch. "Eleanor, you weren't supposed to hear that," he said.

"Why?"

"You know why."

"I know. It's inappropriate. That word again. But is it true?"

"Is what true?"

"That you missed me?"

"Of course it's true. Now go back to sleep."

Eleanor shut her eyes again, and David assumed that the conversation was over. Then she spoke again. "I'm glad it's just the two of us."

David said nothing.

"Shall I tell you why?"

"Go on."

"Because you wouldn't have said something inappropriate if someone else was with us." She waited.

"True," he said quietly.

"But I'm glad you said it."

"Eleanor, Eleanor, please."

"David, I liked doing things with you. What is wrong with that?"

David didn't answer.

"Unless you didn't like being with me," she whispered.

"Eleanor. Stop it."

"So can we do things together again. Things that we both like, if we're discreet?"

"Eleanor, it's not just about being discreet." David said quietly. "It's about being wise."

"As apart from being inappropriate?" Eleanor asked.

"What do you think?"

"It's not as if we're making love or something."

"Eleanor!" David was shocked, and it showed. But it wasn't just that she had used those words. He had had to make himself not consider those actions. But he had been tempted, – sorely tempted – just to wonder, but only vaguely and briefly, that is before he stopped his

mind from dwelling on the subject. "Eleanor," he
repeated, but this time in a whisper, "you shouldn't talk
like that."

"Sorry, David." She said it quietly. "But is it so wrong
to be friends?"

David didn't answer.

"David. I'm sorry about my comment just then, but
being friends doesn't necessarily mean a boyfriend
girlfriend relationship, especially in our situation,"
Eleanor said.

"Our situation?"

"Yes, you being a teacher and me a school-girl. I'm not
stupid, you know."

"Do you have a boyfriend?" David asked.

"No."

"Why not?"

"Why not?" Eleanor repeated.

"Yes, why not?" David repeated.

"Because … ," Eleanor began. "Hey, isn't that rather
personal? Suppose I asked you? Oh, no – that wouldn't
be right."

"Eleanor, good friends can speak about anything. Good
friends only want the best for each other. Jenny and I
talked about being left alone, and we both agreed that
remarriage was fine – should we find someone
appropriate – I certainly wouldn't have wanted Jenny
to be alone. So, in answer to your unspoken question, I
haven't met anyone appropriate yet."

"I didn't mean to pry. Anyway, isn't it still too early?"
Eleanor asked.

"Eleanor, do you want the best for me? If you know of
a suitable female, then you should introduce us."

"So we can be friends?" Eleanor said.

"Yes," David said, and paused. "In fact, I'd like to

think of you as a special friend."

"Special friend?"

"Yes, friends that want the best for each other. Friends that can talk about anything. Friends that can enjoy doing things together from time to time. But," he paused and looked at her briefly, "because of the circumstances, we will be very, very discreet. Now let's change the subject. Tell me more about your visit to Romania now you are awake again."

At that moment David spotted a food wagon, so he slowed, indicated, and pulled into the lay-by.

"Why are we stopping?" Eleanor asked.

"Breakfast." he said, smiling at her. "For both of us." Fifteen minutes later, with coffee and a bacon-bap inside both of them, they set off again. This time Eleanor closed her eyes and laid her head back, and within minutes, she was asleep.

Chapter 2

Sudden Loss

David had often wondered how he would cope with bereavement. Both his parents were still alive, and in such good health that the idea of them passing away in the near future was never considered. But it would have to happen one day, he knew. Did people cope better with death if it was sudden and unexpected compared to, say, an illness that finally took its toll. A sudden death would come as a shock. There would be no goodbyes. It meant no sad time leading up to the final step and one would have only good memories. On the other hand, would it be better to have time to prepare oneself for the inevitable loss? Because they had children, David and Jenny had made wills, but of course they didn't expect they would be needed for a very long time. David had sometimes joked that if anything were to happen to Jenny, then the first thing he would have to do would be to ask Jill, his daughter, how to work the washing machine. Oh, and the oven. Jenny was emphatic that he would need to remarry, and he had assured Jenny that he would not want her to be alone, especially as he reminded her, she couldn't re-washer a tap.

But it did happen, and much earlier than they had anticipated. They had two months notice, well, the doctor said three months, but he was being optimistic. Jenny was surprisingly well for most of that time. In fact, she had time to write copious notes on how he was to manage the house. She gave David a new birthday book with all the relevant birthdays marked in it. She organised who was to sort out her clothes and shoes, and which charities were to benefit. David refused point blank to let her teach him how to cook and use the washing machine. It had not been part of their life, and it wasn't going to be part of it then. Fortunately, for both of them, a good number of friends at their church had stepped in with casseroles and cakes. And another friend had taken some ironing, much to Jenny's shame. David said he would learn when the time was right, which meant, when she was no longer with him.

For the two months he had tried to be positive. Jenny certainly was. She was sad to leave him alone, but she knew that their two children would support their father. Her last three days were spent in a coma, with the Macmillan nurses giving their support. On the day she died, he seemed to be in a trance himself. The undertaker came and went. The house was empty – or so it seemed. Daniel, his son, helped him with the inevitable rounds. Undertaker. Registrar. Local newspaper. Phoning people. He even took some of the phone calls on behalf of his dad. Friends at the church organised the post-funeral refreshments. The funeral came and went. People said it was a very nice service. Daniel and Jill together read out a eulogy, partly written by Jenny herself, and then modified by the two children. The post-committal gathering was enormous. Jenny was well known and loved by many, and David had so many people shake his hand and express their condolences, that even that became a blur. He was glad when Daniel steered him out and took him home. Jill arrived, with her husband, and they sat talking about Jenny until David suddenly realised that it was late.

"Jill. You're still here. Shouldn't you be getting back to the baby?" he said. Jill's husband looked relieved, but kept quiet.

"Whenever," she replied, quietly.

David stood up. "No. Keith, thank you for bringing Jill," he said to Keith. "Now please take her home."

They left ten minutes later. That left just David and Daniel.

"She was a good mum," David said.

"She was, Dad, she was," Daniel agreed.

"She gave you a good hiding that time you swore at her."

"Then she washed my mouth out with soap," Daniel said, and they laughed.

"If you find a wife who's even half as good a wife as your mum was, you'll be in clover." He paused. "But don't tell her that – in fact, never compare your future wife unfavourably to your mum. You'll be in the dog house. So long as she can cook, you'll be fine."

Daniel kept quiet; his mother had been a good cook, but he fancied he would want more than just cooking in a wife. Such a subject was not appropriate. "Yes, Dad," he finally said.

Daniel left the next morning, leaving his father feeling quite bleary. David had always been quick to get to sleep. He was also quick to wake up, and had been known to do a spot of gardening in his pyjamas before breakfast in the summer months. Now that changed. He could not get to sleep quickly, and as a consequence, he was always tired in the mornings. Jill made frequent visits to see how David was coping. He was coping, he assured them. His week-day life was based on school, but the days seemed to pass in a blur. He got up, went to work, came home, made a simple meal, did some marking, and went to bed. He was a geography teacher, and if it hadn't been for the fact that he had already become a popular and established teacher with classes in which one didn't muck about, life would have become very difficult. He was living on his reputation and the good will that he had banked over the years. But now there was no joy in his work. He told no jokes. He rarely smiled.

At weekends he followed a routine he had devised. Saturdays were house-keeping days. Washing machine on for first load. Visit to supermarket for weekly shop, which included some fresh fruit and vegetables – potatoes and carrots, apples and bananas. Always the same. But runner beans would be added when in season. Sometimes he bought tomatoes and a lettuce, at first only because he knew that Jenny would want him to. Back home, empty washing machine and do second wash, if needed. Then prepare dinner. Clean house – that took him back to his teenage years where he vacuumed the whole house for his mum for his allowance. Eat dinner. Then it was back to the kitchen to plan and partially prepare the weeks evening meals. (His midday meals at school were based on rolls filled with cheese or corned beef, another carrot, a tomato and if available, a lettuce leaf – or two.) These evening meals were usually based on pasta or rice, meat from a can, carrots and (frozen) peas. The rice and pasta were cooked on the Saturday, separated into batches, allowed to cool, and then frozen. That way, once back from school, he only had to heat the component parts rather than cook them. Brilliant things, microwave ovens, he thought. Even better than sliced bread. His proper oven, as he called it, did get used occasionally on a Saturday or a Sunday. To heat a certain brand of steak and kidney pie. He hadn't a clue, or the inclination to make a roast dinner. Puddings, or sweets as some people called them were always the same. Yoghurt and cereal, or rice/semolina/tapioca from a can. After a while, he added grapes to his fruit purchase.

Saturday nights were hard, and spent alone at home with the TV for company. Sometimes he took himself to the cinema, and then regretted the waste of money – unless it was a film he particularly wanted to see. Sundays were again different. There were two church services. Sometimes he was invited out for Sunday dinner – and he did appreciate the Sunday roast. He decided to dig out his old bike and use it. It was a bit of a shock to the system, but he got into the habit, weather permitting – and it had to be very bad to stop him – of going for longish bike rides. Long depends on the person doing the measuring, and David set himself between six and ten miles. He could daydream as he rode, remembering some of the good times. He thought that the exercise also helped him sleep better that night.

He had a faith, and in his heart he believed that Jenny was now in a better place, and that one day they would meet again. Mind you, he knew the teaching that in heaven there would be no marriage, and he did wonder what it would be like to meet his wife in a non-marital situation. Because of this, he believed that re-marriage on earth would not be a problem in terms of life after death but even so, he didn't expect to remarry. He couldn't imagine wanting to live with anyone else, and for a long time, he felt no need to remarry. His libido had died along with Jenny, or so it seemed. How much of this was due to grief, and how much was due to tiredness, he didn't know. It just didn't bother him – until one day at a bus stop he realised that he was looking at a woman with more than just academic interest. It shook him, and immediately he felt guilty of entertaining lust. It wasn't really lust, but it could have moved in that direction. But he also felt disloyal to Jenny's memory. It was then that he knew he would never remarry. Not that he knew even how to chat up a woman, as the expression was. The problem was that he was beginning to experience the feelings of being a man. And the apostle Paul said it was better to marry than to burn. All very well for the apostle – but there was no one that David would want to marry anyway. He had many happy years to remember and dwell on, so why introduce new memories?

Then something happened after about three months. One of the old ladies at church asked how Jenny was because she hadn't seen her around that morning. It was well known that the old lady was very forgetful, maybe even moving towards dementia, and she meant no harm. David knew that, but he couldn't stop what happened next. He felt himself welling up. Turning away, he went up to the balcony and found a quiet corner. Now he couldn't stop himself. He used his handkerchief to muffle the sound, and sat there sobbing quietly. He had been there for several minutes when he was disturbed by a discreet cough. It was a girl, and he knew her name was Eleanor, although her friends had shortened it. Eleanor was holding a cup.

"Mr Anderson, would you like a cup of tea?" she asked quietly, before he could say anything. "When Mum's gran died, Mum said it helped," she added.

David took it and she turned to go. "Don't go," David said.

Eleanor paused.

"How did you know I was up here?" David asked. "Does anyone else know?"

"No, I don't think so."

"So how did you know I was up here?"

"I heard what Mrs Cuthbert said, and saw that you were hurt. I don't think she meant it," Eleanor replied.

"I know she didn't. It's not her fault," David said, feeling embarrassed.

"I'll leave you now," Eleanor said, and this time she did go.

David sat sipping the tea. Tea was not a drink he made at home, and in fact, he usually didn't like tea at all. But somehow, it did help, and he was grateful to Eleanor for bringing it, all the more so as he didn't really know her. He remembered her baptism, mainly for the way she had spoken. Baptism can be a problem in a Baptist church in the way that confirmation can be in the Anglican church. It can become the expected thing to do at a certain age, especially among a group of young people. Sometimes he felt that the testimonies sounded a little artificial, but then he felt guilty of being judgemental. He had noticed that some candidates were no longer with the church a year or two later. Sometimes it was what people called church-hopping, but for some it was because nothing serious had taken place inside them. Eleanor's testimony had not been composed of the stock phrases that tended to be used, and there was something about it that had impressed him at the time. It had struck him that she was obviously very mature for her age. On the other hand, maybe it was because she was a girl. There was certainly a difference between the two sexes in his school.

He finished his tea, but didn't go back down until he judged that most of the congregation had vacated the premises. Then he walked down and made for the toilet in order to wash his face. By the time he came out, he felt almost normal. Nobody seemed to notice him as he left the empty cup by the kitchen door, slipped out and went home. He felt a little guilty that he had not shown his appreciation properly, but he decided that he would thank her that evening. But she wasn't there that evening, and by the time a week had passed, he thought it best just to say nothing.

That was the only time that he broke down in public, well almost in public and Eleanor was the only person who knew. There had been evenings alone at home when things got on top of him, and he would then cry for a while. As the weeks passed, these sessions became less frequent. Then after four months of being a widower, something began to nag at him. He began to consider his future more seriously. According to actuarial data, there were still many years ahead of him, God willing, as the pastor sometimes said, and he wanted to do something that was more worth-while than teaching kids about people, places, cities, lands, mountains and rivers. He couldn't enthuse about those things any more. This led on to him feeling depressed, something that he had never experienced before, and which bothered him. Should he seek medication, or counselling? Then the crying sessions began again.

James, the church pastor just happened to arrive one evening and witnessed the situation. Of course he thought it was grief, and addressed David accordingly.
"No, I'm not crying for Jenny, James. I've come to terms with that – at least I thought I had. And I think I'm coping reasonably well," David said. "I just feel, well, useless, I suppose."
"Useless? But you have an important job."
"Is it really that important – learning which river starts where and ends where?"
"Come on, there's more to geography than that."
"Okay, I suppose there is. It's just that I can't see the point right now."

The Pastor paused. "Do you need to do it. I mean, do you need the," he hesitated, "the income?"

"That's another thing. I do need an income, but not as much as I did. Jenny's death meant that the mortgage was paid off."

"Could you go part-time?" James asked.

"I don't know. I'm head of department but maybe it might be possible. Why do you ask? How would it help me?"

"Well this isn't widely known but Mark, my assistant pastor, wants to take some time off."

"And?"

"Well, Mark would be happy, happier, if he thought someone could stand in for him – not for all of his work – maybe a couple of days a week. I would be very, very happy if it was you."

"Are you serious? I mean I don't have any theological training."

"And did Peter? Anyway, I didn't mean preaching or teaching. Mark works part-time in the church. He is also a qualified accountant, so he works two days a week at home on that. He is the church administrator, again, part time, and finally, yes, he has been to bible college, so he helps me with the pastoral work. Two of the church elders can help with the pastoral aspects. We need someone to cover his admin responsibilities."

"Can I think about it?" David said.

David made his decision quickly. His first step had been to have a chat with his head-master about moving to teaching part-time. The headmaster had been expecting to receive David's resignation, having noticed, and not without sympathy and understanding, that David wasn't the man he had been. Furthermore, it was almost the end of May, the deadline for resignations.

"Oh, well," he said, thinking at the same time. "Look, I'll have to have a chat with Symes, about whether he thinks he could timetable you in a part-time capacity. So what will you do with yourself if it is possible? Some people would say that keeping busy is one way to deal with one's problems."

"Actually, it was my pastor who suggested the idea," David said. " He thinks that he can find me plenty to do, especially as our assistant pastor is having a break."

"Okay, but what about when he returns?"

"We've talked about that. I shall find something else, but in the voluntary sector. Who knows, I might want to become a full time teacher again - that's if you'll have me."

"Of course I would, David. When you asked to see me, I was half expecting you to hand in your resignation."

"Even that had crossed my mind," David said. "but I think this is the best thing for me, at the moment."

The headmaster called David back two days later.

"David, just to let you know how things stand. We've had an application for a history post, and the applicant has stated that he is a humanities graduate, and would be happy to teach some geography. Symes thinks he could reduce you down to three and a half days – that's if you don't mind taking on a young teacher to cover your junior classes. Could you still manage a department on three and a half days? I would also expect you to be at heads of department meetings and staff meetings."

"Of course," David replied.

"And when is this pastor chappy thinking of going off?"

"August. For six months."

"Six months? Does that mean you'll want to come back in the new year – Easter?"

"No, no. I think I should give it a year, don't you?"

"And what then?"

"To be honest, I don't know. Just knowing that it might now happen is making me feel better already."

"David, it's not settled yet, so don't get too excited."

"I realise that, Headmaster. Let's hope it does work out."

A few days later, it was settled. The new teacher would teach both history and geography, and David would work three days a week.

Chapter 3

A New friendship

As soon as it was settled, it was as if an elephant which had been on David's shoulders had decided to move on. On the one hand, he still had a career to hang on to, but on the other, he didn't feel that he was tied so strongly to it. He knew he was much too young to consider early retirement. The only other alternative would have been to resign from his job, but he didn't have the courage, let alone the will to do that. This seemed a good compromise. The six months with his church would keep him occupied, and following that, he would have time to think about his role in life. Meanwhile, he had the end of term to think about - examinations and reports.

It was a week later when David met Eleanor again. He had gone into town on a Saturday by bus – mainly because he wasn't sure about the parking situation – and was therefore on the bus home. A group of school girls got on, giggling and laughing. It wasn't the noise they were making that got his attention, it was that they were wearing uniform on a Saturday. The pupils at his school were loath to wear uniform on a school day, let alone at the weekend. As he was about to return to his free newspaper, one of the girls turned. Their eyes met, and with a little start, he recognised Eleanor. She recognised David at the same time, smiled, and raised her hand in a greeting. Taken aback, he nodded rather curtly, and then dropped his eyes. The reason for his surprise was that only a couple of months earlier, a similar situation had occurred, but with another teenage girl from his church.

The girl must have known who he was, but having made eye contact, she then looked away and moved past him.

When David looked up again, Eleanor had turned back to her friends and was talking to them. He heard the bell ping for someone to get off the bus, and then realised that it was the passenger next to him. But once the bus had stopped, he noticed that Eleanor's three friends were also among the leavers. Eleanor tuned round and smiled at him again, and then walked towards him.

"May I?" she asked, pointing at the newly vacated seat. For a second, he froze. "Yes, of course," he replied. Eleanor slid onto the seat next him. "Car problems?" she asked.

"Car problems?" David replied, puzzled by her question. "No. Oh, you mean why am I on the bus. It's hard to park in town on Saturday afternoon so this was easier. What about you?"

"School do," she said. with a grimace.

"On a Saturday afternoon?"

"Yes. Bit of a pain, actually, what with exam revision as well."

"Exams?"

Eleanor stared at him for a moment. "Weren't you listening on Sunday? The Pastor prayed for the people who'll be doing exams."

"Oh yes. Sorry, it hadn't clicked. So, which exams?"

"Mr Anderson, do you know what year I am in?"

David hesitated. Did teenage girls want to be thought of as older? His own daughter had always wanted to be thought of as much older than she really was. How old was she anyway? "Er, year twelve, or do you call it lower sixth?"

Eleanor laughed. "I'm sixteen, and doing my GCSEs."

"Oh," he said, relieved that she hadn't taken offence. "So what was this do?" he added, partly to change the subject. David nearly missed his own stop as he then found himself listening and chatting to Eleanor as though they were old friends as she told him about her afternoon. "See you tomorrow," she called to him as he moved towards the exit.

David felt quite strange as he walked home. Part of it was that he had been chatting to a female in a natural, relaxed and familiar way – something he was quite unused to. However, it was the fact that this female was a sixteen year-old girl. He taught sixteen year-olds, and there was no way that he could feel so familiar with them. Yet when he remembered how Eleanor had brought him that cup of tea, then it didn't seem so odd. She was obviously a very mature young lady.

David biked to his church the next morning feeling slightly apprehensive. Part of him wanted to continue the conversation with Eleanor, yet part of him felt it was foolish, if not inappropriate even to think about it. However, he didn't even see her until after he was in his seat, and Eleanor then entered with her friends. In a way, David felt relieved that he hadn't had to meet her face to face. He didn't know that Eleanor was going to take part in the service, but he already knew that she had a good voice, and that she sang with one of the boys in the youth group. This time he found that his attention was riveted. The boy played a guitar, but he knew that Eleanor could also play. The morning service was followed by coffee, and some people tended to fall into groups. Eleanor was with a group of her friends across the hall, and David smiled to himself as he thought about her remark as he had left her on the bus. A typical throwaway comment meaning nothing? He took his empty mug to the kitchen hatch, and was then engaged in a brief conversation. Turning round, he then nearly bumped into Eleanor as she brought her cup to the hatch. She spoke first.

"Hello, Mr Anderson," she said brightly.

"Hello, Eleanor," he replied. He paused. "Eleanor," he added, "I did enjoy your singing."

"Thank you," she replied graciously. Then there was a silence, possibly an embarrassing silence as David wondered if he should have made the comment. "Oh, Mr Anderson, I meant to have said yesterday," she added, and then stopped.

"Said what?"

"I was with Mum on Friday after school. We went to the cemetery – my mum's nan is buried there." She stopped, and David waited. "It's none of my business, but when we walked around, we saw your wife's grave."

"Go on," he said quietly. He thought he knew what was coming.

"The flowers need replacing. Sorry, I know it's none of my business."

"Flowers?" he said, wondering what she was talking about.

"Yes, they had died."

David stared at her. "Eleanor, I haven't put any flowers there recently. I'm waiting for the headstone to be put in position. I thought that's what you were referring to."

This time it was Eleanor who paused. "I'm sure we had the right grave," she said quietly. "Both Mum and I noticed, I mean, we both read the name on the brass plate. Perhaps someone has moved them."

"I'll go and check this afternoon," David said.

"I'm sorry, I didn't mean to intrude," Eleanor said.

"No, thank you for telling me. I wonder where the

flowers came from. I don't have any to replace them. Was it a vase, or a jar?"

"Just a small jar. Mr Anderson, would you like me to bring you some? I'm sure Mum wouldn't mind."

"That's very kind of you, but I don't want to put you out."

"It's no trouble, honestly."

"Sure?"

"Yes, really. Shall I bring you some after lunch?"

"Well, that would be very kind of you. Thank you."

David ate his lunch feeling apprehensive again. He couldn't remember the last time he had been visited by a single female. Still, she was only bringing some flowers. But who had put the other ones on the grave? Unless Eleanor and her mum were mistaken. Maybe he should ask Eleanor to show him – then he would know, especially if the unknown person had left a note. After lunch he just pottered around, waiting, and still wondering about the mystery flower person. He didn't have to wait too long though, and the sound of his door-bell brought him back to the present time. Eleanor was standing on his door-step, holding her bicycle and panting slightly.

"Hello, Mr Anderson. Sorry I'm late. Do you think these will do?" she said, holding out a small bunch of flowers.

"They're very nice," David replied. He didn't know much about flowers, apart from the common kind – daffodils, tulips, roses, daisies and buttercups. Oh, and carnations. He did like carnation evaporated milk. The garden had been Jenny's preserve, apart from mowing the lawn. The lawn had been his pride and joy. "Look, I've been thinking," he continued. "Are you sure about the grave?"

Eleanor paused. "Well, I was. Do you think I made a mistake?"

David shrugged. "I can't say. Can you describe where it was?"

"I could show you, that is, if you didn't mind."

"Are you sure? What about your revision?"

"I'm okay with that – so long as we don't take too long. I'm on my way to see a friend."

David slipped Eleanor's bicycle into his garage and they left, in his car.

"Are you sure that your mum doesn't mind?" David asked, indicating the flowers, now on Eleanor's lap.

Eleanor giggled. "I didn't actually ask her. I just picked a few from here and there."

"Eleanor!" David gasped.

"Well, it was very small jar. She won't miss just a few." She turned and grinned at him. "Do you think I should take them back?"

"Perhaps I should arrest you for theft," he said.

Eleanor laughed again. This time it was as though something stabbed him. It brought back memories – memories of laughter, but from Jenny. He had to grit his teeth and hold onto the steering wheel tightly. He felt vulnerable again, just like that time in the church – no more Jenny. They had talked about being the one left alone, and Jenny had made it clear that she hoped he would find another person to share what was left of his life. She had reminded him of this in those last few weeks, but he had dismissed the idea. If the presence of a mere school-girl stirred up memories, how would he cope if he met a single adult female? Would he ever have another relationship? Would he ever want another relationship?

"Are you all right?" Eleanor asked, noting his silence.

"Yes, I'm fine," he said, turning and smiling at her. Thank goodness she was only a girl, he thought, feeling at ease again. No complications. Pity she's so pretty, especially when she smiles.

It was a ten minute or so drive to the cemetery. David parked, and they walked across together. David suddenly stopped. "Water. We need water." he said.

"There's a tap in the corner, Mr Anderson," Eleanor replied. "I'll go."

But she didn't. When they reached the grave – and it was the one that Eleanor had seen – there were no flowers – not even an empty jar.

"I don't get it," Eleanor said. "There were definitely flowers here on Friday."

"Sure?"

Eleanor turned to David. "Yes, I am sure. I'm not stupid, Mr Anderson," she said quietly.

David laughed. "Calm down , Eleanor. I didn't say you were."

"You probably think I am though."

"It was probably some people messing about. I have a very high opinion of you, so don't put yourself down."

"Do you?"

"Yes. Now let's go back. Perhaps you will let me have the flowers instead. I mean, you can't take them home, can you? Oh, and another thing, please don't keep on calling me Mr Anderson. I do have a first name. It's David."

As they walked back to the car park, David explained why there was still only a wooden cross and not a proper stone to mark the grave. "I've got to go in this week and choose a stone. Oh, and tell them what to write. Then they will put it in place."

"Have you decided what you want on the stone?"

"I think so. They will leave a space for when it's my turn."

"In the same grave?"

"Yes, you can have up to four coffins in one grave."

"Four? Is that in case you remarry?"

David laughed. "No. I imagine it's for children. Although I suppose that might happen in some cases. Yes, come to think of it, I think I've seen it on old tombstones. The second woman was born too early to be a daughter. Mary, born, say, 1800, and died say 1830. Joseph born 1801 and died 1870, and then Martha, born 1810 and died 1890."

"I suppose it's logical. Would I want a second wife in the same grave as me?" Eleanor pondered.

David laughed again. "Eleanor, you wouldn't be aware of it, would you?"

"I suppose not. But if I was the second wife, how would I feel?"

David thought for a moment. "It depends on when you die. I mean, if you then outlived your husband, you could make the decision. If you died before him, he might pop you in the same hole."

"Mr Anderson," Eleanor began.

"Er, David," David interrupted.

"I'm not used to that," Eleanor said, turning towards him.

"Yet," David said quietly. Eleanor didn't respond which made David regret the remark. "Sorry, Eleanor, I didn't mean to be over familiar," he added.

"No, I'll try to get used to it," she replied, and smiled at him. That smile again, he thought.

They walked the rest of the way to the car in silence, and then drove back to David's home, again not talking. David was just about to apologise for his gaff when Eleanor spoke.

"Do you have a vase, er, David?"

"Of course. I have several."

"So you'll be able to look after these," she asked, referring to the bunch on her lap.

"Well, yes, I think."

"You think? Do you want me to do it?"

"Do you have the time, Eleanor? What about your friend?"

"It won't take long. Where are your vases?"

Five minutes later, the flowers were in an appropriately sized vase, and David retrieved Eleanor's bicycle from his garage.

"Eleanor, I really am grateful for your help," he said. "Sorry if I've made you late."

"That's what friends are for," she said, and smiling again. "See you later."

Chapter 4

A New Service

David went back in and sat in his lounge, pondering the situation. He had just been to Jenny's grave, accompanied by a school girl. A rather unusual school girl, well, compared to most of the girls he taught. So mature. But the most bizarre thing was that she had casually referred to him as a friend. Not a special friend, he realised, just another friend. He again compared her to his own pupils. No way could he ever regard one of them as a friend, in fact, he would hesitate to invite one of them into his home, let alone share a car ride. Yes, an odd situation. There was no point in going over it again, so he decided to get some exercise. He managed ten miles on his bicycle, which pleased him, but he found that he didn't leave his pondering at home. "Bother the girl," he thought. "She's got under my skin."

He very nearly remained at home that evening, but his conscience told him not to be silly. In fact, although they were both at the same meeting, their paths didn't cross. Later that evening, his thoughts turned to his next day at school, and he forgot about their earlier trip to the cemetery. The following Sunday at church passed with no contact, although their eyes did make brief contact across the room. She smiled, and lifted her hand in greeting, but that was all. When David went home, his mind was occupied with other thoughts. However, Eleanor spoke to him the next Sunday after the morning service.
"Mr, I mean, David, can I ask you something?"
"Of course. Questions are free, it's the answers that cost." he answered, rather flippantly.

Eleanor looked surprised, and David quickly followed it up. "Sorry, it's one of my school jokes."

"Oh."

"It's okay, you can groan. My kids at school do. Anyway, ask away."

"Well, when I did your flowers, I saw that you had a guitar. Do you play?"

"As apart from it being an ornament, you mean?" he said.

"No, no. I mean what do you play on it?"

"To be honest, I don't play it much now. I played what we called folk music at university, and I used to accompany Jenny. Jenny used to sing when we were young – sometimes we sang together."

"Sing? Where?"

"In our previous church."

"So why didn't you sing here?"

David shrugged. "Nobody asked us. Anyway, why are you asking?"

Eleanor hesitated. "You know Tom, the boy I often sing with?"

"Yes," David replied, guardedly.

"Didn't you notice? His arm's in a sling."

"Oh. I did. But it didn't strike me. What's he done?"

"Fallen off his bike."

"Mountain bike?" David asked.

"No! BMX of all things. At his age."

"You don't sound pleased."

"I'm not. We're meant to be singing again. Except he can't play his guitar."

"But you play," David said.

"Yes, but not as well as Tom. I just play along with him." She paused. "Could you help?"

"Help? How?"

"Play your guitar for us."

David shook his head slowly. "But Eleanor, I haven't played in public for years. Anyway, what does Tom think about it?"

"He's okay." She stood waiting, obviously not taking no for an answer.

"Eleanor, I would need to practise. A lot."

"That's okay, we have the whole afternoon," she said brightly.

"The whole afternoon? You mean it's tonight?" David gasped.

"Er, yes."

"Are you serious?"

Eleanor smiled, and nodded. "We could come to you, if you like."

David took a deep breath. "Okay, but on one condition. We do a lot of practising, and I have the final say."

"That's two conditions," Eleanor said. "But we accept them."

"We?"

Eleanor looked over David's shoulder, and beckoned to someone. It was Tom, standing behind him. "Don't we, Tom?" she said.

Tom stepped forward, looking rather sheepish, and nodded. "Yes," he replied.

Tom and Eleanor arrived together, soon after lunch, but brought by Tom's mum. Eleanor carried her guitar, and a folder. David had already checked the tuning of his guitar.

"When shall I collect them?" Tom's mum asked David, as they stepped inside.

"Oh, in about three hours," David said.

Tom's mother looked askance. "Three hours?"

"No, Mr Anderson was joking. Say an hour," Eleanor said.

"I'll bring them home," David said quickly. He wanted to take as long as it was necessary.

"Sure?" she said, looking worried.

"Yes, and it won't be in three hours, okay?"

David took Tom and Eleanor through to his lounge.

"Would either of you like a drink first," he asked, trying to be a proper host.

"No, thank you, Mr Anderson," Tom said.

"Tom, please call me David, okay? Eleanor?"

"No, thanks, David."

"Right, then, I suppose we'd better get on with it. Why don't you sing it to me first? Is that okay, Eleanor. I mean you're not in public now, are you?"

Eleanor took a sheet from her folder, and laid it on the carpet. David sat back, listening and watching as she played and sang with Tom, with a feeling of relief. It wasn't a complicated arrangement. Even so, David sensed that she lacked confidence on the guitar.

"You don't need me, Eleanor," he said, at the end of the song, mainly to boost her confidence.

"That's what I told her," Tom said. "Right, Elly?"

"It's as David says, we're not in public here," Eleanor replied, quietly. David wondered if there had been some disagreement about him helping them.

"But you don't mind singing in public?" David enquired.

Eleanor shrugged. "That's easier than playing," she said with a smile. "And anyway, Tom also sings."

"All right, let's try it them," David suggested. "Is there a copy for me, or do we share?"

They sat facing each other, and Eleanor shared with Tom, giving a sheet to David. He played along with them, just strumming, and it was noticeable to him that Eleanor played with more confidence this time. They did another two run-throughs, and then David asked about how they would be positioned.

"We assumed that you would stand with us," Eleanor said. "Is that okay?"

"Let's try it then," he suggested, getting up.

"Do you need Tom to hold the music, then," Eleanor asked.

"I'll try without, I think I know how it goes," David said. "How do you lead in?"

"Ah, that's what Tom did. I'm not doing that," Eleanor said.

"Tell me what you did, Tom, and I will try it, then we'll see how it sounds," David said. Ten minutes later, David thought it was good enough to have a break.

"Let's take a break, have a drink, and then have a couple more run-throughs," David said. "Then I'll take you both home."

David left Tom and Eleanor in his lounge, and went out to get glasses of juice for them.

"Can I ask you something?" he asked them, as they were drinking.

"Go on – mind you, even though questions are free, the answer might cost you." Eleanor answered with a grin.

Tom looked at her, surprised at her cheekiness.

"Good one, Eleanor," David replied, with a laugh. He turned to Tom. "Private joke, Tom." He paused. "What I was going to ask was, have you ever sung in harmony?"

"We have thought about it," Tom answered. "But no more than that. I mean, who would sing the tune part?"

"Well, you could try both ways. Eleanor could try something like a descant, or Tom could harmonise with Eleanor singing the melody."

"Today?" Eleanor asked.

"Not today," David said, smiling. "It might also depend

on the song, for example if there was a chorus, just use harmony there. Bear it in mind for another time."

They sang the song again and then prepared to leave.
"Can I look at your guitar," Tom asked.
"Sure."
Tom slipped his arm out from the sling, and David saw that there was strapping round his wrist.
"What have you done?" David asked.
"I fell off my bike," he replied sheepishly.
"No, to your arm."
"It's sprained, apparently. And maybe a hair-line fracture." He held the guitar carefully, turning it over in his hands, noting the controls on the side. "Where's the pickup?"
"In the bridge. It's a piezoelectric pickup, uses a transducer to convert the vibrations into voltage."
Tom handed it back. "Elly said you played folk style. What's that?" he asked David
David tucked the guitar under his arm, and sang a few lines accompanying himself in a finger-picking style. Tom was obviously impressed.
"Could you do that with our song?" he asked.
"To be honest, I'm not sure. I would need more practise by which time your wrist will be mended."
"I don't know about that. Doc said it would be sore for quite a while," Tom said glumly.
"So we may ask you to help again, if you don't mind," Eleanor added.
"We'll see, we'll see," David said. "Come on then."

David was surprisingly nervous that evening, which surprised him. After all, he had accompanied Jenny many times, but that was many years earlier. All he had to do was simply strum – nothing complicated. He stood to the left, and just behind Tom, played his introduction, and then accompanied them as planned. Then it was over. After the service a few people came up to him and expressed their surprise in seeing him take part. The pastor came up to him as well.

"David, you're a dark horse. I didn't know that you played the guitar. Anyway, how did you get involved?"

"Eleanor didn't feel happy playing on her own," David replied, "so they asked me to help." He shrugged.

"But I didn't know you played, so how did Elly know?"

"She'd seen my guitar," David replied casually.

"But why didn't we know about it?" the pastor persisted.

David shrugged again. "When we moved here, you seemed to well blessed, so we just kept quiet. Work and family kept us busy, I suppose."

"Well, now we know, maybe we'll see you again?"

David grunted in what he hoped was a non-committal way. "I may not be needed," he said.

Tom and Eleanor also came and thanked him, and again suggested that he helped them again. This time David said he would think about it. He did think about it, but only very briefly. There was school the next day to think about.

A fortnight later his feet were firmly back on the ground. Lazy children to chase up, examinations to set, and then mark, his car to have serviced, and domestic plans to implement. It was a Saturday, and he had just put his supermarket shopping away when the phone rang.

"David Anderson," he said.

"David, it's Eleanor."

"Eleanor? Hi."

"David, can Tom and I come to see you?"

"See me? Yes, when?"

"This afternoon, if that's okay with you."

"Okay, when?"

"Whenever convenient if that's okay."

"All right, say in an hour and a half?"

"Great. Thanks. See you, then."

Tom and Eleanor arrived exactly on time, on foot, and both carrying a guitar.

"I take it that your wrist has mended?" David said, as he opened the door to them. "Come in."

Tom grinned. "Well, not completely, look." he held up his left hand, and David could see that there was some strapping. "I can play a bit, and it hurts. That's why Elly insisted that we asked you again."

"And is this for tomorrow," David asked.

"No, next week," Eleanor replied.

"Oh. Oh," David said hesitantly.

"Is that a problem?" Eleanor asked.

"I'm not here next weekend. I'm going to my daughter's, then I'm seeing friends after that."

"Oh." This was from Tom, and he was obviously disappointed. "So there's no point in staying."

"Well, now you're here, why don't we have a practice?" David said.

"Really?" Tom said, showing some enthusiasm.

"Actually, he wanted to ask if he could try your guitar," Eleanor said.

"Elly!" Tom exclaimed.

"And ask you to show him how to play with your fingers," she added, grinning at him. This time Tom glared at her, but David laughed.

"No problem, Tom," David said. "Do you want to see my solid as well?"

"You have a solid as well?"

Tom's injury was to his left hand, so although he found the fret-board difficult to manage, his right hand was free to try the various picks that David showed him. Then David showed them his solid guitar and plugged it in before playing some tunes. Of course, the two young people didn't recognise them, but they were both impressed, especially when he asked them to accompany him with chord playing. After some time, they stopped as before for refreshments, then David suggested that they showed him what they were planning for the Sunday in a week's time. Since he did not expect to be present, he left his guitar, and sat to watch. Tom's bad wrist hindered him, which meant that Eleanor's role was more prominent. Eleanor was not comfortable about it, however, David insisted that she was more than capable. "There's something else you could both consider. I still think Tom should consider singing a harmony."

They both stared at him, and Tom spoke first. "What, at this stage?"

"Well, at least give it a try."

"But I don't know a harmony."

David smiled at him. "Tom, I'm about to show you."

Tom picked it up faster than David expected. David sang a few lines at a time, along with Eleanor, and then Tom sang them. It also meant that Eleanor got some more practise, and somehow, time seemed to fly past.

"Oh, look at the time," Eleanor suddenly gasped. "David, I'm sorry."

"It's not a problem. In fact, I've enjoyed it."

"Really?" Tom asked.

"Yes. Anyway, do you two need a lift?"

"No, we're okay, aren't we, Tom?" Eleanor replied.

"Sure?"

Eleanor smiled at David. "It will do us both good. We've both been revising like mad, so the exercise will be good."

They left a few minutes later, leaving David feeling odd. The fact that he had enjoyed his time with the two teenagers surprised him. It was as if they had known each other for years, not weeks. It felt to David that there was no age difference at all, but he didn't feel that they were being familiar. When they left, David was happy that they were prepared for their session in the church service, and he almost wished that he had not planned to go away. He felt that the time spent had been worthwhile, which made him feel good. But on the other hand, he felt empty once they had gone. He solved the problem by going for a long cycle ride.

Chapter 5

An Evening Out

Because of his absence, and then apparently Tom and Eleanor's other commitments, David did not see them for some time until well into the school holidays, but he did hear that they had sung well. When he finally caught up with Tom, he was with a group of the other young people. When he noticed David, he left the group and walked across.

"Hello, Tom," David said. "I hear that it went well."

"Yes, thanks to you," Tom replied.

"Rubbish! You and Eleanor are good. So, how did the exams go?"

"Pretty good, I think. I think Elly was happy with hers."

"Is she around?"

"No, she's at camp this week. She'll be back next Sunday, I think."

"I'm away again." David shrugged. "Maybe after that."

"Well, I know she'll be glad to see you. She was grateful for your help as well."

"I enjoyed helping you both. It took me back a few years, though."

"So what did you do, I mean guitar wise?" Tom asked.

"Not a lot, actually. We had a little group at uni, then at the church we went to. Jenny used to sing, and I played for her. Sometimes I sang with her. That's it."

"Well, I hope we can get together again before I go off to uni."

"Oh," David exclaimed. "So what will Eleanor do then?"

"Find somebody else, or sing solo. She has the better voice – I was just the accompanist."

"Don't say that, Tom," David said.

"It's true. She used to sing at camp, and sometimes when we met up after church – at the ACF. She only agreed to sing in the main service if someone else was with her. I could strum, so it was me."

"But you are, er, special friends?" David said.

"Special friends? What do you mean? We're all friends. Oh," Tom paused as he realised what David was implying. He grinned. "We're not going out, if that's what you mean."

David shrugged. "I just wondered. You did seem good buddies."

"We are. Just good buddies, as you put it. Anyway, I hope there's time for another session together, that's assuming you don't mind?"

"No, I'd like that. You ask Eleanor, and we'll arrange something."

It was just over a week later that David met Eleanor again. She was in town with a friend to buy tickets for a concert. David had gone into town to buy some new guitar strings. This kind of shopping was easy. Drive most of the way in and park by the road in a space with a two hour limit. Then a brisk walk to the appropriate shop, purchase strings, and walk back to car. All over in less than forty minutes at the most. For the girls, buying tickets was only part of their visit. There were other shops that needed to be viewed – even if no purchase was made, or even planned. Then there was coffee to be drunk – at a table on the pavement so that one could look out for friends. David was not looking for friends, or even for a cup of coffee.

"David!"

David was deep in thought. Should he have bought the more expensive strings? Really, he only needed one string – the D string, but he had bought a set of six. On hearing his name, he stopped and looked around before realising that there was obviously more than one person called David. However, on hearing his name called again, he stopped and looked around again, but this time with more care. He saw Eleanor almost immediately – the fact that she was waving her arm did help. He walked across, feeling somewhat embarrassed because he was not used to being greeted in public. One of the reasons he did not linger in town was precisely because he did not want to be recognised. Recognition could, and indeed had been, followed by abuse from a disgruntled past pupil.

"Hello, Eleanor" he said, feeling self conscious and wondering what to say next. He did not need to worry, because Eleanor spoke again.

"Hello, David. I've been waiting to see you," she said, engaging him with her smile.

"Oh?" David replied.

"Are you in a hurry?"

"Um," David replied. He had been in a hurry.

"Oh, sorry," Eleanor said.

"No, no. I'm not – I was far away."

"I thought you were," Eleanor said laughing. "Have you got time for coffee?"

"What, now?" David asked. "I mean with you?"

"Well you could drink it at another table if you don't want to sit with us," Eleanor's friend said.

David looked at her, not sure how to take her comment, but Eleanor laughed again. "Meet Lizzie, David. She didn't mean it. Well?"

"Okay then, can I leave my bag with you?"

David bought his coffee and returned to the table.

"So you're David," Lizzie said as he sat down.

"Yes, I'm David," he replied.

"I was telling Lizzie how you helped us," Eleanor said,

by way of explanation. "It went quite well. Oh, Tom's wrist is better, at least I think it is. I haven't seen him for a few weeks." She laughed. "And it's been ages since I last saw you," she added.

"Yes, it's odd isn't it? I've seen you most Sundays, but without speaking. Now I know you, I hardly see you."

"Well, you can see her this Friday if you wish," Lizzie said.

David looked at Lizzie thinking it was an odd thing for her to say. Eleanor explained quickly. "We're going to a jazz evening on Friday, and there are still tickets available. We've just bought ours."

"Yes, but ..." David began, and hesitated. The idea interested him, but he didn't think that Lizzie was actually suggesting that he went with them.

"It's okay, we understand," Lizzie said.

"Sorry?" David said.

"You don't have to be seen with us," Lizzie added.

"I didn't mean that. Actually, I was assuming it was the other way round."

Eleanor laughed. "Don't be silly David. If you do go, we'll be happy to sit with you. There are people of all ages – in fact, we'll be the odd ones out. Most people are ..."

"Middle aged?" Lizzie said, with a grin.

"I was going to say mature," Eleanor said diplomatically.

"Are you sure?" David said. "I mean, are you both sure?"

"Yes," Lizzie said. "Anyway, it will be too dark to notice how old you are."

Eleanor laughed again. "Shut up, Lizzie!" she said. "I can't take you anywhere."

The talk turned to school, and how they were waiting for their examination results. Then David told them about his new role, and his reduced teaching load. Eleanor asked if

Jenny's headstone was in place, from which Lizzie learnt about David's bereavement. Finally, David suddenly realised his car parking time was almost gone, and he said he would have to rush off before he was given a parking ticket.

"But what about buying your ticket for the jazz night?" Lizzie said.

"Shall I buy it, and you pay me back?" Eleanor asked him.

"That doesn't seem right," David protested.

"Do you have a better idea?" Lizzie asked.

"Shall I bring it round this evening?" Eleanor asked, assuming there was no better idea.

"Yes please. Look, take this to buy it," David said, holding out two five pound notes as he prepared to leave.

Eleanor cycled round with his ticket, as planned, that evening. David had been watching out for her, and opened the door before she knocked. He had already decided that it would not be appropriate to invite her in, even though it seemed to be discourteous, and of course, she had been inside when she put the flowers into a vase

"Eleanor, thank you very much," he said as he took the tickets and change. "Look, I've been thinking. How do you get to the session?"

"Either Lizzie's mum or my mum, and the same way home afterwards."

"Would it help if I took you both in, and home afterwards?"

"Yes please, David. I'll speak to Lizzie and let you know."

It was another strange evening for David, as he thought about the day. Being with the two girls in town had evoked odd feelings. On the one hand, he had been very conscious of being with two young women, actually, two school-girls. What had concerned him was whether he might be seen by his own pupils. Many of them knew about his personal tragedy. What would they think if they saw him? Would they put two and two together and make five? The fact that there were two young women with him should stop any rumours of romance. They might even think that they were his daughters. On the other hand, he still couldn't get over how relaxed he had been with them personally. It was as if they were his own daughters – except that he only had one daughter, not two. And what about the evening that was now arranged. Thank goodness there were two girls. It was almost like a date. It wasn't a date, of course. Goodness, he had still been married a year ago.

David and Jenny had talked about bereavement in their early days, when it had not been considered as a probability. Both had agreed that should one of them be left alone while they were still young or relatively young, then the survivor should be open to remarriage. They had also discussed the meaning of relative in that context. Of course, once Jenny was pregnant, they had started a family life insurance policy to reduce any financial hardship that would accompany such an event, but the term of that insurance had lapsed once their children had attained adulthood. Even so, Jenny had found it hard to accept that her children would have a step mother. On the other hand, she had been adamant that he would need a wife.

"You can't cook, you can't manage a house, and there's the other thing," she had said with a grin. However, when the time had come to plan for bereavement, remarriage was the one thing that was not discussed. Bearing all this in mind, David was grateful that Eleanor was a youngster.

Romance, let alone marriage was obviously irrelevant. He would look forward to a pleasant evening of jazz, with no other considerations.

By the time Friday evening arrived, David was feeling less certain. He had been to the cinema only very occasionally, and not at all to the theatre, since Jenny's funeral. There had been a few films that he had wanted to see, but he had hated going on his own. He knew he would not have attended the jazz concert alone, and so part of him was grateful that he would not be alone. But at the back of his mind their lurked a funny nagging feeling. Should he be going out to enjoy himself without Jenny? Was he being disloyal to her memory? Thank goodness it was with two young women. What added to his confusion was that they were school-girls. What on earth made him agree to go with them, he wondered? On the other hand, if they were women of his own age, what would people think? No, really, he should have been with a couple of blokes, not that he had any single male friends. It had to be a couple, because going with one girl might also be mis-interpreted. What a crazy world.

Eleanor had phoned him, and so he picked both girls up from Eleanor's home just before seven o'clock. The concert was from seven-thirty until nine-thirty, but most concert goers would then probably stay on in town for more socialising in the pubs or clubs. The evening went very well, as far as David was concerned. The setting was fairly informal and intimate, with the four musicians involving the audience. Eleanor sat between David and Lizzie for the first session, and then the two girls sat either side of him for the second session. He bought them both a soft drink during the interval, to thank them, as he put it, for inviting and putting up with him.

"So, will you come to the next one?" Lizzie asked.

"Yes please," he replied, with genuine enthusiasm.

Although he had picked both girls up together, he had to take them to their separate homes afterwards. He was directed to Lizzie's home first, so it was a little after ten when he arrived at Eleanor's home.

"Thank you very much for the lift, David," Eleanor said.

"No, thank you for taking me," David replied. "I've not been out much since," he paused, "since Jenny died."

"But you have been out?" Eleanor said.

"Cinema two or thee times, otherwise just church and bike rides. I go for long rides."

"On your own?"

David laughed. "Yes."

"Where to?"

David named some of the villages, adding. "You see things you wouldn't see if you were driving."

"I don't drive, David," she said.

"Oh, no, of course not. Sorry."

"So what kind of things?"

"Well – last time I stopped on a small bridge to look over at the water, and there was a swan's nest – pretty close to the bridge."

"Lucky you. I wish I could have seen it,"

"I could show you, it's not that far, well, maybe about four miles."

"That's not far! When?"

"Any time. There's no school at the moment. Haven't you noticed?"

"Very funny. Some of us have holiday jobs."

"You let me know when you are free, maybe after work? Anyway, off you go, I don't want your dad coming out to see where you are."

"He wouldn't do that," Eleanor said. "Did you do that?"

David laughed. "Jill's mum did once. Mind you, it was half eleven, and she was only sixteen."

"Like me?"

David looked at her. Whoops. Clang. He grinned. "Yes," he said. "So go home, Miss."

"Yes, Mr Anderson," she said, with mock servitude, "See you on Sunday. Bye. Oh, and thanks again."

Chapter 6

A Bicycle Ride

As he drove home, the magnitude of the conversation hit him. Had he just suggested a date? With a sixteen year old. Surely not. Was she joking? Was he joking? It had just come out – she wanted to see the swan's nest – he knew where it was – he could show it to her. As simple as that. Except that it was a four-mile cycle ride away. He could take her by car – yes, that's what he would do. Anyway, perhaps she wasn't serious. There was another thing. He did enjoy her company – he, an adult, and she, a child. She was a child. She was sixteen – she had said so herself. But when they were together, there was just a comfortable feeling between them. Odd. Like if they were married. This shook him – marriage meant romance. There was no romance involved at all. Just common interests. Perhaps it was time to try and develop other friendships – but friendships among his own generation.

He pulled into his own driveway, still thinking about it. Virtually all of his friends were married. They had been their, that is, his and Jenny's friends. There were a few single colleagues at work, but apart from work issues, they had very little in common. Two men were rugby buddies – David wasn't sure if it was the game itself, or the drinking that went on after the game that was the most important thing. Of the women, Barbara was scary. And Cynthia didn't like men. Then there was his church. There were a group of tweenies, as they called themselves. Basically, between eighteen and, say, twenty something, where the something was approaching thirty. Much younger than he was. And anyway, several were already in relationships. And that's just what he didn't want. But what about Eleanor? Sixteen. Less than half his age – best let things cool. Except that there was nothing to cool. The trip to see the swans was probably a joke. The jazz concert had been a threesome, and he had got on well with Lizzie as well. But it had been a pleasant evening. It was too late to go for a cycle ride, so he watched a late night film – and then regretted it.

He did see Eleanor on Sunday, but only in passing. There was no conversation, and no mention of swans. The following Sunday, several of the youngsters were buzzing, and he realised that they were sharing examination results. He found himself wondering how Eleanor had done, but he didn't feel it was appropriate to interrupt their conversations to find out. The following Sunday, Tom and Eleanor approached him about another singing practise.

"Is this afternoon okay?" Tom asked. "We didn't know ourselves until Friday."

"When is it for?" David asked.

"Tonight," Eleanor replied, with a grimace.

"And do you know what you're singing?"

Eleanor looked at Tom. "More or less," she said. "We had a brief session on Friday night, but we really would appreciate a bit more help."

"This afternoon is fine, but not so early. What about four?"

"Okay," Eleanor said slowly.

"Not a good time?" David asked.

"There's a young people's tea, and we usually meet up at fourish or so," Eleanor explained.

"We'll just have to skip it, or be late, Elly. After all, they did rather drop us in it," Tom said with feeling.

"We may well be finished by four-thirty," David said.

"I'm not so sure," Eleanor replied. She shrugged. "Oh well, if we miss tea, we miss tea."

"I won't let you starve, Eleanor," David said laughing. "Okay, see you later."

Eleanor was right. They did need a lot of practice. It didn't help that they were fifteen minutes late, but that wasn't their fault.

"Whose idea was this song?" Tom muttered. It was now well past four-thirty.

"Yours," Eleanor replied, quietly.

"Shall we give up?" Tom asked.

"No! Let's take a break. Time for a drink and a walk round the garden," David said. "Come on through to my kitchen."

The drink and the garden took over ten minutes, but the break was worth it, and after another fifteen minutes, they were both much happier.

"We ought to go," Tom said. "Thanks again, David."

"Do want to phone for your mum?" David asked him. "You're very late now."

"No, she can't make it. She said to walk," he said ruefully.

"Shall I take you?"

"No, no. Anyway, we've got food with us. It's a bring and share tea," Eleanor said. "So we won't starve."

"You're welcome to eat it here, and go with me later," David said.

Tom's face lit up. "Sure?" He turned to Eleanor. "Is that okay with you?"

Eleanor grinned. "He would have eaten it on the way, anyway."

"We're carrying guitars, Elly – unless you carried my guitar while I ate."

"Huh! No way."

"One condition – if you stay, you help," David added.

Ten minutes later, they returned to the garden carrying trays, and sat round David's garden table. At one stage Tom casually mentioned that this would probably be the last time that he and Eleanor sang together.

"Oh?" David said, surprised by this.

"I'm off to uni," Tom explained.

"So will you continue to sing, Eleanor?"

"On my own? No, of course not," she said.

"But you have a lovely voice, Eleanor," David said. "I think you should."

"That's what I told her," Tom exclaimed.

Elly turned to him. "Okay, find someone to accompany me," she said.

"What about you, David?" Tom said.

"Me?"

"Well, you can play better than both of us. And sing harmonies."

"But I'm not involved with the young people."

"That's not important," Tom said. "Anyway, why aren't you?"

"Because I don't like young people," David said rather facetiously.

It wasn't the most sensible thing to say, and both Tom and Eleanor stared at him in amazement,

"Well, that's not strictly true," he added quickly. "Look, I have teenagers all day, and in many cases not the most charming of kids. It kind of puts you off seeing more of them after school, sorry."

"So is it hard having us here?" Eleanor asked.

"No. It's not. In fact I can't get over how much I've enjoyed helping you both."

"Then you'll help Elly,?" Tom asked.

"Ah," David said quietly.

"Well?" Tom persisted. "Don't you want to help Elly?"

"Of course, but ..." he hesitated.

"It's okay, David. Forget it," Eleanor said.

"You understand, don't you?" David asked her.

Tom stared at them both. "Is there something I should know?" he said slowly.

"No, Tom. Anyway, it won't be your problem," Eleanor said.

Tom shrugged. "Okay."

David changed the subject, and they finished tea. After another rehearsal, he then took them to the evening service. Tom and Eleanor sang well, and David felt quite proud of them. They both came and thanked him again. As they turned to leave, David called to Eleanor.

"Eleanor."

She came back. "Yes?"

"You understood, didn't you?"

"I'm not sure," she said slowly. "Is it because I'm a girl?"

"Eleanor, do you remember the swans? You never came back to me."

"I know," she said.

"Well?"

Eleanor hesitated. "I told Lizzie, and she advised me to leave it."

"Oh?"

"She thought it was odd, you being much older."

"I understand. I shouldn't have asked you. I'm sorry."

"And I really wanted to see the swans. I don't suppose they're still there?"

"I could tell you where to go?"

"Am I being silly?"

"Eleanor, I don't know. Maybe. Perhaps it was me being

silly in suggesting it. At the time I didn't stop to think – it just came out."

Just then, Tom came back. "Still sorting out if you should help Elly?" he asked.

David looked at Eleanor. "It's up to you, Eleanor."

She hesitated slightly. "Yes, okay."

"I think you mean 'yes please,'" Tom said quietly, and chiding her. She coloured up. "Sorry, yes please, David."

David glared at Tom, but Tom didn't seem to notice.

"Fine, so let me know when, Eleanor," David said to her, gently.

"Excellent," Tom said, and moved away again.

David and Eleanor were left together. For the first time, David sensed unease, as neither seemed to have anything to say. Then Eleanor whispered, "I'm sorry, David."

"It's not a problem, Eleanor, really," he replied.

"Do you think the eggs have hatched?"

David looked at her carefully. "Maybe," he said slowly, wondering why she had asked. "Would you like to find out?" he added. If it was just conversation, he thought, then she would let the subject drop, but part of him hoped that she wanted to find out.

She nodded. "Yes, please."

"When?"

"After work tomorrow? Would that be okay?"

"Bike or car? Or shall we see what the weather is like?"

This time she smiled – the Eleanor smile, as he had come to think of it. "I fancy a bike ride," she said. "I haven't had much exercise this holiday, so, bike. Unless it's raining."

It was another unsettled evening for David, and it meant another bicycle ride. But not towards the swans. No, that was for the next day. David spent most of Monday on school work preparation. Non-teaching friends often teased him about the long holidays that teachers had. The fact as far as David was concerned was that he found the work stressful, so part of the holiday was recovering. However, he knew that other people had stressful jobs, so he kept his feelings to himself. Only Jenny had known how stressful. And only Jenny had known how much of the holidays was taken up in preparing lessons. When the children had been younger, she had often taken them out for the day, leaving David to work undisturbed. He thought about this as he worked. Now there were no children at home to disturb him. There was no Jenny either. It seemed that he actually missed her more now there was no school-day to occupy his thoughts.

He prepared himself a quick-cooked meal at mid-day, and went back to his preparation. It was sunny outside, and he was tempted to leave it all and go for a long cycle ride. Two things stopped him. One, he didn't want to go on his own – yet that is what he would normally have done, and two, he would be riding with Eleanor later that day. He looked at his watch and was surprised how the time seemed to be running away. He was suddenly reminded of how he felt the very first time he was waiting for Jenny on their first date. He almost panicked – this wasn't a date. It was a cycle ride with a friend. A friend who was female. A friend who was sixteen. He groaned – how could he have been so stupid? He would take her in his car and get the whole episode over as quickly as possible. Having made that decision, he felt slightly better, and he managed to settle down to work again.

There is a saying about plans, mice and men. David finally became so engrossed in his work, that he lost track of the time completely and Eleanor arrived earlier than he expected. In fact, David didn't even realise that it was her who was knocking on his door.

"Oh," he gasped, and looked at his watch. It was nearly four o'clock.

"I was sent home early from work, so I've come early," she said enthusiastically. "Is that okay? This way, there's more time."

"Er, have you eaten?" David asked.

"Oh, have I come at a bad time. Mum said I could have my dinner later." She paused. "How long will it take us? I've been looking forward to this all day."

"It depends. We could go by car."

"No, let's bike, David. You said four miles, each way, I presume. I worked it out. If we ride at half the speed of a runner, then half an hour each way? Back in just over the hour. Oh, you haven't eaten, have you?" She stopped suddenly. "Sorry, I got carried away."

David looked at her. Her face was glowing with enthusiasm. "I ate at lunch time."

"What did you eat?" she said accusingly.

"Oh, something with meat and rice. It was in a packet and it went into the micro-wave."

"What? Don't you eat proper food?"

"I added peas."

"David!" she laughed, and then stopped. "Sorry."

"Sorry? Why did you say that?"

"It doesn't matter," she said quietly.

David stepped down to her level, and looked her in the eye.

"Eleanor," he said gravely. "I have been married."

"I know that"

"To a woman."

Eleanor giggled. "Obviously."

"No, what I mean is," he paused, "when a woman says

'nothing' she doesn't mean 'nothing'. Eleanor, please promise me this. You will tell me what you meant before you go home."

"Okay," she whispered.

"Right, let's go."

It wasn't a good way to start the cycle ride, and they rode in silence for several minutes. David was wondering if he should call it off, when Eleanor suddenly stopped.

"What's the matter," David asked, going back and stopping next to her.

"David, it wouldn't have been a kind thing to say," she said.

"Shouldn't I be the judge of that?"

"You might be angry."

"I will try not to be. Go on. Please, Eleanor."

She paused. "It was about your diet. I nearly said that you need a woman. Sorry."

David stared, and then laughed out loud. "Oh, Eleanor. Is that it?"

Eleanor nodded.

"You may be right. I'm half expecting my mum to say the same thing," David said.

"No! It's too soon."

"Eleanor, you and Mum may be right. But I agree, it's still too soon to think about it. When the time comes, maybe I'll put an advert in the paper."

"No!"

David laughed again. "Oh, Eleanor. I'm joking. Come on, let's go again."

That broke the ice and they chatted like old friends. Eleanor would have been close in her estimate of the time it should have taken, but it took longer because they talked and talked as they rode. David talked about school work, and also about his new role in the church. Eleanor told David all about her own life. Fortunately, the roads were minor, and the traffic was light. They reached the bridge, rested their bicycles against the wall and leaned over. The eggs had hatched, and there were now eight cygnets. Eleanor laughed when she saw them.

"Now I understand the Ugly Duckling song. They don't look like swans at all, do they," she said laughing. "We should have brought some bread."

"Next time," David said without thinking.

"Next time?"

"Oh, sorry," David said.

"No, I'd like to watch them grow."

"Right, then we'll come back. Anyway, look at the time – we'd better be getting back."

They rode back faster, and David escorted Eleanor to the end of her road, where they said goodbye.

"I really enjoyed this afternoon, David. Thank you for taking me."

"I enjoyed it too. By the way, are we still on for the next jazz concert?"

"Yes, but I don't think you should mention tonight to Lizzie. I don't think she would understand."

"Understand what?"

"She would read more into it – and might even make a snide comment."

"But she's your friend."

Eleanor shrugged. "She's immature at times."

"Well, she was fun," he said.

Eleanor gave David a funny look.

"You were both fun," he said quickly. "I enjoyed that evening. And I enjoyed today." There was an awkward pause. "See you Sunday, then. Bye," he added.

Chapter 7

David the Host

David didn't expect to see Eleanor until Sunday, but on Saturday morning he had a phone call from her. She said that a group of the young people we going out for a pizza, and he was invited to join them.

"But Eleanor, I don't know the young people," he said.

"You know me, and Tom. And Lizzie my friend from school is coming."

"Yes, but I'm not a young person, Eleanor."

"There will be some," she paused, and David heard a giggle, "oldies as well."

"What?"

"Our youth leaders will be going as well," she said.

David knew who they were. "They're younger than me as well," he said.

There was a pause. "I thought you might like to go out, sorry," she said quietly.

"I'd feel out of place."

"Well if you change you mind, you know where to find us, otherwise, see you tomorrow"

The invitation unsettled David at first and he wasn't sure why. It could not be because of Eleanor – after all, he had felt at peace after their cycle ride. It had been a relaxed, but enjoyable time. He had thought about her unspoken comment during the week. It was too early, but would there come a day when he would seek a female companion. He couldn't imagine it – he couldn't even imagine going out on a date with a female. There would be unspoken questions. That had been the nice thing of being with Eleanor, even though she was so much younger. No hidden agenda – maybe because she was so young, and therefore not a threat.

He tried hard to put it out of his mind, but when the evening came, it re-surfaced. Did he want to go out? Should he go out for his own good? Make an effort, as his mother would have said. He had eaten his main meal at midday, and had a couple of sandwiches that evening, so, did he need a pizza? No. That should settle the matter. But did he like pizzas? Yes. So could he eat a pizza? Yes – assuming it was not large. And Eleanor had taken the trouble to invite him – so it wouldn't hurt just to look in. He didn't have to stay – just say hello. He could even buy a pizza to take away.

Next, what to wear? David was a pretty formal kind of man – being casual wasn't natural. He wore jeans only when work needed to be done at home– digging, decorating. He wore tee-shirts and shorts when on the beach. Then he remembered. Jenny had made him buy what she called chinos. They were hanging in the wardrobe, but virtually hidden behind his suits. They were hardly worn while she was still alive, and hadn't been worn since. And the same with the soft leather slip-on shoes. He dressed, and looked at himself in the mirror. Jenny would have been pleased, but then he had a pang of conscience. He was wearing the outfit she had chosen; but to go out without her. For a moment, he thought of returning the clothes to their places in the wardrobe. Suppose it was the other way round. How would he feel? Would he want her to stay at home, or if going out, dress like a frump? No, she had chosen his outfit, and he would wear it – for her.

The pizza parlour looked full from the outside, and David

hesitated. Then he had a thought – being full meant maybe he could slip in and buy a pizza to take home without being noticed. There was a queue, not a long queue, and he took his place, without looking at the seated area. Then curiosity got the better of him, and he slowly glanced around. He spotted his group quickly – there was Eleanor, and Tom, and one, no, two of the leaders, and Lizzie. At that moment, Lizzie happened to look up. Their eyes met, and immediately Lizzie recognised him. She waved, and then called to someone – it was Eleanor. Eleanor waved, smiled, and told Tom, before getting up. She came across.

"David! You came," she exclaimed. "Come and join the group."

"I haven't ordered yet."

"We've ordered too much. Come and share – unless you want something special."

"That doesn't seem right," David protested.

Eleanor turned, called, and then beckoned Tom. Tom came, his mouth still full of pizza. "Tom, have we ordered too much?"

Tom grinned, and nodded.

"Could we spare any for David?"

Tom swallowed. "Too right. Come and join us, David."

David allowed himself to be led across. Tom took the initiative, and introduced him to the others. "Listen everyone, this is David. David has been helping me and Eleanor with our singing."

The response was mainly grunts of acknowledgement, but the two leaders did respond properly. Lizzie also responded in a friendly manner. "Hi, David. Come and sit here," she said, squeezing up to make a place.

"I told David we had too much, and said he could share, okay?" Eleanor announced. There was one problem –

there was no plate for him.

"You can use my plate if you're not fussed," Lizzie said. "Help yourself," she added, as she pointed out what the remaining slices were. David helped himself to a small slice with his fingers. One of their leaders then spoke.

"We appreciate you helping them, David. Thanks."

"Aren't you filling in for Mark?" the other leader added.

"Only part time," David said quickly. "Nothing important."

"I know James appreciates it. He told me," the first leader said. "He said you had gone part-time as a teacher – is that right?"

David nodded.

"I thought of teaching, but only briefly," the second leader said. "I mean, imagine having this lot all day and every day," he added with a grin.

"What about the poor kids having to have you?" Tom replied, in the same vein. There was a chortle of approval.

"What made you come tonight?" Lizzie asked David. David hesitated. Should he tell her that Eleanor had specifically invited him? However, Eleanor had overheard the question, and came to his rescue.

"It was my idea, Lizzie. I thought he might like to meet some of the youth group, like I thought you might like to," she said with a smile.

"Oh," Lizzie replied.

"And our leaders," Eleanor added.

"Right," Lizzie added. She turned back to David. "So how come you know Elly so well?"

"It's a long story," he said.

Lizzie twisted in her seat to give all of her attention to David. "I like stories," she said. "And the night is young." David gulped inwardly. Was this school-girl flirting with him or was it genuine interest?

"Er, it's not very interesting really," he said.

"Let me be the judge, David," she said in a low quiet voice, but opening her eyes wider.

David thought fast. "Well," he began slowly. "Apparently Eleanor and her mother were at the cemetery and they noticed that the flowers on my wife's grave needed replacing."

"Your wife's grave?" Lizzie said, momentarily forgetting about David's situation.

"My late wife's grave," David said. "But there weren't any."

"Then how could they need replacing?"

"That's just it. Anyway, I thought she'd made a mistake, so to sort it out, I took Eleanor back to the cemetery."

"And?"

"We were both right. She had the right grave, and there were no flowers. It seems that someone put them there and then removed them again."

"And that's it? Didn't you play the guitar for her?"

"For her and Tom," David said.

"Oh," she said, momentarily non-plussed.

"Where do you teach, David?" this from the person next to Lizzie. David recognised her, but of course didn't know her name. It seemed to be a genuine and friendly question, and from her poise and manner, he guessed she was older than Lizzie. David told her, and she puckered her face, so David explained it was in a neighbouring town. "And what about you," he replied, partly out of courtesy, but also out of interest. "What do you do?"

"I am at Cambridge," she answered. "Law," she added, as though she was anticipating the next question. David hesitated. He couldn't remember exactly when the last person from his school had gone to either Oxford or Cambridge, but it had been a cause of excitement in the school. Yet here was this girl seemingly taking it in her stride. David found his voice. "And do you want to practice law?" It wasn't a silly question. One of his colleagues had a law degree, and yet he taught English in a secondary school.

"Yes, I want to be a barrister," she said.

"Wow," he said.

She smiled. "My parents say it's what I've been doing since birth – arguing."

Lizzie, who had felt left out of this conversation, now spoke again. "When did your wife die, David?" The change of topic, and also her directness threw him for a moment. The two girls were quite different, even the new girl gave a flicker of surprise. Age – he wondered? However, he told Lizzie, before adding that it was cancer. "I'm so sorry," the older girl murmured. "You must miss her terribly."

"Yes, that's why … " he stopped. He was about to say he was there because Eleanor felt sorry for him – not that she had actually said that, of course. "Yes, I think she would enjoy being here as well."

"Was she a teacher too?"

"No, she was a civil servant," David answered.

"Better than being a rude servant," Lizzie said, trying to be funny.

It was difficult trying to have a conversation with them both, but then Lizzie gave up, and moved to talk to Tom. David continued chatting with the remaining girl until they were interrupted. A discussion was now taking place about whether to have coffee, or move on to the church hall for coffee. The other possibility would have been going to the leader's house, but David gathered that it was impossible that night. He turned to his new friend.

"Is that what normally happens?" he whispered.

"Yes, but her parents are staying there."

"Oh!" He turned and called across to Philip. "Philip?"
Philip looked across. "Philip, my house is available," he
heard himself say.

Philip looked surprised. "Are you sure?"

"Yes, but," he hesitated – he had very little milk in the
house. "I will have to call in at Tesco's first."

Philip still looked dubious, so David called to Eleanor.
"Eleanor, you and Tom know where I live. Look, take my
key and open up for me. I'll be as quick as I can. Oh, can
you put the kettle on, please?"

"David, there is one thing then," Philip said, looking
serious. "Could you take anyone in your car?"

He took Lizzie and the other girl, and one other girl. He
confessed to them on the way that he needed milk – green
top – tea bags, and biscuits, so they split up, leaving
David to park, while each of them sourced one thing.
Then they met up at the till. By the time he arrived home,
he couldn't park on his own drive. There was Philip's car,
Tom or rather, Tom's mother's car, plus one other.
Eleanor was in the kitchen, and had already taken the
drinks order, so the three girls with David then joined in
and helped her. David went into the lounge, now
crammed with bodies.

"Sorry I'm late," he said. "I needed to buy milk. Anyway,
welcome everybody."

They stayed nearly two hours. Philip said that some
people should help David wash up, but David said they
were to leave it to him. However, as he took a couple of
mugs out, he found Eleanor already at the sink.

"Eleanor!" he exclaimed. "You don't have to."

"And you didn't have to invite us here," she replied. She
smiled at him. "But thank you."

David picked up the tea towel. "You know, I nearly didn't come tonight," he said. "Thanks for suggesting it."

"You seemed to be getting on well with Nicola," she said in a meaningful way.

"Nicola? Oh the girl next to Lizzie. Yes, she was interesting."

"And very pretty too," Eleanor added, looking at him.

"Eleanor! She's young enough to be my daughter," David said.

"So you didn't notice?"

"Eleanor, that's not the point," David said. "Anyway, Lizzie's pretty, you're pretty, most girls are pretty."

"Jenny was pretty, wasn't she?" Eleanor said quietly.

"Yes, I think she was, but I was married to her, so that makes me prejudiced, doesn't it? So do you remember her?"

"David, you have photos of her around the house," Eleanor pointed out.

"Yes. But it means I will always remember her as she was. I won't know what she would have become."

"Is that a bad thing?"

David paused, and Eleanor waited. "I don't know, Eleanor, I really don't know," he said quietly.

They stood in silence for several moments, then Philip came through.

"David, thank you again for your hospitality, but we must be going soon. Do you want to come back into the lounge – we normally end with a prayer."

It was another evening where David had a lot to think about. A couple of the girls had asked him about some of the photographs around his lounge. They remembered that a young wife had died some seven or eight months earlier, but hadn't connected it with David. Following their marriage, David and Jenny had moved around.

Jenny had helped with the smaller children in their second church, but by the time he took up his current post, her own growing family took priority over her time. And as David had told Tom and Eleanor, dealing with teenagers at school put him off helping with the teenagers in their new church, especially as that area of work appeared to be adequately staffed. Suddenly, he had come face to face with teenagers who did not remind him of the teenagers he taught. And it seemed that they had all appreciated his hospitality. Suddenly, a great feeling of sadness surged over him. Not just that he had lost his Jenny, but that she would have enjoyed hosting the young people – probably much more than he had done. He made a decision that he would make an effort to learn more about the young people and their leaders.

The next morning at church, several of the young people spoke to him, including Nicola and Eleanor. Nicola stopped him and thanked him, before moving on. Eleanor saw him just as he was leaving.

"Have you recovered from last night, David?"

"Yes, thank you, and thanks again for helping me," he replied. "I can't get over how mature your friends are."

"Huh!" Eleanor laughed. "They were on their best behaviour last night. Philip warned them when you were getting the milk."

"And the tea-bags and biscuits," David added, ruefully.

"Don't you have tea in the house – or biscuits?"

"I don't drink tea. When my daughter comes, she always brings her own tea bags."

"But what about when … " Eleanor stopped.

"Yes?"

"Nothing."

"Eleanor!" David looked at her.

"But what about when Jenny was alive?" Eleanor whispered.

"Oh, there were always tea-bags then. And biscuits."
"And don't you eat biscuits either. I saw you last night eating at least one biscuit," Eleanor said.
David laughed. "That's just it. I do like biscuits – too much. It's better for me if I don't buy any."
"But what about when friends come?"
David shrugged. "I don't have visitors. You and Tom are the first visitors, apart from family. No, James has visited me – he had coffee."
"And no biscuit," Eleanor said with a laugh. "Oh, David, what are we going to do with you?" She stopped suddenly. "Sorry, I didn't mean that. That was rude."
"No, no. If you think I need sorting, go ahead," David said, smiling at her. "All suggestions are considered – but I reserve the right to ignore them," he added, humorously.
"Typical male!" Eleanor said. "See you tonight?"
"No, I'm going to my daughter's this afternoon," he said. "So, next week."

It was a busy week for David. Once back from Jill's, he had his new church responsibilities and then some school-work preparation. When he arrived at church the following week, the first person he met was Nicola. He nearly didn't recognise her – she was in heels and a dress. She greeted him and asked about his week. David said that he had had a good week, and asked about hers. She had had a good week too.
"Bought any more biscuits," she then asked, mischievously.
"I've still got loads," David replied. "You bought far too many."
She laughed. "Sorry, but you did say I could choose."
"When I said a mixture, I meant one of those tins containing a mixture, Nicola. Like at Christmas."
"Haven't you noticed – it's not Christmas? Anyway,

they're usually boring. Crackers or biscuits to eat with cheese. Didn't you like my hobnobs?" Nicola asked, with a put-on pained expression.

"I love hobnobs. That's why I don't buy them. I eat them."

"You're meant too," she replied, laughing. "Come, let's go in."

David normally sat near the back, and alone. It didn't mean he remained alone, people arriving after him were often directed to the vacant seat adjacent to him. However, going in with Nicola meant that he sat with her, and not near the back. Because of her youth and gender, he felt very self conscious about it, but it didn't seem to bother Nicola. David felt better when Tom arrived and sat next to him, however, Nicola continued to chat quietly as though they were old friends. At one stage, David managed to look around. He spotted Eleanor on the far side and they exchanged a smile and little wave. He saw that Lizzie was with Eleanor, and she also waved a small greeting. After the service there was coffee, but David had to see a couple of people – his new responsibilities. Lizzie and Eleanor then came across. Like Nicola, they were both in heels and dresses as David would describe it, but he refrained from making any comment. It did remind him, however, of his own daughter, and of her transition from teenager to adulthood. There had been a few tears and tantrums about what she wanted to wear, but Jenny had handled most of these situations. Lizzie seemed keen to check that he was still going to the jazz evening with them, and David confirmed that he would pick them up as before. David wanted to ask Eleanor if she had been back to see the cygnets, but he remembered that Eleanor wanted to keep it a secret from Lizzie, and he did not have the opportunity that evening either.

It was a bad week weather-wise – not the weather conducive for a four mile cycle ride, but by the weekend, better weather was forecast. David picked Eleanor and Lizzie up from Eleanor's house as arranged to go on to the jazz evening. As before, there was a wide age range, including what David assumed were family groups, so David did not feel uncomfortable being with two younger people. Apart from not being aware of the jazz evenings, David knew that his own children, and even Jenny herself would not have been interested in attending, so in a way, he felt grateful that the girls had introduced him to them. This time, though, Lizzie seemed to be as interested in him as much as the music, and he didn't have the opportunity to talk privately with Eleanor, except for one time when Lizzie had to visit what she called, euphemistically, the ladies room. She had wanted Eleanor to go at the same time, but Eleanor had demurred.

"I don't suppose you've been back to see the cygnets?" David said casually after Lizzie had left them.

"No. Have you?"

"It was raining over my house this week," he said, with mock seriousness.

"Oh, so you're a fair weather cyclist, are you?" Eleanor replied, laughing.

"Yes, next question."

"Are you a wimp?" she said still laughing.

"Most definitely," he said.

"David!" she exclaimed. "Be serious."

David paused. "Okay, would Lizzie be interested?"

"I don't know – ask her. Mind you, I haven't told her that you have already taken me there."

"But when would suit you?"

"I'm not working tomorrow afternoon. I don't know about Lizzie."

David suddenly saw Lizzie coming. "Right. Okay. Let me think about it."

As they were walking back to the car, Lizzie asked David
what he was doing at the weekend. David hesitated.
"Bit of this, bit of that. Shopping in the morning.
Sometimes I cook for the week. Why, what are you
doing?" he replied.
"I thought about going to the cinema," she said.
"What's on?" David asked, mainly out of politeness.
Lizzie told him. "Do you fancy going," she added.
David wasn't expecting this at all, but managed to show
no reaction, although he sensed that Eleanor on his other
side did react. It was one thing going to a jazz evening
with two young women. The cinema was something
different, especially if it was with only one young
woman, and who was also still at school. It was obviously
out of the question, but something made him reply
tactfully. "Actually, I was thinking about an outside
activity. I was talking to Eleanor earlier about some
swans and their cygnets. Would you both be interested in
going to see them?"
"When?" Eleanor said.
"How about tomorrow afternoon?" David said.
"I could manage that, what about you, Lizzie," Eleanor
said, leaning round David.
"Where are they?" Lizzie asked. "And how do we get
there?"
"Out in the country, and by bicycle. I first saw them on a
bike-ride. You do have a bike, don't you?"
"Of course. Okay, why not."
"Good, arrange it between you, and meet me at my
place," David said. "Two-thirty, or soon after. That okay
with you, Eleanor?"

Chapter 8

Another Bicycle Ride

Before separating, Eleanor had arranged with Lizzie to collect her on the way to David's house. By Saturday, the weather had changed completely, and it was a hot and cloudless day. David had completed all his domestic tasks, and had eaten a cooked lunch. He was waiting, dressed in long, but casual trousers, and a short-sleeved shirt. He did have some reservations about the proposed trip, but it had side-stepped the alternative suggestion. He still wondered if he had misunderstood Lizzie about the proposed cinema trip, but he was sure that he had heard right – Lizzie had asked him, a singular you, as apart from the three of them. He would speak to Eleanor about it, but sometime later when Lizzie was not present.

David looked at his watch again. He had suggested two-thirty or soon after and it was now two forty-five, and no girls. Maybe they had changed their minds. Fair enough, he thought, but he thought that Eleanor would have phoned him. Then she arrived, but alone.
"I am so sorry I'm late," she said, as she dismounted.
"Where is Lizzie?" David asked.
"Family!" Eleanor said with feeling.
"Family?"
"She'd totally forgotten that some cousins were expected this afternoon."
"It happens, Eleanor. Don't you ever forget things? Don't let it bug you," David said, to sooth her.
"Huh! It's not that that's bugging me. She tried to get me to stay there with her and her cousins."
"Oh. Look, if you'd rather go back, it's okay," David

said, wondering if that might be the best thing now that Lizzie hadn't come.

"I don't want to, okay?" Eleanor said rather forcefully.

David laughed. "Calm down, Eleanor."

"You didn't hear what she said," Eleanor said.

"What did she say?"

"It doesn't matter," Eleanor said quietly.

"Eleanor?"

"No, sorry, David."

David looked her, and realised that she didn't want to tell him. After all, it was only repeating what somebody else had said and which didn't concern him. "Okay, let's go," he said.

He saw Eleanor relax, and then she grinned at him "Expecting snow, then?" she said cheekily.

"I can see that you're not," David replied. "I hope you don't get sunburn."

"I've got sunscreen on – and I've got some with me," she said, pointing to the basket on her handlebars. "And I've got some water."

"That's a good point. I'll just go and get some too."

Because of the heat, they rode slower than the first time and it was just past three-fifteen when they reached the bridge. They propped their bicycles against the parapet, and leaned against it. As they searched for the cygnets, the water glistened as it reflected the sun's rays. "Where are they, David?" Eleanor asked.

"Am I their keeper?" David asked, with a smile, mis-quoting from Genesis.

"Sorry," she grinned. "So what do we do now?"

"Go back, or go and look for them."

"Where?"

"There's a path down there, look."

They locked their bicycles to some railings and squeezed through a gap that took them down to the river's edge, and then made their way along the path. They had to walk in single file for some of the way until they reached a style. There was a meadow on the other side, so they walked side by side.

"There they are," Eleanor cried excitedly, pointing. "Look!"

They slowed as they approached, and then stopped. Eleanor sank down, and then sat. David sat down next to her, and they sat in silence for a few minutes.

"I wonder how long it takes for them to become beautiful swans, like their parents?" Eleanor pondered.

"They stay with their parents for six months," David replied. "Apparently the parents then chase then away."

"Then what?"

"I suppose they think about their next brood. 'Hey, mummy swan, what say we, er, get together tonight,'" he mimicked.

Eleanor laughed. "Don't be silly. I meant what happens to the poor little swans."

"They find another group to join. It keeps the genetic pool varied."

"Seems hard," she mused. "Aren't they so beautiful? It almost makes me wish I was a swan."

"Eleanor, you don't need to be a swan," David said without thinking. She turned to him, as though wanting an explanation. "Do you want to be kicked out of home?" he added quickly.

They sat in silence, just watching. She was on his right, with the swans now further to the right. David was thinking about his gaff. It was true but it had slipped out without thinking. It was not the kind of comment he would say to one of his female pupils, and he shouldn't have made it then. Thank goodness he had managed to cover himself, he thought. Maybe they should move on. "What do you want to do now?" he asked. "Go back?" "What would you do?" "Oh, I would carry on, but don't feel you have to." "Where to?" "The next village." "And what then?" "Well … " David hesitated. "Is it a secret?" "No, no. There's a little tea shop that I have been known to patronise." "Oh," Eleanor said. She sounded as if she was disappointed. "They do other drinks," David said quickly. "It's not that," Eleanor said. "What is it?" "Nothing. You go on and I'll go home."

David looked at her and waited a moment. Then he spoke. "Eleanor, sometimes I want to shake you!" Eleanor looked startled at this revelation, so David continued quietly. "We had a similar conversation last time. Nothing does not mean nothing. Are we going to sit here until you tell me? Is it me? Did I bully you to come?" "No, it's not you." "Well?" David said as gently as he could. "I didn't think we would be going on. I didn't bring any money." "Eleanor!" David exclaimed. "Well, all you mentioned was the swans. You didn't mention about going on," she said defensively. David laughed. "I never will understand women. Eleanor Jenkins, if you would care to accompany me, I would be honoured to buy you a cup of tea."

Eleanor smiled. "Thank you, kind Sir. I accept."

"And if you're good, I might even include a bun," he said, getting up first. He then held out a hand to help her up, but then withdrew it quickly. "Sorry," he said quickly.

"What for?" she asked, as she scrambled up.

"Nothing," he said.

Eleanor put her hands on her hip. "David Anderson, I could shake you," she exclaimed. "So do I stand here until you tell me?"

"Sorry," David repeated, somewhat sheepishly. "It was holding out my hand to you. I was intruding into your space."

Eleanor looked puzzled. "No you weren't."

"Eleanor, you're a girl, and I'm a man. I would never have dreamt of doing that at school."

"David, do you take your girls on bike rides, and offer to buy them tea?"

"No, of course not."

"So? How do you see me?"

David hesitated. Was she fishing about a possible relationship? No, she wasn't like Lizzie. "Eleanor, for some of the time I feel as if we are, er …" he paused, searching for the word, "I know – contemporaries. I mean that I talk to you as if you are my equal. Oh, that sounds bad. We are all equals. I know, I think of you as an adult – but I know you aren't really. I suppose I think of you the way I thought of my daughter when she was a teenager. Yes, maybe that was it."

"Hence your remark about shaking me?"

"No, that was a figure of speech."

"Of course." She laughed. "To shake me, you'd have to intrude into my space."

About twenty minutes later they reached the village tea shop. David wondered if it might not be open, but as it was still the tourist season, he wasn't disappointed. They chose a table outside and in the sunshine. A lady in a pinafore came out.

"Hello," she said brightly. "Are you ready to order?"

"What would you like, Eleanor?" David asked.

"What do you suggest?"

"Well, I know it's a hot day, but they do specialise in different teas, right?" David said, looking up at the waitress. "A pot of what you recommend, please. Oh, and a couple of scones – with jam and cream, please."

"So, I'm a good girl then," Eleanor whispered across the table behind the departing waitress.

David grinned. "I guess so. Just make sure you keep it up."

"Or?" she said mischievously.

"I might have to invade your space," he said, without thinking.

Eleanor opened her eyes wide at David. "Ooh!" she said.

David looked at her. On the one hand, he was looking at a very pretty young woman, dressed for the fine summer weather, that is, wearing a strappy top, short shorts and sandals. On the other hand, he knew that she was a teenager. A school-girl in fact. He swallowed. Was she flirting? No, she wasn't like that – that would be Lizzie. It was as he had said earlier – she was just behaving the way his daughter would have behaved. He changed the subject.

"So next year is sorted, then?" he said.

"You mean school?"

"Yes. Are you looking forward to it?"

"Oh yes. Well, apart from worrying whether I will cope," she said.

"You'll cope, Eleanor."

"How do you know?"

"Because I know your grades, and I know you, well, I'm getting to know you. I forecast straight 'A's at A level, then a first three years later."

"David, stop it. That's five years away."

"Alternatively, you could be married with three kids."

"No chance of that," she said with some feeling.

"What? Never?" David said in surprise.

"No! I mean not so quickly. My mum had to get married at eighteen – she could have gone to university – and then lost the baby. It's not talked about. I came along years later!"

"Oh," David said. Maybe this was a touchy subject, and best avoided. They sat in silence for a minute or two, and then further discussion was prevented by the arrival of the pot of tea and scones.

"Shall I be mother?" Eleanor said.

David nodded. "Please." He paused, and watched her pour. "And I think you will make a good mother."

"Maybe in ten years time. That's assuming that I find a husband."

"Well, from the way you handle a tea-pot, I'll give you a reference," he said.

"Thank you. I'll bear it in mind," she said with a grin.

David sipped his tea, then he picked up his scone and spread it with cream. Then he added a blob of jam.

"Oh," Eleanor said. "I thought it was the other way round."

"It might be. This is my way." He grinned. "But I don't mind if you choose the wrong way."

"You cheeky man," Eleanor exclaimed. "Who said your way was the right way?"

"I did, just now," he said, picking up his cup. He studied her over his cup, and compared her to Nicola and Lizzie. There was no doubt that all three were attractive girls. However, while Lizzie was very trivial and Nicola was sophisticated and very, very serious, this girl was in between. Yes, a bit like his daughter was. Maybe that's why he enjoyed her company. But why wasn't she out with her friends, or with a boyfriend.

"Eleanor,"

"Yes, all knowing one," she answered, with a grin.

David ignored the sarcasm. "Did Tom tell you what I thought. About you and him?"

"Whether I was his girlfriend, you mean?"

"Yes."

"I'm between boyfriends at the moment. Tom is just a good friend. He has a girlfriend, and by the way, he was quite amused."

"I can't see why," David exclaimed.

Eleanor shrugged. "I wasn't upset."

"But it was a hurtful thing to say,"

"Tom's a boy."

"That's either a scientific statement or a sexist comment, Eleanor."

Eleanor smiled. "Is it?" she said sweetly.

They resisted the temptation to have a second round, but did manage to squeeze a second cup each from the pot by asking for some hot water. While David visited the washroom, the waitress left the bill with Eleanor. She giggled when she gave it to David.

"What's funny?" he asked.

"The lady asked me to give this to my dad."

"So? At least she didn't say grandpa," David pointed out.

"You're not old enough to be a grandpa, are you?"

"I am a grandad, Eleanor. Jill, my daughter has a baby."

"Really? You don't seem old enough."

"I got married to Jenny a year before we graduated, and the twins were born soon after we graduated. I finished my PGCE course the following year."

"Wow."

"Not intentionally. Things don't always follow plans. But we coped, with help from our parents."

"How old are your twins now?"

"I have to think. Twenty."

Eleanor thought for a moment. "So you are over forty?" she said.

"Correct. Is that bad?"

"I don't know. I hadn't really thought about it. I mean, you don't behave like an old man."

"Thanks, Eleanor."

"The thing is, I know you said you see me like a daughter, I don't see you as my father. That's why it was so funny. If it had to be a relative, then maybe an uncle, or an older cousin. There, satisfied?"

"Do I have a choice?" It was rhetorical. "If you need the loo, go now while I settle up. I'll see you by the bikes."

As they rode away, with Eleanor just in front of David, he noticed that her back shoulders were fairly red.

"Eleanor," he called. "You've caught the sun. In fact, you are very red. I know it's too late, but I think you had better use some more sun cream."

She stopped, and twisted her head. "Oh my," she exclaimed. She got off her bike and searched in her basket.

"This isn't going to be easy," she said, putting lotion onto her hand and then applying it to her arms and then behind her neck. "How's that?" she asked, turning her back towards David.

"Pretty good, especially the arms, but you missed a bit

here and there."

"Can you help me then please, David," she said, handing him the bottle. David hesitated. "Please," she added.

"Are you sure?"

Eleanor turned back. "Sorry, is it a problem?" she said.

"No. Yes. I mean no. Oh, Eleanor, I'm not used to this."

"It's okay, I'll leave it," she said, extending her hand for the bottle.

"No! Turn round." David tipped some lotion onto his hand and applied it to her back, but rather gingerly.

"You can rub harder," Eleanor said.

"I'm trying to miss your hair and, er, the straps."

Eleanor bared both her shoulders, lifted her hair, and bent forward. "Okay?"

This time David was more vigorous, partly to get the job done faster. "There," he said, "that will do." He rubbed his palms on his own arms to remove the excess lotion, as Eleanor re-adjusted her straps.

"Thank you, David," she said. "Okay, let's go."

The ride back was slow, with a couple of stops to look at the view.

"David," Eleanor said at the second stop. They were sitting on the grass.

"Yes?"

"Swans."

"Yes?"

"So when do they settle down?"

"I don't know. They take four years to mature fully," David added.

"And do they really mate for life?"

"As a general rule – yes. If a mate is lost then the surviving mate will go through a grieving process like humans do, after which it will either stay where it is on its own, fly off and find a new stretch of water to live on –

where a new mate may fly in and join it – or fly off and re-join a flock."

Eleanor thought about this. Then she spoke quietly.

"David, how long do humans grieve?"

"Do you mean am I still grieving?"

"Are you?"

David thought about the question. It was the first time anyone had been so direct about the subject. Eleanor mis-interpreted the silence. "Sorry, it's none of my business," she whispered.

"No, it's a fair question." He paused, and turned towards her. "Eleanor, there's a passage in the book of Job – the Lord gave, and the Lord has taken away; blessed be the name of the Lord."

Eleanor waited.

"That didn't stop the hurt. And I know where she is now," David said quietly.

They sat in silence again.

"David, you said that swans sometimes find another partner," Eleanor said.

"Eleanor," David said. "We have talked about this before – on the previous bike ride."

"I know. I'm sorry."

"And you shouldn't tease me about Nicola. Do you remember?"

"Sorry."

There was another silence.

"But I want to ask you something," David said.

"Yes?"

"About Lizzie."

"I know what you're going to say," Eleanor whispered.

"Go on."

"She's – er – she's got a thing for you."

"What? Come on, be serious," David said.

"I am! Didn't you ever, er, fancy your teachers?"

"Of course not!"

"Not even the young single ones?"

David grinned. "Well, we did have a young French exchange teacher. Okay, yes, I suppose most of the sixth form fancied her. But I'm not a young teacher."

Eleanor shrugged. "Can I ask you something?"

"Go on."

"Well, suppose it was Nicola?"

"Eleanor!"

"No, listen. Suppose it was Nicola, after all, she is clever, sophisticated, and pretty."

"Still not interested."

"Yes, but why? Is it because she's young enough to be your daughter, as you said, or is it too soon. I mean, let's say, for the sake of argument that you were interested, and so was she, then say allowing for a year's engagement, and that's after a year getting to know each other, then it would be two and a half years after, well?" She stopped.

"Wow!" David said.

"Well?"

"Okay," David said. "I agree that Nicola is very attractive, but she is at university."

"That's not the point."

"Okay, it's the age gap."

"So shall I let Lizzie know that she's too young for you," Eleanor said with a smile.

"I still don't think you're serious. But if you are, then tell her that it's too soon. That will sound better."

David rode with Eleanor to the end of her road, rather than with her to her gate.

"David, thank you ever so much," she said. "I really enjoyed it."

"And me," David said. "See you tomorrow?"

"Yes. Oh, if Lizzie comes, best not talk about today."

"But suppose she asks me?"

Eleanor hesitated, but then spoke, but quietly and slowly. "Remember I said that Lizzie could make unpleasant comments? Well, she did today. First she wanted me to stay with her, but when I said I wouldn't, she said something horrible – that's what I wouldn't tell you. But the gist of it was that maybe I wanted to have an affair with you, sorry."

"Oh, Eleanor," David said. "What did you say?"

"I told her not to be so stupid – and that since you weren't married, it wouldn't be an affair anyway."

"Eleanor, I don't want to spoil you friendship with Lizzie."

Eleanor grinned. "You won't. I was annoyed at first, but I'm not now. It's been a good day."

"But we should be discreet about it – I will be. In fact I won't tell anybody," David said. After all, who could he tell? "Anyway, I'll talk to you tomorrow. Bye."

Chapter 9

Back Down to Earth

David found he was humming to himself as he rode home. It was a good way to end the holiday, he thought. Back to school next week – ugh – although not full time – thank goodness. But first, Sunday. That might be awkward; that's if Lizzie chose to be unpleasant. She certainly would not be told about the tea and cake stop. Nobody would. He had nobody to tell, and so nobody would know. However, David was wrong. As he rode into his drive, his neighbour saw him.

"Hi, David. Good ride?" he called.

"Hi, Mike, yes, a good ride, thanks," he replied, casually, intending to continue in. Mike walked towards him, so David had to stop.

"Where did you go?" Mike asked. David told him, adding that there was a family of swans that he had seen on a previous ride. Mike looked puzzled for a moment. "You must have gone further," he added. "You've been out most of the afternoon."

"Well, I did stop for a cup of tea."

"You and the lady?"

David looked at him steadily. "Of course. I could hardly drink on my own," he said carefully, wondering if Mike would ask who she was. Mike didn't ask any more questions, but David knew that Freda, his wife would probably be more direct the next time he saw her.

"Well, you've had a nice day for it," Mike said lamely.

"We did, Mike. And it was a good day for gardening, by the look of it," David said, indicating Mike's lawn. "I should have cut my lawn. I'll do it after tea. See you."

It wasn't just his neighbour who was interested. His daughter phoned after tea, explaining that it was because she knew that he would be out all the next day visiting an old school friend.

"Bother!" David exclaimed, before he could stop himself. He had totally forgotten.

"That's nice."

"No, I didn't mean it like that," he said quickly.

"So how did you mean it, Dad?"

"Oh dear, it's just that my last words to someone this afternoon was that I would see her tomorrow."

"Did you say her?" Jill asked. David gritted teeth – this time the "bother" was in his mind.

"Yes, it was someone I know at church," he said as casually as he could. "I helped her and a chap with their singing. Remember, Mum used to sing?"

"Were you singing this afternoon?"

"No, not this afternoon."

"What were you doing, then?"

"We went to see some swans."

"Swans?"

"Yes, swans."

"With this couple you sing with?"

"I don't sing with them."

"Okay, but with them?"

"With one of them."

There was a long silence. Finally. "With one of them?"

David sighed. "Yes, Jill, with one of them."

"With the woman? Did her husband mind?"

"Jill, it wasn't like that. She's not married."

"Oh-ho! What's going on, Dad?" Jill said, now intrigued.

"Jill, Jill! Calm down. Nothing is going on. I told her I'd seen a nesting swan, then with it's brood, so we went to see how they were getting on. Satisfied?"

"So is she, I mean was she a friend of Mum?"

"Jill, what is this? It was just a bike ride, all right?"

A pause. "Then I can't hear bells?"

It took a few seconds for the significance to sink in. Then David exploded. "No you can't hear bells. I presume you mean wedding bells?" he said vehemently.

"Sorry, Dad," she said contritely.

There was a silence, and David regretted his outburst.

"Jill, there is nothing going on, but," he paused, "but if there was, how would you feel?"

Jill did not answer, and David wondered if he had upset her. Then she spoke, slowly. "Dad, Keith and I have talked about, I mean about you finding someone."

"And … ?"

"Well, I didn't expect you to move so fast … "

"Jill! I have not moved at all." David said, interrupting his daughter.

"Sorry, I meant that I wouldn't have expected."

"What does Keith feel?" David said.

"He thinks it will happen, sooner or later."

"Why?"

Jill laughed. "Come on, Dad. What do men need?"

"Jill!" David exclaimed, somewhat shocked.

"I didn't say it, Keith did."

"Okay, but if it did happen, one day, how would you feel?"

"Dad, how can I say?"

"Come on, dear. You have talked about it. You must have feelings."

"Dad."

"Please, dear."

Jill took a deep breath, wondering if she should say anything. "All right, but please don't be upset." Another pause. "On the one hand we would both be pleased for you – I can't even start to imagine how I would cope if Keith passed away."

"Of course you can't, dear," David interjected quickly.

"But," Jill continued slowly, "how would I feel with someone taking Mummy's place?"

"Would she be taking her place?" David asked.

"That's it. Would I see it like that? I hope I would like her."

"Darling, can you see me liking someone who you didn't like?" David said. "Maybe I should bring any prospective step-mother to you for inspection first."

They both laughed at this. Then David spoke again.

"Seriously though, Jill, if it did happen, when would be the right time?"

"That's easy. It would be when you met her."

"But just suppose, hypothetically, that I met someone today, no tomorrow now, would that be too soon?"

"Are you still grieving."

"Yes and no. When I put the phone down tonight, it will hit me that your mother was not here to talk to you. When I was looking at the swans this afternoon, I was not grieving, sorry."

"Dad, you don't have to apologise to me. Did it help being with someone?"

David paused. "Yes, my dear, it did."

"Then it was good that you were with someone." Pause.

"Dad, I heard what you said earlier – that nothing is going on, as I put it. But could something develop?"

"No, not in this case," David replied, quickly.

Jill let the matter drop. However, she was pleased to hear that her father was beginning to get out and about, but she did wonder why he was so adamant that nothing could develop in this situation. Was this woman unsuitable, and if so, in what way. She wasn't married, but she might have been. A divorcee? A widow with a family? Odd.

As David had said, once he had put the phone down, he experienced a feeling of loneliness and sadness. It didn't help that school was due to start in the next week, but everything that he needed to do had been done, so he couldn't lose himself in work. Then he remembered that he had to mow his lawn. After that, he phoned his mother to confirm his visit. Then he watched television – for too long. It was in an advertisement about suntan lotion that he suddenly found himself remembering how he had rubbed the lotion into Eleanor's back that very afternoon. It was a vivid recall. For years, he hadn't touched another woman except Jenny. He could still feel the softness of Eleanor's skin under his hands. He shook himself and stood up quickly, feeling confused. Why had it suddenly comeback. He wished he hadn't done it – not that he had done anything to be ashamed of. It had been a good deed, that's all. Bother the girl. He was thinking about her again. A mere slip of a girl. He grinned suddenly. Actually, she wasn't a mere slip of a girl, she was an attractive young woman. But did that make it better? Step back, he told himself. Yes, maybe it was good that he was seeing his mother the next day.

David had no appetite for breakfast on the morning of the first day back to school – not that breakfast was anything substantial. Cereal and coffee. But even with milk, the cereal still seemed dry. Then he realised that it was his mouth that was dry and not the cereal. The first teaching day of term had been preceded by an in-service day – a day originally taken, along with four other days, from their annual holiday. When parents had to make arrangement for their children on these days, they inevitably made comments about even more days off for the teachers, not realising that the children had no fewer school days in the year – it was the teachers who had five extra working days.

The first in-service day always began with a full staff meeting. The timetable had been finished before the end of the last term, but sometimes it needed tweaking at the start of the new term due to some unforeseen circumstance. There were none. New colleagues were introduced, one of course was going to teach some geography, which meant a second meeting between David and the new teacher. The new teacher would also teach history and some games, which meant that he, it was a he, would also need to see the heads of history and games. David looked around, looking at the faces of his colleagues, and wondering if they were experiencing the same sinking feeling in their stomachs that he was feeling. This was his first new year as a single man, or rather, as a widower. He remembered going back home after the same day a year earlier, and having a moan to Jenny. She had laughed and told him he always said the same things – standards were falling, expectations were higher, the budget, that is, his departmental budget was frozen. Well this year, it had been increased, but apart from that, he was already experiencing the same feelings. And there was no Jenny to listen to his moans.

He hadn't taken lunch, and of course the school kitchens were not in use, so he joined some of his older colleagues and went to a local pub for lunch. It probably wasn't a good idea – for two reasons. Everyone was being pessimistic about the school, and it's future. In fact, it was two of his colleagues, with well meaning questions about how he was coping, that reminded him of his situation. Despite a good, and indeed, even encouraging meeting with his new, and seemingly very young colleague, he went home feeling depressed.

Jill phoned in the evening, just a brief call, mainly to see how the first day back at school had gone.

"You make it sound as if I was a sprog," David said. Jill knew that this was the term used for new boys at David's school.

"I said the first day back, not your first day, Dad," Jill said.

"I know, my dear. Actually, it wasn't a teaching day."

"Oh. Was it one of those in-service days? The ones you resent?"

"Officially – yes. But nothing was organised for us. Apart from having to give up a day of holiday, it was useful. Remember how I used to go in one day early – but never for a whole day. Anyway, I've got a new colleague in my department, so it was useful seeing him. And I got all of my class lists sorted out. Tomorrow is my first proper day."

"Shall I phone tomorrow to see if you've survived?"

"You can do, love, but I'm pretty well sorted now. Of course, I've also got my church work still."

"So no problems then?"

"Well … " David hesitated.

"Go on."

"Nothing much really. It's just that Marilyn, you remember mothering Marilyn, asked me how I was coping – that is, without your mum. I thought I had been coping, but suddenly, in the school environment, it brought everything back. We were having a sandwich in the Wagon Wheel at the time. Then old Curruthers, he asked the same thing – well near enough. It's odd, some peopled ignored it at the time – didn't even ask about the funeral, let alone how you and Daniel were coping. But to ask me just out of the blue just threw me."

"What did you say?"

"Can't remember exactly. I mumbled something. But I was tempted to say that I'd just got engaged to a young teacher."

"Dad! That would be untruthful." Jenny exclaimed, rather shocked.

"I know. I didn't say it."

"Wishful thinking?" Jenny asked, quietly.

"Jenny!" It was David's turn to be shocked.

"Well, you know what people say – there's many a true word spoken in jest."

"Then just for the record, Jenny, I don't know any young single female graduates."

"But you have just met … "

"Jenny!" David spoke rather louder than he intended. "Enough."

Jenny bit her tongue. She nearly replied to tell him not to be so touchy, but thought better of it. "Sorry, Dad," she said, hoping that she did sound contrite. But why was he so touchy? Best let the subject lie for a while. "Speak to you next Sunday, then, Dad. Have a good week."

The week went much better than David had anticipated. Lessons in the first week could include a degree of administration, but as David had already prepared his class lists and mark book, he jumped straight into teaching and setting homework. It was intended to keep his pupils on their toes, and to set out the standards he expected. Of course on top of that, he had his church work, and by the end of the week, he felt exhausted. But it was a good feeling, a feeling that something had been achieved. Apart from the two questions on the first day, he had not had the time to think about his situation, that is, his loneliness. He had, however, been reminded of Eleanor. It was a new girl in year twelve – the year that some schools called the lower sixth – and he first saw her from behind. There was something about her, or about the way she was standing, and for a moment, David thought it was Eleanor. He felt his stomach lurch. What on earth was she doing here, he thought. Then he realised, and the moment passed. However, later in the same day, she turned up in one of his teaching groups. David looked at her as she left – yes, there was a similarity. But apart from her rear view, there was nothing else about her to remind him of Eleanor. One of her preoccupations appeared to be her finger nails. And that was when she wasn't fussing with her hair. David soon assessed her as lacking in organisational skills – she had to borrow a pencil when he asked them to make a quick sketch. Then, from one of the questions that she asked, he doubted whether her academic abilities were suited to his course. For a moment, he wished he could do an exchange, and have Eleanor in his class at school.

Saturday was spent, as had become usual for him in the school term, in shopping, planning and preparing his meals for the week ahead, and cleaning. He looked forward to the Sunday as a day of rest. Jill had phoned him on the Friday night to ask this time about his first full week.

"Actually, it went much better than I had anticipated. Having school and my church work really kept me busy."

"Not too busy, I hope."

"What do you mean by that?"

"Did you manage to see your friend?"

"What friend?" David asked, genuinely puzzled.

"Your lady friend – the one you took to see the ducks."

"Swans," David corrected her.

"Yes, that one."

David paused. "She was at church this morning, and yes, we did speak, Jill," he said slightly irritably.

"Sorry, Dad," Jill replied, quickly.

"It's okay. No, I've hardly had the time to think of anybody else, let alone myself. I had to catch up housework and cooking yesterday, and I'm enjoying a restful day today. So what about you and your family?"

Jill took the hint, and they talked about her family.

Chapter 10

Eleanor Is Asked To Sing

At the end of the first week back in school, David was
looking forward to the first Sunday of term as a rest day.
However, bearing in mind his absence from church the
previous week, and his parting remarks to Eleanor, he
was concerned that he might have upset her. This was
based on his experience of girls at school who took
umbrage very easily. His male pupils did seem to have
thicker skin than his female pupils. He had experienced
girls not responding to his teaching because he had felt
the need to reprimand them over some issue, even a
trivial issue. However, there was no problem or
embarrassment. Lizzie was with Eleanor and they both
came across to speak to him at coffee time. David greeted
them both, and asked about their first week back at
school, and then they continued to chat in general terms
about their week, as they asked David about his first week
back as well. Of course, no mention was made about
David and Eleanor's cycle ride. The other thing that
struck David was that Lizzie seemed rather subdued, but
he felt he didn't know her well enough to make a
comment. Eleanor excused them both saying they had to
meet Lizzie's parents outside, and after a few more
minutes, David left as well.

That Sunday evening the youth group were going to meet
at someone's house after the church service, but Eleanor
first came to find David.
"Where's Lizzie?" David asked.
"Why?"
"I wanted to ask you. Was she all right this morning? She

seemed a bit odd, well, down. Not her usual self."

"I had a word with her," Eleanor said.

"A word?"

"Okay, after she apologised to me for upsetting me, I said that when she was with me, there were two groups of people she ought not to flirt with. Married men and widowers who were still grieving."

"You didn't," David gasped.

"Well, you did say that I should say something."

"So did she ask you about last Saturday?"

"Yes, and I told her that you bought me a cup of tea. So, how was your first week back?"

David blinked at the change of topic. "As expected. Actually, I thought of you this week. I had this batty sixth-former, who paid more attention to her nails and hair, than to what I was saying. I just wished that I could have swapped her with you."

"Do I take that as a compliment?" Eleanor asked, with a smile.

"And I'm sure that she fluttered her eye-lids at me," David continued.

"David," she said. "Like this?"

"Eleanor! Stop it. Someone might see."

"So long as it's not Lizzie," Eleanor said laughing.

"Eleanor," David said reprovingly.

She took a step back and put her hands behind her back. "Sorry, Mr Anderson," she said in mock humility, and looking down at the floor. Then she looked up and fluttered her eye lids again.

"Eleanor," David whispered urgently, and looking around to see if anyone had noticed. "What's got into you."

She grinned. "Sorry. Actually, I came to ask you something serious." She paused, as someone called her name from the other side of the hall. She turned and waved. "Just coming!" Then she turned back to David. "I have been asked to sing again."

"Good," David said. "With Tom?"

"Tom can't make it. I said I wasn't happy to sing on my own, so it was suggested that I ask you to help."

"Me?"

"Well, Phil knows that you helped us both before."

"Oh, Eleanor, what do you think?"

"It's up to you," she said, "but you did say you would." Her name was called again. "Got to go. Can I phone you, David?"

David's mind was in a spin for most of the evening. It wasn't the actual accompanying that bothered him, well, it did a bit, but with practice, he thought he would not find it too difficult. After all, he had accompanied Jenny. No, he still had reservations about whether he should accompany Eleanor at all. It would mean practising together – presumably just the two of them. Was he being stupid? After all, only a week or so earlier they had been together for most of the afternoon – alone together. But out in the country – and on bicycles. They could have been seen, but according to the lady in the tea-shop, they were father and daughter. The thing was, if it had been a school situation, giving extra help, or something like that, a one to one situation would have been frowned on. Only a few years earlier, one of the girls at his school had shown promise at table-tennis, and the best person in the school to coach her – a member of the games staff – was a man. All their practice session had to be in hall at lunch-time, and they found it hard to concentrate on their game. It wasn't just people walking past. It was people wanting to watch them play, which was quite off-putting for the girl. The situation with Eleanor wasn't quite the same. In a school situation it wasn't always the safety of the girl, but the worry about whether false accusations would be made against the teacher. In a private situation there was also the reputation of the girl to consider. In this case, if he refused to help her, then she wouldn't sing at all. Thus, any arrangement would have to be very discreet.

Eleanor phoned after school on Tuesday. "David, it's Elly, Eleanor."
"Hello," he replied.
"Have you decided?"
"Eleanor, I still think we should talk about it," he said
"Okay. When?" she said. "Philip needs to know."
"Of course," David said.
"Shall I come round after dinner? Would that help?"
"Today?"
"Is it a bad time?"
"No, no. Okay, come after dinner."
"Okay, see you later."

Eleanor arrived soon after seven. David had some work to mark, but he could not settle himself to make a start. In fact, he was ready for her at least thirty minutes before she arrived.
"Come in, Eleanor," he said. "Coffee? Or a cold drink?"
"We had a pot of tea last time we had a drink together," she pointed out.
"Sorry, would you rather have tea? I do have tea in the house since that pizza evening."
"Don't you usually drink tea then?"
"Hardly ever. Only if I have to," he said, without thinking.
Her face fell. "Oh. I'm sorry about making you drink tea the other day."
"No that was different. It was a special occasion."
"Special occasion?"

"Yes, the sun was shining, the sky was blue, the grass was green, the river was enchanting, and," he paused. "I was with a very special young lady, my newly adopted daughter."

"Oh, David," she laughed. "That was very poetic."

"Well, so what would you like now?"

"Just a cold drink, please. But if … " She stopped.

"Yes?"

"Nothing."

"Eleanor! That's against the rules."

"Sorry."

They stood in silence, as David waited. "Okay, I was going to say that if we went to the tea shop again, I would like a pot of tea for two again," she said in a rush.

"And I would like that too," David said quietly. Then he went to his refrigerator and took out a carton of juice. "This okay?"

David waited until they were seated.

"Eleanor, when you first asked me, one of the considerations was whether I was still good enough. It's quite some time now since I accompanied Jenny."

"You're better than Tom, but don't tell him I said that," Eleanor replied.

"Of course I wouldn't tell him that, Eleanor. Anyway, he's not that bad, and he's still improving. No, my main concern is where and when we would practice."

"Is that a problem? Weren't you happy having Tom and me here?"

"That wasn't a problem at all. There were two of you."

"You mean me on my own is a problem?" she asked.

"Eleanor, it's back to this age difference problem. If I were sixteen, no problem. If you were thirty-ish, no problem."

"It wasn't a problem last week. Or were you embarrassed

being with a teenager?" Eleanor stood up. "You said you enjoyed it."

"Eleanor, please. I did enjoy it. Please sit down. Listen, it's your reputation – a young woman visiting an older man."

Eleanor sat down and stared at him. "Are you serious? What about now?"

"Okay, do your parents know you're here?"

Eleanor hesitated. "I told them I had to pop out and see a friend from church about some singing."

"See," David said. "And did you tell them you were with a man old enough to be your dad?"

"No, why should I?" she said defensively. "What's that got do with it. Look, if you don't want to help me, just say so."

"Eleanor, calm down! I'm very happy to help you. I just want you to be aware of the situation. I mean, people could talk."

"Gossip, you mean."

"Okay, gossip. We must be careful not to fuel their gossip," David said.

"How?"

"By being discreet. Not telling people that you came here to practise."

"I suppose we could go to the church," Eleanor suggested, tentatively.

"That's true. Would it be open?"

"That depends on the time, I suppose. Sometimes they open early in the evening if there's a young people's tea. In fact, there is this coming Sunday."

"And are you singing this Sunday?"

"No, the Sunday after," Eleanor said.

"Right, we'll meet there this Sunday and find a quiet room. What do you think?"

Eleanor hesitated. "Tom and I tried that. It wasn't easy –
people kept disturbing us. And I don't like people
watching me – until I know what I'm doing."
"So, it's back to here?" David said.
"Only if you don't mind."
David took a deep breath. "Okay. We'll fix the time on
Sunday morning. Do you know what you're singing?"
"Ah," Eleanor said, looking worried.
"Ah? I don't know a song called ah" David said,
attempting to be humorous.
"I haven't thought of a song."
"Oh. What do you usually do?" David asked
"Tom usually suggested a song. He has more ideas than
me."
"And Tom's not here. Great. So, Eleanor, the ball is in
your court. I'm not very familiar with the modern songs."
"What did your wife sing?" Eleanor asked.
David laughed. "Oh, you wouldn't like that. My
generation would call them golden oldies."
"What are they like?"
"Well, I suppose they rhyme, to start with," David said.
"I've got some albums with those kind of songs
somewhere." he walked across to his HiFi. There were
some albums on the shelf above it. "Have you seen one of
these things?" he added, indicating the turntable.
Ellie walked over. "My grandparents have a thing they
call a record player and little vinyl records which they
call forty-fives. Why are they called that?"
"Because they spin at fort-five revs per minute," David
said, as he began flicking through the albums on the shelf.
"Bother, they're not here. They must be up in the loft."
"Oh," Eleanor sounded disappointed.
"I could go and look," he said tentatively.
"Could you? Now?" Eleanor's face lit up. "Can I come
too?"

David's loft had a loft ladder, so it was easy to reach. Once inside the loft, Eleanor saw that it was organised. The old albums were on a shelf at one end, but in a rack made of plywood boxes so that they didn't all fall over. "These were mainly ours, and those are some that I picked up in a jumble sale – a kind of car-boot sale, but indoors. Usually for charity. I also found some in a skip." David said, pointing at the opposite end. He picked out a couple of albums from the first end and handed them to Eleanor. She saw that one was titled "Gospel Songs" and that the other was in a similar genre.

"Can I hear them?"

"Oh. Look, I suppose we could play it downstairs. I've also got some songbooks somewhere."

"What, up here too?"

"No, under the keyboard. Come on, let's go back down."

"Oh."

"Do you want stay up here?"

"I just wanted to see what else there was, sorry," she added, looking at the shelf.

David grinned. "There's quite an eclectic mixture. All kinds. Rock, jazz, folk, country and western." He picked an album. "Django Reinehart, guitar player. Lost a finger. And this one, trad jazz. Pity you haven't got a turntable, otherwise you could borrow them. Right now I think we should make a start on finding a song, Eleanor. We might find something in one of the songbooks. Come on, perhaps I'll let you look at them another time."

David played snatches from the two albums, and they looked through the songbooks that he located. It took fifteen minutes before Eleanor found something she liked. It was something from one of the songbooks, and it had the guitar chords. David played it on the keyboard using one hand, and then Eleanor tried singing it, but accompanied by David, again on the keyboard.

"I like it, David, but I'd like to hear that one on the record
again, do you mind?" she said.
David played it, and Eleanor scribbled down the words.
This took several goes, and finally, Eleanor sang along
with the record, this time with David on the guitar.
"How do you know which chords, David?" she asked.
David shrugged. "They just feel right," he said.
"I'd need to have them written down."
"I'll work on it, Eleanor, but not today. Stick with this
one," he said, indicating the original song. "That will do
for today. You can take my songbook home and finish
learning it."

Eleanor paused before she left. "David, I do like the other
song, I'm bound to be asked to sing again," she said.
"And could you think about looking out for more songs,
please, David?"
"Are you sure? Do you think you should wait until you
have actually sung this one?"
"No. I'm happy with it. Mind you, I suppose that if
nobody else likes it, then I won't be asked to sing again."
"Is that what you want?" David asked, surprised by this.
"I thought you thought of it as a service. You do have a
gift, you know."
"Do you think so?" she asked.
David looked at her. "Are you fishing?"
"Fishing?" she asked, looking baffled. "Oh, you mean for
compliments? David! No!" she exclaimed. "Did you
think I was?"
David hesitated.
"You did, didn't you? Well, I wasn't, okay," Eleanor
said.
"Eleanor, I didn't say that," David protested.
Eleanor shrugged. "See you Sunday," she said, and
mounted her bicycle.

Chapter 11

Eleanor Sings Alone

David worried about his tactlessness for the rest of the
week, wondering how Eleanor would react on Sunday.
He didn't think she would bear a grudge, but he knew
how different boys were from girls. He thought that boys
were much more thick skinned, at least they were in his
school. In the end, he did not manage to speak to Eleanor
until after the service. He walked across, ready to
apologise, but to his surprise, she gave him a very warm
smile as he approached her.

"Still okay for this afternoon?" she said, catching him off
guard. He looked around quickly, hoping that she had not
been overheard.

"Eleanor," he gasped. "Shush."

She put her hand to her mouth. "Whoops. Sorry," she
said, and then grinned. "I didn't actually say what the
thing was, did I?"

"No, but best to be discreet, Eleanor. Remember?"

She put on a straight face. "Sorry, David," she said
meekly. Then she looked around. "What time, then?" she
added quietly.

"What time is your tea at the church?" David asked.

"About half four to five, we chat first."

"Well, you decide how long you need, and come when
you want. I often talk to my daughter after lunch on a
Sunday, so not before three-thirty"

"Okay, see you after three-thirty then," she said, and
smiled again. There was something about the way her
face lit up when she smiled. David was about to apologise
for his comment on the Wednesday, but the smile, and the
realisation that the two of them together might be noticed

stopped him. After all, he would see her again later.

Jill phoned much later than usual. There had been some crisis, not a serious crisis, in her family, and of course she had to explain. Jill made no reference to Eleanor, or rather, to any female until the doorbell rang two minutes after three-thirty. Jill heard it, and stopped in mid-sentence.

"Is that your lady-friend arriving?" she then said, partly to tease him. David interpreted the word 'lady' as being an adult female "I don't have a lady friend," he replied, separating the two words, and speaking somewhat tersely, as he walked towards his front door.

"All right, woman friend," Jill replied, quite affably, and not put off by his brusque manner.

"Jill, behave," David said, as he opened the door, putting his finger to his lips. Unfortunately, Eleanor, holding her guitar in one hand and a bag in the other, didn't notice.

"Hi," she said brightly. "Sorry, am I too early?"

David covered the mouthpiece with his hand. "No, Jill was late." He uncovered the mouthpiece. "Sorry, Jill, I've got a music practice now," he said.

"With a female?" Jill had obviously heard Eleanor's voice.

"Yes, Jill, with a female."

"Is she a pretty female?"

"Jill!" David expostulated.

"Well?" Jill said, unabashed. "Come on, Dad, don't be coy."

David hesitated. "Can I tell you another time?" he said, trying to make his voice sound disinterested.

Jill laughed. "Go on, Dad. Go and make music with your, er, woman friend. Bye."

David put the phone down, and turned to Eleanor. "Sorry

about that. She phoned later than usual. Coffee – or cold?" he asked.

"No, I'm sorry. I interrupted you."

"By pressing my door bell? Don't be silly. Anyway, coffee or cold?"

"Cold, please."

"Okay, go on through."

By the time David had poured out a juice, Eleanor had unpacked her guitar and was standing with the strap round her neck.

"Are you in a hurry," David asked.

"I wanted you to hear me first. I'm nervous about it."

David put the drink onto the coffee table, and faced her.

"Okay, but I need to say something first." Eleanor suddenly looked worried, wondering what he was going to say. "Don't look so worried – it's not about you, it's me. I want to apologise for my unworthy comment last Wednesday."

"It's okay," she said quietly.

"It's not. I happen to think that you have a lovely voice, and I enjoy hearing you sing."

"Do you mean that?"

"Eleanor, I would not have said it if I didn't. Okay, off you go."

Eleanor had learnt the words, tune and chords perfectly. David waited until the end.

"Eleanor, you don't need me at all," he said.

"I do, I do. I was nervous, couldn't you tell?"

David smiled. "Okay, yes."

"So how was it, really. Be honest."

"Word perfect. Tune perfect. Chords perfect." he paused. "You were breathless, slightly. Try again, but after the drink," he added, sternly.

"Yes, Mr Anderson." Then she laughed.

Five minutes later, she sang it again. "How was it this time?" she asked.

"Word, tune, and chord perfect again, Eleanor."

"Anything else?"

"Well … ?" He hesitated.

"Yes?"

"Eleanor, I'm not an expert."

"Yes, but there is something, isn't there?"

"Maybe you could work on your breathing," he said tentatively.

"I know. The trouble is, I'm also trying to remember the chords. Oh, and I'm still nervous."

"Right, this time, you sing and I'll play."

Eleanor handed her guitar to David, and took a deep breath. Then she sang, as David strummed.

"Fantastic," David said, when she finished

"So that means I do need you, doesn't it?" she said triumphantly. She paused. "Please," she added.

David laughed. "Okay, yes, at the moment. I'll remind you of this when you make the big time, and you no longer need me."

"That won't be for a very long time, if at all," she replied.

"You mean I could be stuck with you for a long time? Oh dear – how will I cope?" He grimaced.

"Stop being horrible."

"Sorry," he grinned. "Right, back to work, woman."

David made Eleanor sing it again, twice.

"Right, I think you've got it, Eleanor. That's it. What time is your tea at the church?"

Eleanor looked at her watch. "Oh, not for a long time. Do you want me to go?"

"Where would you go?"

Eleanor shrugged. "Home, probably."

"Then back to the church for your tea?"

"Yes, why?"

"Would it be easier to stay here?"

"And could I listen to your music?" Eleanor's face lit up. "Or are you busy?"

"You can listen," he said with a smile. "Right, back up into the loft"

"Are you sure you don't mind?"

"No, not at all. Come on, then."

David followed Eleanor up into the loft.

"So what are you interested in," he asked.

"I don't know. I think it was just seeing so many records. I've seen then in charity shops. What do you suggest?"

"Eleanor," David laughed. "What do you like?"

"Do you mean what CD's do I buy?"

"No, you won't find much of this stuff on CD's in music shops, although I know you can get quite a lot of old stuff on CD now. I mean, what are your tastes, generally?"

"You know I like jazz."

"Right." David picked out two albums. "This is a lady called Ella Fitzgerald and this is a band. That should be enough for today."

David settled Eleanor into his lounge. He had a few other things that he had to do, so he showed her how to use the turntable and left her to listen. Twenty minutes later, he slipped quietly into the room and sat in an easy chair. Eleanor was listening to Ella Fitzgerald. She smiled at him, but said nothing and continued to listen. As David sat waiting for the record to end, he couldn't help his mind start to ponder the situation as he had done after the very first time she had been in his house. All the time he had been helping her, he had felt that he was in a pupil-teacher situation. Now they were just two people again –

but of different gender. And far apart in terms of age. He thought that he would probably have been uncomfortable if Eleanor had been much nearer to his age. In some ways, he thought, the age gap was a blessing. There could be no complications. However, as far as other people were concerned, that was the main reason to be discreet.

The record came to the end so he got up and lifted it from the turntable.

"Well?" he said, looking at his watch.

"Wow," she said, and standing up. "Thank you."

"You're welcome. So how are you off for time? Do you want me to run you there?"

"No, I'll walk. Thanks again." She moved towards the door.

"Hang on," David said. "What about next week? We ought to have another practice."

"Okay. Same time?"

"Same time." David said. "And I'll bring another record down. Oh, and I'll look out for some more songs, for the future."

David used the week to write out the words and chords by listening to the Gospel album. He also practised a finger-style backing to the song that she was planning to sing. When he saw Eleanor on the Sunday morning, he didn't tell her that he intended to use this style but he did confirm that she would not be using her own guitar.

"So I'll bike round," she said. "And are you still happy if I come at three-thirty?"

"Yes, yes, of course," David replied. When Eleanor had originally suggested the same time, that is, three-thirty, he had agreed. Last week she had had the young people's tea to go to after the practice. With hindsight, he thought that it would have been better to delay the rehearsal, and he

had intended to suggest that. However, he was caught out
by her question and so he was ready for her at three-
thirty.

"Hello, Eleanor, put your bike round the back," he said.
"What's in the bag?"

"My tea – sandwiches," Eleanor replied.

"Your tea?"

"You said I could listen to your records. There's no
young people's tea, so I thought I would stop and eat it in
the park on the way, after finishing here."

"Don't be silly," David said. Eleanor looked at him, taken
aback by his reaction. "You'll have your tea here. Not
sitting by yourself in the park."

"Are you sure?"

"Yes, but on condition you help," he said. "That is, unless
you don't want to," David added, wondering if he had
been too bossy.

"You mean put the kettle on?" she said laughing. "Okay.
I accept your offer, kind Sir," Eleanor said smiling at him.

David decided to get straight on with the practice, and
took Eleanor straight into his lounge. He picked up his
guitar.

"Stand over there, Eleanor. I want to try out a new
backing. Are you ready?"

"I think so. I'm still slightly breathless."

"Do you want to wait?"

"No. I'm ready."

"Okay, I'll play eight bars, then come in."

David began the backing, and nodded at the appropriate
time. Eleanor came in on time, but not confidently.
However, as the song continued, her confidence gradually
improved, and she finished well. She looked at David.

"Well?" she said.

"What do you think?" David countered.

"I felt, well, exposed. Partly not having a guitar to hold, and also because of the different style."

"But are you happy to try it?"

"What do you think?" she countered.

"Eleanor, it does expose you, but I think you're exposable. Okay, you weren't comfortable at first, but you got better. Let's just practise a few starts."

"Where will you be tonight?" she said.

"Probably standing, or maybe sitting, to the side of you. Why?"

"So I'll be on my own?"

"No, I'll be near you, Eleanor," David said patiently.

"David, I like your backing, but I don't think I'm ready for it. Can we go back to the first way please?"

"All right. Am I pushing you too hard?" David asked.

"I don't know. Maybe it's nerves again. I didn't really want to sing with Tom when he first asked me – but at least there were two of us singing. By the time I got used to that, he went off to uni," Eleanor said ruefully.

"Okay, let's have two more goes, and then have a break. I'll play much louder, but I want you to pretend that I'm in the next room and can't hear you very well. All right?"

With David now leading her with his guitar, Eleanor sounded much better.

"Much better," David said, after the first attempt. "This time I want you to try something slightly different. Put your hands on your tummy, and try and sing from under your hands."

"What? I mean, pardon," Eleanor said.

David smiled. "What I mean is, use your diaphragm." Eleanor grinned. "I know. But when I'm standing up there in front of all those people, my tummy feels like jelly."

"I do understand, Eleanor. I really do admire you for

singing, and I feel bad making comments."

"I want you to comment, David, otherwise there's no point in me asking you to help me, is there?"

David shrugged. "You were pretty good before I got involved, Eleanor. It's not just your voice that I enjoy, it's the way your face lights up as you sing. You feel the words, don't you?"

Eleanor smiled. "Yes, maybe."

"There is one small improvement that I would like to see, but I won't be able to," David said.

"What's that, and why won't you?"

"You don't make eye contact with the people," David said.

"I know," Eleanor replied quietly. "Do you want me to?"

"What I want doesn't count. Do you want to?"

Eleanor laughed. "Want to? Or ought to? I know I should – it's not easy."

"I agree. Shall we leave it then?"

"No. Remind me tonight, and I'll try."

"Okay. And we'll take a break now," David said.

"But what about my tummy?"

"Later. I'd like you to listen to this."

David showed Eleanor the album, and put it onto the turntable. Last week it had been a female artist, this week it was a jazz band – traditional jazz. As they sat listening, and without speaking, David again pondered the situation. Bizarre was the word that sprang to mind. Very strange or unusual. He wondered how long it would continue. And yet Eleanor seemed quite relaxed – quite at home. Was it just a novelty – having the attention of an older person? He rejected that theory because she seemed equally self assured and relaxed among her peer group. She didn't need the extra attention. She was quite remarkable. He remembered the quiet way in which she

had brought him that cup of tea – oh, ages ago now.
Mature, way beyond her years. Maybe that was why she
was between boyfriends, as she had once told him.
Judging by some of the boys he taught, she was obviously
much too mature for them. But one day she would find
someone – or someone would find her. And he would be
a very lucky man, David thought. Then he found his mind
taking a strange line – he hoped that wouldn't be too
soon. He mentally reprimanded himself, telling himself
not to be so selfish, and then tried to concentrate on the
music.

"Well?" David said, when it came to the end.
Eleanor wrinkled her face. "Not sure," she said. "Lizzie
would have liked it."
"Oh," David said. "Are you suggesting that I ask Lizzie
to join us?"
"No," Eleanor replied quickly. "Anyway, I'm here to
practise my singing."
"That's true. Right, let's have another session."
"Slave driver," Eleanor said, but with a smile. "Are you a
slave driver at school?"
"That's an interesting point. Should I be?"
Without realising, the subject moved onto schools – their
respective schools. Then, because David was now part-
time at school, it then moved onto his church work. And
then onto other church related topics.
"Hey, look," David exclaimed suddenly. "Look at the
time. It's tea time. Eleanor, can you go and put the kettle
on while I put the record away? Oh, sorry, would you
rather have a cold drink?"
"No, tea will be fine," Eleanor said without thinking.
"Will a mug be okay, or do you need a cup and saucer?"
"Oh, David, I forgot. Sorry. Coffee will be fine."

"No, we'll drink tea – you're a guest. But you must make it."

Eleanor laughed at him. "David, a guest shouldn't have to work."

"Okay, you're not a guest," he said. "Go!"

Eleanor made a mock curtsey. "Yes, Mr Anderson, Sir. Whatever you say." She grinned at him and went to the kitchen. David joined her and made himself a couple of sandwiches while Eleanor made the pot of tea, then they returned to the lounge. David remembered the Gospel record that Eleanor liked, and put it onto the turntable. He lowered the needle at the position for the song that Eleanor had liked.

"And here are the words and chords," he said, handing her a sheet of paper. "Just in case you get asked again."

"In case we get asked, you mean," she replied, smiling at him.

"Eleanor, it's you they want," David pointed out. "You don't need me."

Eleanor smiled at him, but said nothing. She picked up her mug of tea.

Eleanor had ridden her bicycle to David's house, however, because the weather had changed during tea without them realising, David said he would take her in the car. There was one advantage – it allowed David to have one more practice with Eleanor.

"Eleanor, have you ever noticed politicians wave to their friends – they often point, then smile and wave."

"Yes," she replied, looking puzzled. "So?"

"Don't you ever wonder if they have really seen a friend in the crowd?"

"No, I just assumed that they had," Eleanor replied. "Why are you asking me?"

"This evening, you will have friends in the congregation.

Does that bother you?"

"No, it's the people that I don't know that make me nervous."

"Good! You are going to sing just to your friends – ignore the rest. When you go out the front, just look for a few friendly faces. Smile at them, and then sing to them. We'll try it now, before we go, okay?"

David made Eleanor walk to the far end of his lounge, and then pretend to look for her friends. He waited, and Eleanor waited. Finally she spoke.

"What are we waiting for, David?"

"When you are ready, then you tell me."

"Okay, I'm ready."

"Ah, but you won't say that tonight, will you?" David said.

"So what will I do?"

"You will walk out, look around, smile, and then when you are ready, you'll turn to me and nod, or smile. To let me know you're ready, okay? Then I'll play your intro. So, let's try it. Oh, and don't forget to look at your imaginary friends – there, there, there and there." David pointed to various part of his lounge. Eleanor had to walk there again, look around, and smile, and then she looked at David, and nodded. David began immediately, and quite loudly. Eleanor came in on cue, and they continued to the end.

"Well done!" David exclaimed. "Well done. Okay, let's go."

They separated at the church. Eleanor went to talk to her friends, while David unpacked his guitar, and found a quiet corner to sit. As the congregation began to arrive, Philip saw him and came across.

"I just want to say thank you for helping Ellie," he said.

David shrugged slightly. "It's a privilege," he said.
"What is she singing?"
David smiled at him. "'Fraid you'll just have to wait and see, Philip. I just hope that I don't ruin it for her."
"Sorry?" Philip said.
"I'm playing while she sings."
"I'm sure it will be fine," he said. "Well, see you after."

Philip was followed by Eleanor. "Do you want to come and sit with me, David. It will make it easier."
"Are you sure?"
"Yes. And it will help calm my nerves," she added.
"Are you nervous?"
"Yes, a bit. You're not, I suppose."
"I am apprehensive," he admitted. "That's why I'm sitting back here."
"I'd rather you sat with me. Please?" She smiled.
"Okay."

Because he knew that he would be taking part, David could not really concentrate on his primary reason for being in church. He was thinking about his accompaniment. However, despite Eleanor's nervousness, and David's apprehension, it was good – both her singing and his backing. She paused and looked around, before turning to him and nodding slightly. David played his introductory chords loudly, but then as she sang, he gradually softened his backing, as well as moving slightly away. There were four verses. As she began her last verse, David switched to his finger style. Eleanor noticed immediately, and glanced at him. David just smiled and nodded, and hoped she would not give up. She didn't, and her final words were confident and clear. David then followed her back to her place.
"Why did you do that?" she whispered, as they sat down.

"Because you are very good," David whispered back.

"I very nearly stopped."

"Ah, but you didn't, did you? In fact, you got stronger. Well done."

Eleanor shook her head, but didn't reply. David smiled to himself, and turned his attention back to the service.

When the service came to the end, a couple of Eleanor's friends came across. David slipped past them and went to collect his guitar. As he was putting his guitar into its case, Philip came to speak to him.

"David, I just want to say thank you again for helping Elly," he said.

"No problem," David said. "As I said, it was a privilege."

"Well," he hesitated.

David looked at him, wondering what was coming.

"Yes?" he said.

"There's a joint youth meeting in a couple of weeks or so."

"And … ?"

"I'd like her to sing," Philip said.

"On her own?"

"That's the problem. Tom won't be here, and she won't sing on her own."

"I think I can see where this is leading," David said with a smile. "What did she say?"

"Would I ask you to help again. Well? Oh, it's on a Saturday night, by the way."

"I can't see a problem. So, I'd better go and see Eleanor about it. I presume she knows which Saturday?"

David waited until Eleanor was free, and walked across carrying his guitar.

"So you have another booking?" he said with a smile.

"Only if you will help. I said I wouldn't do it on my own."

"Which means choosing another song, and practice sessions," David added.

"Do you mind? I thought I could use that song from the record, if that's okay with you."

"Next Sunday afternoon then? Look, you needn't bring your tea, I can provide tea."

"Are you sure? I don't want to be a nuisance."

"You won't be. Right, see you next week then." He turned to go.

"David?" It was Eleanor.

He turned back. "Yes?"

"My bike's at your house. Had you forgotten?"

"Oh!"

"So, David," she said in a sweet voice. "May I have a lift, please?"

David grinned. "Only if I'm forgiven."

"Bully," she said, and smiled back.

Chapter 12

Two Interesting Questions

David expected that once Eleanor had collected her bicycle, she would then rush off to join her friends at the after church get-together with the other young people. However, having extracted her bicycle from his garage, they continued to talk, standing by his front door.

"Eleanor!" David suddenly exclaimed after over half an hour had passed. "Look at the time. I've kept you from your meeting. I'm sorry."

"It's too late now, anyway," Eleanor said.

"What will you do? Go home?"

"Then they'll ask me why I'm early," she said with a grimace.

"Are you asking if you can stay here?" David said with a smile.

"Only if it's not a problem. I won't get in your way,"

"Come on; let's put your bike away again. Then you can make the coffee."

David thought Eleanor would ask him to play the song on the record, but after drinking their coffee, they just kept talking. Suddenly she gasped. "David! Now I'm late. I must fly."

Back on his own, David sat and pondered – as he had done before. In fact, it seemed that it was becoming a habit. It was odd, he thought, very odd. Maybe even weird. Was it himself who was odd by being friendly with a youngster? Or was it the youngster who was weird by being friendly with the older person. They just seemed to get on so well, and yet they were poles apart. Work wise – teacher and pupil, chronologically – he could be her father. And then there was the question of their gender – opposites. In fact, the age difference was an advantage here. If Eleanor had been in the same age cohort as him, there might well have been other complications. Romantic complications. With Eleanor, there were none. The only problem was that other people might not see it like that. Fine – it just meant that discretion was needed. He would have another word with her – assuming that their friendliness continued.

Eleanor arrived on the Sunday afternoon, as arranged, but with her tea in a bag, despite having been told by David that he would provide the food.

"Eleanor. I said I did have food." David said.

"I know. But Mum asked if I was coming home for tea after the practice. I thought that if I said I wasn't, then she'd ask why. So, I've brought my tea to the practice – especially after what you said about being discreet."

"You mean that your mum doesn't know that you are here?"

"I didn't say where the practice was," Eleanor replied, "and she didn't ask."

"So where does she think you are?"

"Probably at the church."

"And she can't phone up to check," David added. "Oh, Eleanor."

"It's only for a couple of Sundays," Eleanor said and shrugged. "Unless … "

"Unless what? Unless you get asked to sing again?" David said.

"Unless we get asked, you mean," Eleanor countered, stressing that she was including David.

"Do you know something that I don't know, Eleanor?"

"Well, there might be something at an old folks home."

"We'll see," David said. "Right, let's make a start. Tell me about this do."

Eleanor explained that it was an evening meeting for the teens of several churches. It consisted of a spiritual part, followed by a social part. There would be lots of singing, maybe a video presentation, and finally a speaker.

"But why have you been asked to sing?" David asked.

"Several churches get asked. Tom and I sang, oh, six months ago, so they asked us again. They didn't know that Tom was at uni, so then it was suggested that I sang on my own. No chance!"

"Do I make that much difference?"

Eleanor nodded. "Yes."

"But I thought I'd seen, I mean heard, other people sing last year?"

"Yes, Lyn, Sue and Verity. But Lyn and Sue are now at uni. I suppose I could ask Verity. Oh, and we'd still need a keyboard player. Verity doesn't play the guitar."

"Right, we'd better think of something," David said. "Do you have a song in mind?"

"Yes, that song on the record. You gave me the words and chords, remember?"

"Which means you could play the guitar?"

"But not on my own. And anyway, I haven't brought it with me," Eleanor said.

David picked up his guitar and handed it to Eleanor. "So borrow mine," he said.

Eleanor stared at him. "David," she said. "Not on my own."

David sat down next to Eleanor. "You won't have to, Eleanor," he said quietly. "But I want you to practise with my guitar at the moment. Please?"

"Okay," she whispered.

"Good girl," he said.

She looked up quickly. "That's patronising, isn't it?"

"Sorry, Eleanor," he said. "I didn't mean it like that."

"Were you in teacher mode?" she asked.

He nodded. "I suppose so."

"Then I'll be a good girl – just for you," she said, but with a big grin. "Okay, Mr Anderson, Sir, what do you want me to do?"

David stood up and walked to the far end of the room.

"Okay, Miss Jenkins, when you're ready."

David listened while Eleanor played and sang.

"Eleanor, you've been practising that, haven't you?" he said, when she finished.

Eleanor smiled. "Yes, but not a lot. I like it, don't you?"

"Yes, but isn't it dated?"

Eleanor shrugged. "Okay, but they won't know that, will they." It was a statement, not a question. "Anyway, it's my choice," she added

"Fair enough. Now try it again, but slightly slower. Oh, and louder, as if you were at church."

"David – I'm not singing on my own!" Eleanor said firmly.

"I know, Eleanor, but I can't look at you if I'm next to you, and playing, can I?"

"Okay."

This time, as she sang, David sang a harmony line, but quietly to himself.

"Well?" she asked.

David hesitated.

"Not good?" she asked, looking worried.

"No, you are good, Eleanor – good enough not to need me."

"David!" she said. "Anyway, what were you singing just now?"

"Oh, just a simple harmony," he said.
"Please can we sing it again, and this time, you sing properly."
"Eleanor!"
"Please, David."
"Oh, all right."

Eleanor handed David's guitar back to him, and they took up positions, but this time closer and facing each other. David strummed the introduction and nodded at the appropriate point. This time they sang together, and to each other. For David, it was almost like being with Jenny again, except that the face in front of him was not Jenny's. However, the need to concentrate, and keep his voice down stopped him from being distracted. As they finished, it was Eleanor who reacted first.
"David. That's it." she said excitedly. "Well, what do you think?"
"It was okay," he said guardedly.
"David, please can we do it together?"
"I don't know," he said slowly.
"You don't know? What was wrong?"
"Nothing was wrong, Eleanor. Sorry, it just took me back."
"Oh!" she gasped. "Sorry. I'd forgotten."
"Forgotten what?"
"It's okay."
"Eleanor," David said quietly, and then waited.
"Tom told me that you used to sing with ... ." She hesitated. "It's okay, I understand if you don't want to sing with me."

David unwrapped the guitar strap, and sat down.
"Eleanor, I enjoyed singing with you. It's not what you think – but I must admit, it did take me back. No, look,

this do you're preparing for is for young people, isn't it? That's why they have asked you. I don't think I should be involved at all."

"So if it was for the old people, would you sing with me?"

"Hm," David said.

"Okay, I'll do a deal with you. I'll sing and play on my own this time if you will join me if we get asked to sing at the old-folks home. What do you say?"

"When would that be?"

"Some time in November – it will be a Sunday afternoon. Well?"

David took a deep breath. "Okay, assuming that I'm free. When will you know the date?"

Eleanor clapped her hands together. "Oh David. I haven't actually been asked yet, but thank you. I'll find out tonight."

David decided that they had done enough practice. He took Eleanor back into his loft and she picked out two more albums, which she played on his turntable. Then it was time for tea, David suggested that she added hers to his. "I mean, that's if you don't mind," he added.

"Is that so you can share my cake?" she replied, with a straight face.

"No, no," David replied, quickly. "Sorry."

"David," Eleanor replied. "I'm joking."

David looked at her. "The thing is, Eleanor, I invited you to tea, but I didn't think to buy a cake."

"Or even make one?"

"Eleanor," David exclaimed. "I wouldn't know where to start."

"Start by having lessons."

"Who from, and when?"

"I'll buy you a recipe book," Eleanor said. "Okay?"

David grinned – there were books somewhere around. "Anyway, can you make a pot of tea?" he said. "I can't do that either."
"Tea? You don't drink tea. Oh, it's to use up the tea-bags."

After tea, which included the beverage, tea, they listened to some more music, and then it was time for church. Eleanor found out from James, their pastor, that he did want her to sing at the old folks home, and told her the date. She told David, and he noted it. Before going home, they arranged to practise the following Sunday afternoon. When Eleanor arrived at his house the following Sunday afternoon, he confirmed that he would be free to sing with her. They then had a run through of Eleanor's current song ready for the following Saturday.
"I wish you would come, David," Eleanor said.
"Don't you think that I would feel out of place, Eleanor?"
"Why should you? There will be other leaders there."
"As old as me?" he said.
"Don't be silly," she said. "You're not old."
"Eleanor!"
"Well, I don't think of you as old." She shrugged. "It's up to you, but it would make me feel more confident. You came to the pizza evening, didn't you? And I seem to remember that you got on quite well with Nicola."
"Eleanor, behave, or I definitely won't come," David said.
Eleanor smiled at him. "Sorry, David."

For the rest of that week David knew that he would go. Partly because Eleanor said she needed him, but partly because he wanted to see and hear her sing. He didn't offer to take her because he assumed that she would go with the other young people in the church. When he arrived, he sat in his car for a while watching other people still arriving. He was looking to see how many leaders there were – there didn't seem too many. Finally, he made his way in, hoping to find an inconspicuous place to sit. He was greeted at the entrance and asked which church he came from, and on giving the information, he was shown to where his young people were sitting. Before he could quietly ignore the steward, Eleanor spotted him. She stood up and waved, beckoning him across.

"You came," she said, smiling. "I've saved you a seat," she added, indicating a vacant place. As he sat, she leaned close. "Thank you," she whispered.

David settled himself, and looked around. He saw Lizzie, who gave him a little wave. Then Nicola, and then Tom. He turned back to Eleanor.

"Tom's here," he whispered.

"I know, I've spoken to him."

"But couldn't he have sung with you?"

"And when would we have practised? He only came home this morning."

"So why is he here?"

"David! Didn't you ever go home in term time? I bet his mum's pleased to see him."

"And so is that girl," David said, indicating a girl who was sitting very close to Tom.

"That's Ali, his girlfriend," Eleanor grinned.

David could sense Eleanor's nervousness during the meeting. He wanted to hold her hand to give it a comforting squeeze, but of course, he didn't. At last it was Eleanor's turn. She walked out, picked up her guitar and hung it from her neck. As she stood still, David felt his own heart beating faster. Eleanor looked around, before her eyes came back to David. He smiled back, and nodded. She took a deep breath, and began to strum her introduction. David kept his eyes on her now, willing her to be confident. Then she began. He could tell she was nervous from the slight quaver to her voice, but it actually enhanced her singing. He caught her eyes again, smiled and nodded, and then flicked his own eyes from side to side to remind her. This time though, she held his gaze, but as she sang, he felt her confidence rise. Then, as she paused before the final verse, she smiled, and then calmly looked around. She finished the song and stood still. Everyone applauded as she then removed the guitar from her neck and stood it against the wall, the applause continuing as she walked back to her seat. This time David did take her hand, squeezing it briefly, as he congratulated her.

"Well done, Eleanor. I said you could do it," he whispered.

"But I'm glad it's over," she replied. "I was too nervous to eat before I came out tonight."

"Maybe it will be easier next time," he said.

"Maybe, but it's both of us next time, remember?"

At the end of the meeting, David assumed that he would quietly leave. However, first Eleanor insisted that he had coffee, and a biscuit. David then assumed Eleanor would want to be with her friends, but she stayed with him, and insisted on introducing him to some of her friends. Nicola recognised him of course, and joined them for a chat. Tom came across to congratulate Eleanor, and to talk to David about guitars. Just then Lizzie came across to ask Tom and Ali if they wanted to go to a burger bar with the others.

"When do you go back to uni?" David asked Tom.

"Tomorrow, straight after lunch, unfortunately, why?"

"Well, I'm off home, but if you wanted to come round for a few minutes afterwards, we could strum a few chords? But don't feel obliged."

Tom grinned, and looked at his girlfriend. "Would you mind, Ali?"

"Won't it be too late?" she asked.

Tom turned back to David. "How about now?"

"All right, but what about the girls," David asked.

"Ali?" Tom asked.

"I'm easy, what about you," Ali then said to Eleanor.

Eleanor looked at David, not sure if she was included.

"Would you mind, Eleanor?" David asked.

"Mind?" she asked, not sure if he meant mind being left on her own.

"Mind keeping me company, Elly," Ali said, laughing.

"Oh. But how will I get home?"

"I can take you home, I've got Mum's car," Tom said to Eleanor. "So, yes please," he said to David. Then he turned to Lizzie. "Sorry, Lizzie. I'll catch up with you tomorrow, okay?"

"And I'll have to get my guitar, oh, and let Philip know that you're taking me now," Eleanor said.

"And I can see that she gets home, Tom," David said to Tom.

As they drove, David remembered that Eleanor hadn't eaten, so he suggested that he should make her a sandwich as soon they arrived.

"That would be nice, but Tom wants to talk to you," she said.

"Okay, how about you making it?"

"Would you mind?"

David laughed. "Eleanor, would I suggest it if I didn't mean it? You know your way around my kitchen. Mind you, I think you will have to defrost the bread. Oh, I bought some crumpets, could you toast them for all of us, please?"

"Sure you don't want me to bake some cakes while I'm at it?"

David turned and looked ather, not sure for a moment how to take it, but she grinned at him. "Joking," she said.

"Didn't you offer to teach me how to make cakes?" he said.

"No! I said I would buy you a cook-book," she replied.

"I wouldn't know how to use a cook-book."

Eleanor laughed. "Don't tell lies, David! You're not a helpless male, are you?"

He shrugged. "I did help you with the singing."

"Okay, I'll teach you how to bake a cake – but not tonight," she said.

Tom and Ali were already outside David's house and waiting in his mum's car, so they followed David and Eleanor into the house. Tom asked if he could borrow Eleanor's guitar, went with David into his lounge.

Eleanor told Ali that she was going to the kitchen to make a sandwich, and asked if she would help.

"David suggested that I should toast some crumpets as well," she added. "Fancy a toasted crumpet?"

"How come you know your way round David's kitchen?" Ali asked, a few minutes later. "Or should I not ask?"

"Sorry? What do you mean?"

"Is something going on – with you and David?"

"Ali!" Eleanor gasped. "Of course there isn't."

"Well, you seem very friendly," she said pointedly.

"Ali," Eleanor said. "David has been helping me with my singing – now that Tom has gone to uni. We practise here on Sunday afternoons. Originally both Tom and I came, that's how Tom knows David. Anyway," she added quietly, "David's wife hasn't been dead for a year yet, so don't talk like that."

"Sorry," Ali said.

David and Tom were strumming together until the girls brought in refreshments. Besides buttered toasted crumpets, they had made hot chocolate drinks. Over the refreshments, Tom took the opportunity to tell Eleanor that he had appreciated her singing, particularly as she had been alone at the front. Eleanor explained how David had persuaded her to sing on her own earlier that evening by agreeing to sing with her at her next singing outing. They continued to chat – about singing, about music and then about Tom's course at university. Suddenly David noted the time.

"Hey, look at the time. I know it's early for you uni bods, but oldies like me need to rest our brains. And I'd better get you home, Eleanor."

Eleanor gathered up the mugs and plates, and took them back to the kitchen. Tom turned to David.

"Do you especially want to take Eleanor home or would you like Ali and me to take her, David?"

"Would you mind?" David replied.

"Of course not, it's just that I wondered if … " He hesitated, but didn't notice Ali glaring at him.

"If … " David repeated.

Tom glanced in the direction of the kitchen, and then lowered his voice. "If there was something, er, special between you two?"

David stared at him for a moment. "Good gracious – no, of course not. Whatever gave you that idea?" he uttered.

Tom was embarrassed. "Sorry. Stupid boy," he said, referring to himself. He stood up, and apologised again.

David smiled at him. "Forget it," he said. "Anyway, she's younger than my own kids. What ever you do, don't talk like that to Eleanor." David picked up Eleanor's guitar

and walked to the door. "Eleanor," he called, "leave the plates. Tom's going to take you home, okay?"
As David saw them out to Tom's car, Eleanor turned back to David.
"David, when do we prepare for the old-folks? Do you want me tomorrow?"
"When is it?" David asked.
Eleanor gave him a strange look. "Four weeks tomorrow. It's on your calendar – remember?"
"Oh yes. Um, let's have a week off, what do you think?"
"All right. See you at church tomorrow then. Bye."

David walked back in, locked up, and went into his kitchen to wash the mugs and plates. He was relieved that Tom and Ali were taking Eleanor home. He had volunteered to see Eleanor home himself mainly to save Tom and Ali the trouble. He smiled to himself as he thought about Tom jumping to the wrong conclusion with his question. Typical male, he thought, as he recollected that he had the same thoughts about Tom and Eleanor. He had noticed the look that Ali gave Tom and guessed that Ali would give Tom a good telling off. At least they wouldn't say anything to Eleanor – he didn't want to frighten her away. He was running a bowl of hot water, and had just picked up his detergent bottle. He stopped, with the bottle in the air, the water still running.
"My goodness," he exclaimed to himself, aloud, and staring at his reflection in the window in front of his sink. "What am I thinking? So I don't want to frighten Eleanor away? Come on David. This a temporary arrangement. Pull yourself together man."
He looked down, and suddenly realised that the bowl was too full so he closed the tap quickly. Then he pulled the blind down, wishing goodnight to his reflection in the process. He put Tom's question out of his mind as he

added some detergent and began to wash the plates and mugs. It was just too silly. But he did wonder why he had suggested to Eleanor that they had a break. He had assumed that they would meet – it was probably a reaction to Tom's question. He would see Eleanor the next morning, so he could suggest that they did meet as usual. But would that give the wrong impression? No, best leave it.

David would have been very surprised if he could have eavesdropped Tom and Ali's conversation, not long after. They dropped Eleanor off, and then Tom drove to Ali's house.

"Tom," Ali said, after a few kisses. "That question you asked David – I had already asked Eleanor."

"What?" Tom exclaimed, shifting his position to look at Ali more closely. "What did she say? Did she deny it?"

"Oh yes. And she reminded me that David had lost his wife, oh, not that long ago."

"Yes, I remember. But, Ali, what made you ask?"

"I'm not sure. Maybe the way she was looking at him at the rally? Body language and all that. It was the way she knew her way around his kitchen that really tipped the scales, as it were."

"So what was her reaction?" Tom asked.

"She really did seem surprised by my question. But I think she coloured up – maybe she does have a thing for him, but in secret. So why did you ask?"

"I just sensed that they were very, very friendly. But then I felt a right fool, Ali."

Ali laughed. "Supposing we are both right?"

"What do you mean? No. Eleanor wouldn't lie."

"But David might? Is that what you mean? It happens, Tom. It was only in the papers a few weeks ago, remember? That games teacher, and his pupil. No she wasn't his pupil, but she was in his school. He got suspended."

"Eleanor's not in his school, Ali."

"So?"

"Ali," Tom laughed, "calm down. My goodness, you'll be writing for Mills & Boon next."

"So why did we both get vibes? We both asked the same question."

"Because we hope other people feel the way we do," Tom said, and kissed Ali again. They dropped the subject.

Chapter 13

Mistaken Identity

David saw Eleanor the next morning, as expected, and did not suggest that they met for a practice after all. Eleanor, however, reminded him that there was another jazz night the coming Friday, and asked if he wanted to join her and Lizzie again. David said that he would like that, and as before, offered to supply the transport. After lunch, he had his usual weekly conversation with his daughter. Suddenly she asked him about Eleanor, although, of course, she didn't know her name.

"I meant to have asked, Dad, how did the singing go?"

"It was okay," David replied.

"Last night, wasn't it?"

"Yes," David said.

"Tell me about it."

"There's not a lot to tell. It was a youth thing – several church groups."

"And were you singing?" Jill asked.

"Of course not, Jill!" he exclaimed.

"Sorry, but I had the impression that you were – I thought you said you were."

"I was coaching this girl. She used to sing with one of the lads, but he's gone off to uni, and she needed helping."

"Dad?" Jill said after a pause. "Is this the same person you went to see the swans with?"

"Yes. Why do you ask?" David replied. "Is it important?"

"You tell me. Why didn't you mention it before?"

"Jill, I have been involved in helping a couple of the young folk. One, the female, said she wanted to see the cygnets that I had mentioned. So, I showed her. I could have taken her by car, but we went by bike. It was nice

weather and biking is considered greener and healthier."
"And there's nothing in it?"
"Jill!" David exploded. "She's just a teenager."
"Calm down, Dad," she laughed. "My goodness, it was only a question."
"An inappropriate question, Jill, all right?"
"Sorry, Dad."

David felt very unsettled after the phone call. He had a novel, half read, but didn't feel interested in it. Part of the reason was his loneliness as a widower, which he recognised, but another factor was the absence of Eleanor. This was something he didn't recognise. However, the two questions, the first from Tom followed by a similar question from his own daughter only added to his discomfort. His usual solution was a cycle ride, but it was raining. It wasn't just ordinary rain – it was very, very heavy rain. Much too heavy and dangerous to cycle in. His mind went back to the question – and there was only one question – the same question asked by three different people. What on earth would Eleanor have thought if she had known? He was thankful that Jill and Eleanor were unlikely to meet, and he felt he could trust Tom to say nothing. Anyway, Tom would be at university very soon. That fact made him feel better. However, his eyes then just happened to glance across at his Hi-Fi, with a few albums propped up by it. Immediately, his thoughts turned back to Eleanor, wondering what she was doing. He pulled himself together, and made himself a cup of coffee. Then, on an impulse, he dug out his Wellington boots and waterproofs. It was too wet to ride a bicycle, but not for a walk. It did help, and by tea-time, he felt back to normal.

Throughout the following week he found his thoughts

turning towards Friday – or rather, towards the jazz on Friday night. Apart from enjoying the music, he knew that it was good for him to get out of the house. Going for cycle rides also got him out of the house, but apart from the two trips with Eleanor, they were not social activities. No other people were involved. That hadn't bothered him, but he knew he should make some kind of effort to be with people in general. He wondered if he would go on his own to the jazz if Eleanor and Lizzie said they were both unavailable – probably not, he admitted to himself. What he didn't think about was what he would do if only one would be free to go.

Eleanor was standing on the path outside her house, so David assumed he would then have to drive to Lizzie's house. Picking Lizzie up from her house was not a problem in itself, it was a question of time. Eleanor jumped in and buckled up.

"So off to Lizzie's now?" David asked, after they had exchanged greetings, and he was pulling away.

"No. Lizzie phoned to say she had a migraine – and she particularly wanted to go tonight," Eleanor said. "She'll be upset, so best not talk about it on Sunday."

"Unless she asks," David said.

"Yes, but don't make a big thing about it," Eleanor said.

"Of course." He paused. "So are you sure that you want to go on your own – I mean without Lizzie?"

"Sorry. What do you mean? I won't be on my own, will I?"

"No," he replied slowly.

"Oh. You mean, just with you?" she said. "David, is that a problem – I mean, for you?"

"No, it's not a problem for me. It's just what people might think."

"Did you worry what people might think when we went to see the swans?" Eleanor asked.

"No, I didn't at the time," David admitted.

"So why now?" Eleanor hesitated. "David, has somebody said something?"

"Well," David began.

"Was it Ali – you know – Tom's girlfriend?"

"No, it wasn't Ali, it was Tom."

"Tom?" Eleanor asked, surprised

"Yes, he made some kind of comment – but it was inappropriate, and I told him so."

"What did he say?"

"It doesn't matter," David said cautiously.

"David!" Eleanor admonished.

"Yes," he answered, innocently.

"You know the rules? What did he say?"

David waited a moment. "Okay. He asked if there was something special between us – but I soon put him right. Oh, and I told him not to say anything like that to you."

"Ali more or less asked me the same question," Eleanor said quietly.

"Oh?" David said.

"I pointed out that you hadn't been a widower very long. I think she got the point."

"People tonight won't know that."

"Are you seriously suggesting that people tonight might think we're a couple?" Eleanor asked.

David shrugged.

"Does it matter? After all, no one knows us," Eleanor said. This time David didn't respond at all. "You don't want to be seen with a child," Eleanor whispered.

"You're not a child, Eleanor," David protested. "And may I remind you that I took you to see the swans?"

"Out in the countryside, if I remember," Eleanor said.

"I'm talking about tonight. What is the problem?"

"I'm thinking of you, Eleanor – you don't have to sit with me."

"Don't be silly, David," she said gently. "Have you finished? What people think doesn't matter, so stop talking like that."

David stopped.

The evening went as expected. Although David felt strange at first being with only one girl instead of two, it did not affect his enjoyment of the music. By the end of the evening he suddenly realised that he wasn't missing Lizzie at all. However, it was as they were leaving that he experienced a shock. There were two couples exiting just in front of them, and in both cases the couples then held hands before crossing the road. Forgetting who he was with, David reached for Eleanor's hand.

"Shall we cross here, Darling?" he said, as took her hand. It was the voice that replied that shook him.

"Pardon?"

David spun round. "Oh my goodness," he gasped, dropping her hand as though it were red hot. "Eleanor. I am so sorry."

Eleanor recovered first. "Yes, why not?" she replied. "May I take you arm, kind Sir?" she then added, tucking her hand through his arm. They crossed the road in silence, and apart from a quiet 'thank-you' from Eleanor as she withdrew her hand, they continued walking in silence. Suddenly David stopped. "Eleanor," he began. Eleanor put her finger to her own lips. "Shush," she said. David was nonplussed for moment. "I still have the music going round my head, David," she said.

"But … ," he began again. This time Eleanor put her finger to his lips, holding it there until she thought he had got the message. Then as she removed it, she tucked her hand through his arm again and gently moved him along.

There were no more words until they reached David's car, got in, and drove away. Suddenly he pulled to the curb, stopped the car, and turned the engine off. Eleanor waited.

"Eleanor, I need to explain," he said.

"You don't need to explain anything, David," she replied quietly.

"But I want to," he said.

"You thought I was Jenny, didn't you?" Eleanor said.

"Yes, and I am so sorry."

"Don't be silly."

"I'm not being silly," he protested.

"David, I took it as a compliment."

"What?"

"Remember what we were talking about? It meant that you had forgotten that you were with an embarrassing schoolgirl."

"Eleanor!" David said, raising his voice. "I never thought that at all. I didn't want you to feel embarrassed."

"Well, I'm not, so that's the end of it. Mind you," she paused and giggled. "Suppose it had been me with the migraine?"

"Sorry?" David said, not seeing where the conversation was going.

"You would have taken Lizzie's hand."

"Oh no," David gasped. "That would have been terrible."

"But it didn't happen, did it?" She paused. "So can we go home now, please?"

Nothing more was said until they pulled outside Eleanor's house. Eleanor turned to David.

"Thank you again, David. I've really enjoyed tonight – more than you can imagine," she said, laughing. "Your face when you took my hand – even in the street lighting I could see it clearly. You looked horrified."

"I was," David said. "I still feel terrible."

"Would Jenny have enjoyed it?"

"It wasn't really her thing, but I enjoyed it. I am really grateful that you and Lizzie introduced me to it."

"Even though we're only girls?"

David switched on the internal light and looked at her. He could see that she was teasing him.

"Go home, woman," he growled.

Eleanor opened her door, then paused. "Are we meeting this Sunday to make a start on our next singing engagement?"

"Oh yes, of course. I was going to ask you about that. Right – usual time and place?"

"Are you sure. Actually, there's a young people's tea at the church, so I will go on to that, if that's okay."

"You do whatever's most convenient, Eleanor, okay?"

"Okay. Thanks again. Bye."

As David drove home, his head was still spinning. There were so many thoughts in his mind. It wasn't just Tom's question – it was the fact that according to Eleanor, Ali had asked the same question. He was sure that he had not given Tom, or Ali any reason to ask such a question. Then a further thought struck him. Did anybody else think that way? Surely not – at least, he hoped not. He went over the times that they had been alone together, one by one. On the bus? To the cemetery? To see the swans? But that was ages ago and Tom wouldn't have known anyway. Talking together in church? No. Singing practices – ah. But who knew about them? He wished he had pursued the matter further with Tom – something must have prompted him, but what? His mind moved on to wonder how Eleanor herself had reacted to Ali's question – not that he actually knew her reaction. But Eleanor didn't seem to be greatly affected. According to her, she had merely reminded Ali that he was not long bereaved.

Trains of thought are not always predictable. David suddenly found himself wondering what it would be like to be in a relationship with Eleanor – after all, apparently Tom had considered it a possibility. And so had Ali. No, silly idea. But, then his mind reasoned in hypothetical mode – suppose he was Tom? No, not Tom, but a boy like Tom. Yes, he would be very interested. He would want to get to know her better. He smiled to himself – he did know her better. Suddenly his heart lurched. He had first met Jenny when he was Tom's age. A feeling of guilt swept over him. Was he replacing Jenny in his head. Were his thoughts really hypothetical? What were his feelings towards Eleanor? Now he went cold. Eleanor was a child, and he was a middle aged man. Sure, yes, he was very fond of her, but in a totally innocent way. In a fatherly way, even, he thought. Yes, that's why his heart lurched when she smiled. It still did that whenever Jill visited with his grandson. Yes, another reason why there could not, in fact, should not be what Tom had euphemistically had called 'something special' between them. However, at the back of his mind was the feeling that Tom had not shown any sense of disapproval. Nor had Eleanor in the way she had spoken about Ali's question. Did people find such a relationship acceptable – or was it just young people. Young people did seem to accept things more readily than his own generation. Then another thought struck him – suppose he had been seen that evening by one of his own pupils? How would they have reacted? He almost wished he had been seen just to find out.

Just thinking about school caused his thoughts to move on, by which time the music was also going around in his head. Saturday was the usual busy day, interrupted by a phone call from Jill. Keith needed to visit David's area the next day. It was a work related emergency that needed Keith from about midday, and Keith had suggested that he drop Jill and their son at David's for the day.

"I know you'll be at church, Dad, but we can let ourselves in. Tell you what, I'll bring Sunday lunch as well. What do you think – you haven't seen the baby for a while, have you?"

The sudden nature of the suggestion caught David out, and he hesitated. Jill noticed, and continued. "Sorry, have you made other arrangements? The thing is, Keith didn't know about it until this morning. It's an emergency, but he's not needed quite yet. Normally, he would go on his own, of course, but as it's not that far from you, he suggested that we see you. It was just an idea, not to worry."

"I think it's a great idea, Jill," David said. "Especially your idea about dinner."

"What about your music practice – don't you have a practice in the afternoon?"

"I can cancel that," David said.

"No, no, Dad, don't do that. Keith doesn't know how long he'll be. He could finish halfway through the afternoon. How long does the practice take?"

"It varies, depending on things. It could be half an hour, or an hour."

"Don't cancel it, Dad, okay? Or we won't come."

"That's blackmail, Jill," David said.

"Dad. What a suggestion," Jill said, and laughed. "Okay, see you tomorrow."

Eleanor saw David after the service the next day to confirm their singing appointment. David had wondered if he should cancel or delay the practice, but it was the enthusiasm in Eleanor's voice and the look on her face that kept him silent on that subject. He returned home to find Jill well and truly in control. The table was laid, and there was a good smell. David kissed Jill, and commented on the smell.

"I cheated. It's a ready meal, sorry. The smell is part of the packaging, I think. But the pudding is real. I cooked a crumble last night. It's in the oven."

"So where is his nibs?" David asked, referring to his grandson?

"In the lounge, in his travel-cot, Dad. He can crawl now, so he has to be imprisoned, I'm afraid. You can take him out, so long as you watch him. I don't want him climbing up the bookcase."

"That's because he knows where the intellectual books are," David said. "He obviously takes after me. Anyway, what's Keith doing for lunch?"

"Sandwiches," Jill said. "But I'll save him some crumble. I've got a spare crumble to leave with you."

"Really? Oh, Jill, that's good of you."

"It's about time you learnt to cook properly. That was the only mistake Mum made – letting you off learning to cook. Perhaps you could join a cookery class."

"Yes, dear," David said, and left the kitchen. He picked up James, and spoke to him. "Hello, James. Your Mum has been bullying me, what should I do?" On not getting a sensible answer, David tried actions rather than words. James liked being bounced on his Grandad's knee.

After dinner, and more grandad/grandson time, Jill moved the travel-cot to the dining room, and put her son down for a rest. She then sat with David in his lounge, chatting.

Eleanor arrived at three, but of course was then surprised when David said he had company.

"Come in, Eleanor. My daughter is here, but don't worry, she knows about our practice."

Eleanor looked confused. "Did you know they were coming?" she asked.

"Yes, it was arranged yesterday, why?"

"Then you should have told me this morning," she answered, as Jill came into the hallway.

"Jill, this is the young lady I told you about," David said to his daughter. "Eleanor, meet my daughter."

They exchanged greetings, and then Eleanor turned to go.

"Eleanor, you don't have to go," David said.

"No, don't go," Jill added. "I knew about the practice, and I told Dad that I wouldn't come if he did cancel it," she said. "Sorry, will it inhibit you, me being here? I could take James for a walk in his buggy."

Eleanor looked at David, unsure of what to do. "Eleanor, please stay," he said. "That's if you don't mind Jill being here as well."

"Okay. But I didn't tell you, they want two songs this time."

"Where are you singing, Eleanor?" Jill asked, as they moved into the lounge.

"At an old people's home," Eleanor replied.

"And what are you singing?"

"We haven't decided yet. That's the first thing," David said. "So, any suggestions, Jill?"

"An old-peoples home? Hm. Golden oldies, I would have thought. What did my great-grandma used to sing? I know, Blessed Assurance, The Old Rugged Cross, oh, and the slave traders hymn."

"Amazing Grace," Eleanor said. "But I don't know Blessed Assurance, how does it go?"

Jill smiled. "I can't remember all the words, but I do remember the chorus." She paused, then she sang.

"This is my story, this is my song,
Praising my Saviour all the day long;
This is my story, this is my song,
Praising my Saviour all the day long."

"It was written in the eighteen hundreds," David said. "I do know that. And I have heard it sung."

"Do you know how it begins," Eleanor asked Jill.

Jill thought for a moment.

"Blessed assurance, Jesus is mine!
Oh, what a foretaste of glory divine!
Heir of salvation, purchase of God,
Da da da da dah dah, da da da dah."

"I'm sure you could find the words, Dad," Jill said to David. "Sorry I can't help more," she added, speaking to Eleanor.

"No, you have helped. Can you sing it again, please? David – guitar?" she added, looking at David.

David picked up his guitar, chose a key, and nodded to Jill. This time, the forth line came back to Jill, as David strummed the chords. Then, to Eleanor's delight, David joined in the chorus, but with a harmony.

"Will you be able to get the words?" Eleanor asked. "And can I write them down? I mean the ones you remember," she said to Jill.

"Do you like it then?" Jill asked, as David got up to go and find pen and paper.

"Yes. Sometimes we get asked to speak about," she hesitated. "About our faith."

"Testimonies?"

"Yes. I think this song says what I believe. It depends on the rest, of course."

"From what I remember, one of the verses talks about angels and visions, but yes, the song is a very personal song. I think the old people will like it. Ah, Dad," Jill said, as David returned. "Eleanor is wondering if it's suitable."

"For the old people, or for her?" David asked.

"Both."

"I think the old folks will like it, and I know it's what Eleanor believes, so, yes, very suitable I would say."

"What about the bit with angels and visions?" Eleanor asked.

David thought, then picked up his guitar. "It's coming back – I think."

> "Perfect submission, perfect delight,
> Visions of rapture now burst on my sight;

a pause

> Angels, descending, bring from above
> Echoes of mercy, whispers of love."

He put the guitar down. "Okay, rather whimsical? Poetic? What do you think? Shall we sing it again?"

Four or five minutes later, Eleanor had the tune in her head and the words in front of her.

"Okay, Eleanor, ready?" David said.

"Yes, but you have to sing too, remember?"

"Eleanor," David said.

"We had an agreement. Remember?" she said quietly.

"An agreement?" Jill asked, intrigued by this information. Eleanor turned to her. "Yes, I used to sing with Tom, and your dad helped us. Tom's gone to uni, so I have no one to sing with. I sang on my own last time on condition that we sang together this time. Right?" she added, looking at David for confirmation.

Jill said nothing, but mentally gasped at the young girl's apparent hold over her father, especially as he nodded agreement. David picked up his guitar, strummed an intro, and then nodded to Eleanor.

They sang just the two verses and choruses, including the Da da da da dah dah where they didn't know the words. Then they both looked at Jill.

"Wow!" she said. "I think they'll like it."

"Did you like it?" David asked her.

"Well, it' not my cup of tea, but you were both pretty good."

"Right, one down, one to go. I'll find the rest of the words later," David said

"How about 'Amazing Grace' for the other one?" Jill asked. "And this time, Dad, you sing the melody, and Eleanor, you sing a higher accompaniment. Have you got the words and music?"

David found the music, but Eleanor looked puzzled.

"I'm not sure how you mean," she said. "Can you show me?"

David looked at Jill. "Can you demonstrate?" he asked her.

"Okay, you start, and I'll come in," Jill answered.

Eleanor's eyes were on Jill, as they sang the first verse, with Jill singing the harmony that she suggested. "And again, please?" Eleanor said, as they finished. This time, Eleanor joined in, but quietly as she concentrated on the her part.

"What do you think," David asked Eleanor.

"It's pretty high," Eleanor said.

"It's basically this line, but sung an octave higher," Jill said, showing Eleanor the music. "Here, you hold the music. Can you read music?"

"Yes, to a recorder," Eleanor said. "But this will help."

"Right, let's go all the way through, then," David said.

It wasn't easy, with three of them sharing the one copy, but after the first two verses, Jill withdrew leaving

Eleanor singing the harmony on her own. At first, Eleanor felt vulnerable, but by the end, her confidence had returned. Jill applauded.

"That was good – well done. I think the old people will really like it," she said.

"Thanks, Jill. And we didn't even wake up the little man," David said.

"Little man?" Eleanor said.

"My grandson, James. He's having a rest. So, cup-of-tea time, Eleanor?"

"You don't drink tea, Dad," Jill said.

David looked embarrassed. "I do sometimes," he said.

"But I always have to bring my own tea-bags," she exclaimed. "Is there tea in the house?"

David just nodded, and Eleanor kept her eyes down.

"I'll go and check on James," Jill said, getting up.

"Sorry," Eleanor whispered, after Jill had gone out. David grinned. "Don't be silly. So, are you going to make it? Oh, I've bought a box of different kinds of tea-bags – I mean different kinds of tea. You'll see it in the cupboard – you can choose which one."

Eleanor stayed on a while, since it was too early for the church tea, talking to Jill while David played with James. When it was time to go, she picked up the music for their second song in order to practise he lines with her recorder. David said he would probably not be out that night – it depended on Keith's call-out, so they arranged to meet as usual the following Sunday.

"And I'll have the words to Blessed Assurance, Eleanor. Bye."

"Well, well," Jill said, as David rejoined her in his lounge.

"Well, well?" David echoed.

"Quite a young lady, Dad."

"Yes, she is," David agreed.

"Talented."

"Yes, she does sing well," David said.

"Oh, I didn't only mean singing. She's doing pretty well at," Jill paused, but only briefly, "school."

David wasn't sure about the pause, so he ignored it.

"How do you know?" he said.

"We were chatting. Didn't you notice?"

"Yes, I did actually. Thank you for being kind."

"I wasn't just being kind – she was interesting."

"Yes."

"And very pretty… "

"Jill!" David spoke sharply.

Jill looked up and opened her eyes wide as though totally innocent. "Yes, Dad?"

"Jill, was that necessary?" This time he spoke gently.

"Dad, is there something you should tell me?"

"No, of course not," David replied.

"So there's nothing going on, I mean between you and this girl?"

"She does have a name, Jill."

"Just answer me, Dad."

"There is nothing going on, Jill. Tell me, why do you ask?"

"I'm not sure. The way she knows her way around here?"

"She's been here several times, in fact, along with the other young people as well."

"There's something else. It was the way you two were together – you were, um, so relaxed together."

"Oh." David hesitated. "Jill," he said slowly, "suppose I said there was something? What would you say?"

"What?" Jill exclaimed. "So there is something."

"There isn't. I just wondered what your reaction would have been if there was, that's all."

Jill thought for a moment. "I don't know. My first reaction would have been to tell you not to be so silly – sorry, Dad. I mean, she's only sixteen – she told me."
"You mean you asked her."
"Okay, yes."
"Why did you?"
Another pause. "Well, I was intrigued. Men do fall for young women, and I wondered how young she was. I must admit that I didn't expect her to be so young, I don't think I was as mature as that at sixteen."
David shrugged. "So a romantic liaison is hardly appropriate, right?"
Jill grinned. "One does hear of such things, Dad. But I wouldn't expect it with you. But maybe you should take care with Eleanor. Young girls can be very vulnerable, and there's what other people might think. Oh, that's Keith arriving, isn't it?" Jill jumped up and went to the door. Nothing more was discussed, and his family left after tea.

Chapter 14

Another Booking

David and Eleanor had their first practice session on the following Sunday. David had taken his daughter's comments to heart, and had every intention of keeping his time alone with Eleanor as short as possible. Eleanor already knew her harmony lines when she arrived, and since David had acquired the words and music to 'Blessed Assurance' they soon had it learnt. Ideally, Eleanor should have gone home at that stage, but as she had brought her tea with her, David didn't have the heart to tell her to leave. She also asked if she could listen to more of his music, assuming that he didn't mind. David said he didn't mind, so long as she didn't mind him working in his study at the same time – not that he had work that needed doing. Eleanor also took it upon herself to make a pot of tea, as she had done the previous week, but then she made a few sandwiches for David. David took her to church in his car, but made sure that they were early so as not to be seen together by too many people. Once there, he took himself off to the church office. This more or less set a precedent for the two following Sundays, the second of which was their final practice, or so David expected.

The appointment at the home was three thirty, and David had assumed that they would meet there. However, on the Sunday morning Eleanor asked if they could have another quick practice before going. This was at David's house, so then he took her in his car. Their two songs were separated by some other items, namely by someone reading a psalm, and another person reading a poem.

Someone played a medley of hymn tunes, and then a man gave a short spiritual talk. David thought that he was more nervous than Eleanor, and wondered how their performance was received. The whole meeting took less than thirty-five minutes, and then they were served tea and biscuits where they were expected to socialise. David noticed that Eleanor seemed to be very relaxed as she moved around and chatted to some of the residents. David hadn't expected to socialise and found this part even harder than singing, and was glad that it was almost over. It also meant an end to Sunday afternoons with Eleanor, and he had to admit to having mixed feelings. On the one hand, he had enjoyed her company, but on the other hand he still remembered his daughter's remarks. It was for the best, he told himself, and anyway, the jazz evenings were still acceptable, assuming Lizzie went as well.

The first problem arose just before they were preparing to leave. Eleanor was talking to the assistant warden, and they beckoned David across.

"I was just asking Eleanor if you also sang secular songs," the assistant warden said.

"I said we hadn't actually sung very much, and that you had stepped in because my previous partner had gone to uni," Eleanor said.

"Well, you were very good," the assistant warden said.

"Thank you," David replied.

"The thing is, we also have an afternoon entertainment in the week. You know, sometimes a little demo on flower arranging – more for the ladies. Sometimes it's old-time singing. Sometimes someone comes in to play music – a keyboard, or a big violin thing – a cello. Sometimes it's pictures, well slides – we even have one of those new-fangled projectors."

"Should I put my name down – to be a resident, I mean,

when the time comes," David said, attempting to be funny.

"Ha, ha," the man said, but not actually laughing.

"Actually, I was wondering if you could fit in a visit – to sing to us."

"In the afternoon?" David asked.

"Which afternoon?" Eleanor asked.

"Wednesdays."

"Sorry, I'm at work," David replied. "I'm a teacher."

"Could you make – er … " the man asked, looking at Eleanor.

"I'm Ellie. Sorry, I'm at school. And I would need David anyway."

"What about sometime in the Christmas holiday? My name is George, by the way."

"Can we let you know," David said. "As Eleanor said, we are quite new at this game."

George looked disappointed. "We could change the day to suit you," he said.

"We'll let you know," David said, thinking it was better than just refusing point blank, after all, his singing days were over. "I must take Eleanor home."

"I take it that you aren't keen to go back to the home, David," Eleanor said, as he drove her home.

"Are you?" David said.

"Yes, I think it's a good idea. And I quite enjoyed it."

"What about the nerves?"

Eleanor shrugged. "Not as bad as I expected."

"So would you go on your own?"

"Not to sing, David, you know that."

"So what is good about it?"

Eleanor twisted in her seat to face him. "Okay, why were we there in the first place? Just to entertain?"

"No," David said.

"But that's how they saw us. Didn't you see the glazed look on their faces when Roger spoke, or when Juliette read that psalm? They switched off. We were, to quote, church people, end quote. Nice to listen to when they sing, but not to take seriously. We're not ordinary people, David, we're Sunday people. So if we met them in a non-Sunday context, they could see that we are normal people."

She turned back to a forward position, as David took it in.
"You don't agree?" she said quietly.
"Actually, I do."
"So?" She waited.
"Eleanor, I stepped in because you lost Tom, well, originally because Tom hurt his wrist. It wasn't meant to become a big thing. I certainly didn't anticipate singing at an old peoples' home, did you?"
"Tom and I sang there, oh, last spring. Look, if you're not happy, fair enough."
"That's emotional blackmail, Eleanor."
"No, David, I didn't mean it like that. If it sounded like that, I'm sorry."
"My mistake," David said. "And you really wouldn't go on your own?"
"You know I wouldn't."
"What about Tom. He'll be home."
"David! And when would we prepare? What would we sing?"
"Okay, and what would we sing? I don't follow the pop world."
"But that's just it, David," Eleanor, now speaking with enthusiasm, "you've got all those records in your loft. We could find something there, surely?"
David gave in. "All right, Eleanor, I'll go through the records."

"Thank you, thank you," she exclaimed, twisting round to face him. Then she giggled. "It's a good job you're driving," she said.

"Why?"

"I nearly kissed you!"

"Eleanor!" David exclaimed.

"It's all right, I've calmed down now," she replied, smiling. "You're quite safe now."

David dropped Eleanor off outside her house, and then drove home. Doubts began to assail him even as he drove. "But she was so enthusiastic," he told himself. "And it's for the right motives." But what about nearly being kissed? "Typical girl reaction", he told himself, thinking of how the girls would make little screams and wave their hands before hugging, when they were pleased. He did see the point about some of the old folk switching off, but on the other hand, they had listened quite intently to their, or rather, Eleanor's singing. They did seem to appreciate it, and they had certainly appreciated the way that she circulated and talked with them. There was no doubt that she had a gift, and it was not up to him to stand in the way of her gift being used. Somehow, this helped, and by the time he reached home, he felt much better about it. All it left was for him to start searching through his record collection.

Eleanor was already sitting with her friends when David entered, but seeing her with her friends suddenly raised doubts in his mind about their arrangement. She was with other young people – she was a young person – and he wasn't. He was a middle-aged man – a single man. Mind you, he thought, maybe it was a good job he was single. What wife would be happy to see her husband spending time with a teenage girl. If he was a teenager as well, then there would be no problem. Like with Tom. Except that unlike Tom, he wouldn't be immune to her charms. At that moment, Eleanor turned and saw him. She waved her hand and smiled, and for no good reason, his heart lurched. Immediately, he felt guilty – guilty because he had been thinking about a relationship between them, albeit, one between them as teenagers. What was his brain doing? He pulled himself together. That settled the matter – he could not go ahead with the singing. But how on earth could he tell her, let alone explain? With that on his mind, he was distracted from the service, which in turn caused further feelings of guilt.

The service ended, and he again rehearsed in his mind the words he needed to say to Eleanor. Thus, he didn't see that she was coming across to him.

"David," she began with obvious excitement. "Mum and Dad asked me about this afternoon."

"Yes," he answered carefully.

"Well, then they said would you mind letting them hear us sing?"

"Oh, when?"

"Tonight."

"Tonight?" David echoed.

"Unless you're busy?"

"But don't you have a young people's thing?"

"Only if you can't make it ..." she waited.

"All right, if you're sure."

"Oh, David, thank you. Say when."

"No, you say when. We can go as soon as you say."

It was obvious that David had to take Eleanor, and he wondered if people noticed them leaving together.

"Eleanor," David said, as they pulled up outside her house. "Perhaps you should introduce me as Mr Anderson."

"Really?"

"Well, like if I was your teacher."

"Okay."

Eleanor's parents seemed pleased to see him. As requested, Eleanor introduced him as Mr Anderson, who taught Geography. While Eleanor went to collect her guitar, they offered him a drink, however, David declined, hoping that his stay would be brief.

"It's very kind of you to help Eleanor," her mother said.

"It's been a pleasure, Mrs Jennings," David replied.

"She's been practising hard, that's why we said that we would like to hear her. She said the old people seemed to appreciate her, and she's quite excited about being asked to go back."

"Ah, well, it's not been confirmed," David said.

"Yes, she said you had to let them know – it's finding a suitable day in the holiday, right?"

Before David could answer, Eleanor came in with her guitar, which she handed to David. "What one first?" she said.

"You decide," David answered.

"Okay, Blessed Assurance first."

They stood at the end of the lounge and sang both songs. Eleanor's parents applauded at the end.

"I knew the second one, but not the first one," Eleanor's mother said. "Where did you get it from?"

"Jill said something about your grand-mother singing it, didn't she, David," Eleanor said.

"So what are you going to sing next time," Eleanor's father asked.

David hesitated, but Eleanor answered quickly. "We haven't decided yet, that's the first thing. David has quite a collection of old records – and he has the thing to play them on," Eleanor said.

"We had one, didn't we, dear. But you said we should get rid of it," her father said, addressing himself to his wife.

"So you managed to hang on to yours then. Lucky you'"

David looked embarrassed. "I'm a hoarder," he said.

"Mind you, I've noticed that some old albums are being released on CD now. And someone at work said that you can copy an old record onto a CD, if you know how. Needs a computer, apparently," Eleanor's father said.

"Yes, so I hear," David said. "Well, if you would excuse me, I should be going."

"I'll see you out, David," Eleanor said. "And we have to arrange our first practice."

"Yes," David said.

"Next weekend is out, so shall I pop round in the week? We need to find something – or some things to sing first, don't we. And will you tell that man – George wasn't it?"

"Yes, all right."

"You don't seem very enthusiastic," Eleanor said.

"Sorry, " he said quickly. "Things on my mind."

"Oh, so is it still okay to sing?"

David looked her and could see the potential disappointment in her face. He pulled himself together.

"Yes, Eleanor, it is okay. I will speak to George. So, what night this week?"

As he drove home, David felt annoyed; not with himself, but with Eleanor. He felt that he had been manipulated into singing again. It wasn't just that it meant finding some appropriate songs, and maybe, several at that. No, it also meant spending a lot more time with the girl, when he was trying to distance himself from her. For her own good, he told himself. So far, three people had made comments, one being his own daughter. Then he had a twinge of conscience. Had Eleanor really manipulated him? Perhaps he was being too hard – the reason she wanted to sing was because she wanted to witness her faith. Her motives were pure. In fact, her character reminded him of the comment that Jesus had made about Nathaniel – 'Behold, an Israelite indeed, in whom there is no deceit.' No, she was a lovely person, and the problem lay with himself. "Pull yourself together, man. She's a teenager who just happens to have a radiant smile. It wasn't just for you," he said, speaking aloud to himself. "Stop being stupid."

Despite giving himself a good talking to, he still felt unsettled later at home. In the end, he went up into his loft, and browsed his long playing records. He wondered how many songs they would be expected to sing. What type of songs? Would Eleanor expect him to sing? Probably. It was cold in the loft, and he didn't stay up there long. Once down, he picked up pad and pen. On the left hand side he planned to make a list of genres. On the right, he decided to put down any actual titles that came to mind. Then he paused for a moment as he recalled the records in his loft. Folky. Jazz. Old pop. Another pause – what kind of folk music – traditional or modern? World War I, or II's era. Jazz, well he had those records with Ella Fitzgerald. Old pop – Cliff? Everly Brothers? or Bing Crosby, Perry Como or Frank Sinatra? Perhaps he had better go to a music shop. Yes. That would be a start. That and a selection of records from his loft. Although his list was still blank, he felt much better. He even felt a twinge of excitement, and he had had no problem so far with Eleanor. Yes, perhaps he had been silly. Why should he think of her as being different from one of his own sixth-formers.

By Thursday evening, the evening he had arranged with

Eleanor, he had spoken to George, and had been shopping twice. He had also spent well over an hour browsing on the internet. Often, one search led him onto other names, names that he did recognise. He was amazed by the sheer number of songs that some artists had recorded. The bad news was from George. When David had asked what was expected, George had replied, without hesitation, that an hour would be fine. David had nearly choked on the phone.

"An hour? George, that's the first time we've sung more than one song, and only the third or forth time we've sung together."

"Oh, so what do you suggest?"

"No more than fifteen minutes, and if that isn't enough, then I suggest we leave it."

"Half an hour," George said.

"George, we've only sung Christian songs, so there's the problem of knowing what to sing in the first place. I can't commit us to filling half an hour, sorry."

"Do you tell jokes?"

"What?"

"Or play an instrument – or show pictures?"

"Pictures? What kind of pictures?"

"Holiday slides go down very well. Have you been to anywhere interesting?"

"I crossed America, oh, several years ago – by bus."

"Great. So sing, and show pictures. You say they are slides – can you digitise them?"

"Digitise them?"

"Yes, get them onto a computer. We have a video projector."

"Oh my," David said. "I assumed that I would bring my own slide projector."

"Well, you can I suppose. So it's settled. An hour?"

"No, George. But maybe half an hour. Anything extra will be a bonus. Yes or no?"

George agreed, and also confirmed that it would be in the school holidays. When David put the phone down he had mixed feelings. A whole hour? No chance, but maybe half an hour. Some singing and some slides. In some ways, it was exciting. Even exhilarating. But also worrying – were they up to it? What would Eleanor think about fifteen minutes of singing? He grinned to himself. He would tell her they were expected to sing for an hour and watch her reaction. It suddenly struck him. Just a few days earlier, he had been dreading it, and had hoped to avoid it. And for different reasons. He did find her an attractive young woman. Well, he would behave – no, silly word, he would make sure that their relationship was professional – after all, professional dancers managed it, and they had to cope with quite intimate situations.

Eleanor arrived at seven-thirty, and brought her own guitar.
"How did you get here? You didn't walk, did you?" David said, as he suddenly realised that it was dark outside
"No, Mum brought me," Eleanor said, turning and waving to a car that was waiting in the road. "She said to phone her when we're done. I had no idea how long it would take."
"I can run you home, if you like. It'll save her the trouble. Do you want to tell her?"
"Okay, thanks. Oh, she's going."
"Never mind. Right, how are you? Coat?"
"I'm okay, but what about you." Eleanor said, handing David her coat. "You didn't seem keen, did you, so?"
"I've spoken to George," David said, following her into

his lounge.

"And …?"

"He suggested an hour," he said casually, as he sat down.

"What?" she gasped.

"And I said fine."

"David! You didn't."

David laughed. "No, I didn't. I said fifteen minutes."

"Fifteen minutes? Can we manage fifteen minutes?"

David shrugged. "If we can't, then we can't. I've been thinking, and I've been shopping."

"Shopping?"

"Yes, I've bought a selection of song books, mainly old songs – some very old traditional pre-First World War songs, some Wartime songs, and a Burl Ives song book. Do you have any ideas?"

"I'd like to try a jazz number – Ella Fitzgerald – or do you think that's too ambitious?" Eleanor replied.

"No, not at all. I'm not so sure how well I could back you though. Would that make a difference?"

"Oh," Eleanor said.

"I said how well – I'm sure I could manage something," David said, trying to be positive.

"I asked Mum and Dad and they asked how old the old people were."

"Well, it's sheltered housing cum a residential home apparently. Say sixties-seventies-eighties?"

"They wouldn't know about World War I songs, David."

"I'm not sure. Some of those songs are timeless now. Do you know 'It's a long way to Tipperary'?"

Eleanor thought for a moment. "I don't know it, but it does ring a bell," she said.

"And what about 'We'll meet again' – Vera Lynn?"

"I've heard of Vera Lynn. That's Second World War."

"Okay, Clementine? On Yonder Hill? Barbara Allen?"

"No, no, and no."

"I knew an old woman who swallowed a fly?"

"What?"

"It's in the Burl Ives song book," David said.

"Oh, David, I'm beginning to regret this now," Eleanor said glumly.

"Look, let me get a paper and pen, and we'll makes notes. First question, do we stick with one genre, er, style, or mix them up, and second question, one era, or across a time scale?"

"No, first question, how many," Eleanor said. "Five? Or more than five?"

"No, let's make a list first, then pick from the list. We may not even make five, or," David paused, "We may find it hard to limit to five."

"Huh! Some hope."

David got his pad, and a pen, and sat down again.

"Genre," he said.

"Can you explain, David?"

"Okay. Traditional folk, modern folk, pop, humorous, ballad, country and western, and of course, jazz. One kind only, or a mixture?"

"What do you think?" Eleanor asked.

"Well, by not tying ourselves down to one particular genre, it will be easier to find songs."

"And the same then, if we don't stick with a particular period," Eleanor said.

"Exactly. Right, let's start with one of the song books," David said, getting up again, and moving to his keyboard. He propped the first book, 'Traditional Folk Songs' up above the keys. "Sit here, and we'll go through it together. If you recognise anything, tell me and I'll play it. Ditto if I see something."

It took three quarters of an hour to finish two books – the

traditional folk songs, and a book of 'Wartime Melodies', but they did have six song titles written down. David looked at his watch.

"I think we should call it a day, soon, Eleanor. Copy out the list and take it home and ask your parents what they think. Oh, and take the Burl Ives book too – they may recognise some of the songs."

"We don't have a keyboard, David."

"I meant by name, oh, and ask your grandparents. We still haven't looked at modern folk songs, or pop songs, I mean old pop songs. Should we look at Bob Dylan, Elvis, Cliff, Buddy Holly, The Everlys? And going back further, Perry Como, Petula Clark, Jim Reeves."

"How do you know so many names?"

"I've been on the internet. If you browse the charity shops, you'll see the same names – especially Jim Reeves. Come to think of it, we could probably do a whole session using Jim Reeves. Anyway, write down those names, and see what they think."

"I'd still like to try an Ella Fitzgerald song – do you think I'm being silly?"

"No, I'd like to hear you. Look, where do your grandparents live, the ones with the record player? Could you borrow it?"

"Why?"

"Because you could then borrow my record of Ella," David said.

"Oh, really? That would be fantastic!"

"Well?"

"Well what?" Eleanor said.

"So could you?" David asked. "Could you borrow it?"

"Probably. I'll tell them it's important."

"Right, one last thing. George really did suggest an hour, and I said we couldn't do an hour. So then he asked if we could do something else to fill the time. Tell jokes, or play a musical instrument. The last idea was for me to show some pictures, you know slides."

"Do you have any?" Eleanor asked.

"Well, yes. We went across America years ago. The problem is that he wants to use a computer to show them. Do you know anybody who can, I think the word is, scan them?"

Eleanor thought. "I know what you mean, our geography teacher has his slides on a computer. I could ask him how he did it."

"Okay, then. We'll call it a day. I'll get the record for you, and take you home. Hopefully, your parents can suggest some more songs. If we could manage ten, then I think that would be plenty."

David had expected to start that very first Sunday, but Eleanor had told him she was unavailable. The reason became clear the following Sunday – it had been her birthday weekend.

"Oh," David said. "Why didn't you say?"

Eleanor looked embarrassed. "Sorry," she said.

"So, big party?" David asked.

"No, it was a family do. Both grand-parents – oh, and I've got the record player. I think I know one of the songs, but I'm not sure how good it sounds. Oh, I asked about the slides thing at school, and the teacher said he had bought a special slide copier for his computer."

"Oh," David said. He had meant to ask his colleague in the staff room.

"But," Eleanor continued, her face showing enthusiasm, "I was telling my other grandpa about this booking and the need for someone to copy your slides and guess what? He has a slide copier."

"Your grandpa!" David exclaimed.

"Don't sound so surprised. My grandpa is quite with it

when it comes to technology."

"Sorry," David said.

"Anyway, he said he could do it for you."

"Really?" David gasped.

"And there's more good news," This time she waited.

"Yes," David said cautiously.

"I asked them about songs. They knew some of those old ones, but they also suggested some more. I have a list of over a dozen. Have you heard of, oh, Perry Como – Catch a Falling Star? Dad suggested a song by a lady called Tammy something. I've got it written down, but I don't have the music. Other songs were 'Blowing in the Wind,' and 'Bridge Over Troubled Waters,' which I have heard. So?" she ended up breathlessly.

"Fantastic – all we have to do is learn them," David said. "But first, let's hear your jazz number."

Eleanor looked worried. "I'm not convinced about it, David."

"But do you like it, I mean, do you like singing it?"

She nodded. "But when Ella sings it, she has a backing group."

"Never mind, let's give it a go."

"On my own?"

"Eleanor, I don't know it, so yes, please – then we'll have a drink, then we'll start work. Okay?"

Eleanor stood at the other end of the room. She was nervous and to start with, her voice was shaky, but she knew the words and the melody.

"Well?" she said.

"Eleanor, that was good," David said.

"Come on, be serious. It was better at home."

"That's because you're nervous. Okay, it's not up to Ella's standard, and you were shaky to start with, but you got better. If I could do some kind of backing, would that help?"

"Yes, please."

"Then I'll need to borrow my record back. Right, let's have that drink, and then we'll start work."

Working involved them going through the list, and moving between his keyboard and his computer. Some of the songs were in his books, but some they had to find on the Internet. Then they had to download the song, and if possible print out the music as well as the words, before trying them out orally. In some cases they were fortunate in that they could actually listen to someone singing the song. It was fairly intense, and before they realised, over two hours had passed. Eleanor noticed first.

"David, look at the time," she gasped.

"It's not late," he replied.

"Didn't you hear this morning, it's young people's tea, and I told Lizzie that I would be there."

"Do you want me to take you now?"

"What do you think?"

"Well, I was hoping that we would agree on a final list today – then we can both start learning them, or at least get familiar with them. What about after church? Could we finish then?"

"No, I can't do that today."

"Well, you decide, Eleanor."

"Let's carry on then. Oh, there's one other thing. I would like to include just one Christian song, what do you think?" Eleanor said.

"Fair enough. Have you got one in mind?"

"Yes."

"Well?"

"I'll sing it to you at the end if there's time, okay?"

"Okay. Right, so where were we?"

It was another hour before they had finalised their list. Besides the list, there were two copies of the words and, where appropriate, music. There were now eleven songs, all old, and most of them new to Eleanor, although David could recognise their titles. Some were quaint, some were funny – such as the one about the old woman who swallowed a fly. Some were corny – and some needed to be modified, according to David, so that the song about someone being the only girl in the world talked about by a boy. David said the older men would like it when sung by Eleanor.

"All we have to do now is to learn them," Eleanor said.

"And work out the harmonies," David added. "Plus work out a backing for Miss Fitzgerald."

"Are you still sure about that one?"

"Yes and no. Yes about you singing it, not so sure about my contribution, but we will definitely aim at it. I'll need to borrow my record back."

"Okay, I'll lend you your record," Eleanor said, laughing.

"And what about your Christian song?" David asked.

Eleanor looked at her watch. "Is there still time?"

"We'll make time," David said.

It was unfortunate that by making time for the extra song, and then making tea, that they were late for church. Not very late, but the first hymn had started. Normally David would have slipped into a single seat near the back but they were ushered by a steward as a pair. David did wonder whether their arriving together and then sitting together was noticed by some people.

"Whoops," David whispered. "We'd better not be late again."

"And I hope Lizzie doesn't make a scene."

Chapter 15

David Learns to Cook

The end of term was always a busy time for David – end of term examinations, marking, and then reports. It meant that David had little time to think about Christmas. Because this would be his first Christmas on his own, Jill had already planned to have him for Christmas Day. Daniel, now in his third year at university, had told David that as he expected to spend Christmas with his girl-friend's parents, he would like to bring her to meet him some time after that. David had agreed immediately, and without really thinking about it. She would have to take them as she found them, he reasoned. Jenny would have worried about it – what food to prepare, what would this girl think of them, and much more, David thought. From what Daniel had said so far, it seemed that this girlfriend was extra special. This fact alone would have both excited and worried Jenny. David's main reaction was sadness in that if Daniel had found the right girl, then Jenny had missed the joy of knowing her.

Despite David's initial reservations, he was now looking forward to the performance at the old people's home. He was past thinking about their relationship now. They were just two people, comfortable in each other's presence, with no other motive apart from rehearsing. He still compared Eleanor to other girls – such as Lizzie (who had made quite a fuss that time when Eleanor had missed the young people's tea) or Samantha, the vain girl in his class. Once or twice he had wondered what they would do after the session at the home, but he had deliberately chosen not to think about it. However, he had managed to check out his slides, and select a sample for Eleanor to give to her grandad.

The rehearsals with Eleanor had gone well, and with no more late arrivals at church afterwards. On the last Sunday before Christmas they did a complete run through, including the introductions to each song. David had already spoken to George at the old people's home, and they had agreed on a day between Christmas and the new year. He also said he would be bringing a computer disc of pictures. Because they had added three more songs, making a total of fourteen, David and Eleanor had decided to sing seven, then have a break for the slides, before singing the final seven. Eleanor's jazz number was in the first section, and the second section ended with her Christian song. It was a Sunday afternoon, and there was a carol service at the church that evening, so David took Eleanor and her guitar home. Her parents were then going to accompany her to the carol service. David lifted Eleanor's guitar from the back seat, and handed it to her. "Well, Eleanor, we are just about ready. How do you feel now? Nervous?"
"Excited. And nervous. I wonder what they will think. What about you?"
"I don't know. I've had a lot on my plate at school."
"Oh, I'm sorry," Eleanor interrupted.
"No, no. Doing this has been a distraction from school – sorry, that came out badly – I've actually enjoyed it. Anyway, off you go. See you tonight at the carol service. Bye."

The carol service was always well attended – in fact it was usually crowded. Although his parting words were that he expected to see Eleanor that night, once he was home, he had second thoughts. He thought he wouldn't be missed if he did have a quiet evening at home. Maybe it was because he was a man, but David had never been so enthusiastic about Christmas as Jenny. It was Jenny who had organised the children's presents. It was Jenny who had investigated and bought the tree. And put up the decorations. This year there were none. And he hadn't even bought any presents, but that did bother him. What on earth did one buy a daughter? He tried to think of last year, but it now seemed a very long time ago. Jenny had been ill, but not too ill to organise. It had been a matter of pride to her that everything had been normal, and David had gone along with it. Clothes. It came to him. That was it. Jenny had bought Jill a blouse. Well, he would go into town on the Monday and browse. Then there was Keith and Daniel. Bother. Jenny would have sorted it by now. Daniel would be happy with a cheque, but Keith? He would have to phone Jill – in which case he could ask what she would like. Maybe he could ask Eleanor? Yes, good idea, he would go to the carol service.

The carol service wasn't just crowded– it was overflowing. David was tempted to go home again, but then Nicola stopped him.
"Are you trying to escape, David?" she asked, laughing at him.
"Well, it is rather crowded," he replied.
"Isn't that a good thing. I mean, isn't that the whole purpose to have visitors? There is an overflow room, that's where I'm going. Coming?"
"You're right," David said. "Sorry."
"You don't have to apologise to me. Anyway, how are you?"

There were refreshments after the carol service, and it was natural for David to go there with Nicola. It was also very crowded, and several people came up to talk to Nicola, which made David feel slightly redundant. However, Nicola made sure that David was involved. She would remind them, if appropriate, that it was David's house they had moved on to after the pizza evening. Suddenly David saw Eleanor and her parents. They were coming across towards them.

"Elly!" Nicola exclaimed as they arrived

"Nicky!" Eleanor said at the same time.

The two girls hugged, before Eleanor introduced her parents to Nicola. "And Mr Anderson you know," she added.

After they had shaken hands quite formally, Eleanor's mother mentioned the forthcoming performance.

"Eleanor tells me that you're ready for the old people, Mr Anderson," she said.

"Please call me David," he replied, "and yes, I think we're as ready as we can be."

"Old people?" Nicola asked.

"David and I sang at the Sunday afternoon service that the church did for them, so they then asked us to do a session on our own."

"What, a whole service?" Nicola gasped.

"No," Eleanor laughed. "We sang at the service, that's all."

"You both sang – together?"

"Yes. I used to sing with Tom, and David helped us, remember? Then Tom went off to uni, so David helped me. After we sang at the service, they asked us to go back on our own."

"Why didn't you tell me?" Nicola said, turning to David. David shrugged. "Sorry. It didn't occur to me."

Eleanor's mother looked confused. "Are you two not together?" she asked, referring to David and Nicola.

David hesitated. He thought it was obvious that Nicola was much younger. He looked at Nicola, who then answered. "No, Mrs Jenkins, I'm at university, but we are friends."

"David lost his wife earlier this year, Mum," Eleanor said quietly. "Don't you remember, we saw her grave, oh, earlier this year when we went to your nan's grave."

"Oh," Eleanor's mum said, then again. "Oh."

Eleanor looked at her. "Oh?" she asked.

"No, nothing. I'm sorry, Mr Anderson, I didn't realise." David wasn't sure how to react, and for a moment, nobody spoke. Then Eleanor's mum spoke again. "Right, it's nice to meet you, Nicola, and you again, Mr Anderson. Well, Eleanor, I think we should be going. Okay, Len," she said, turning to her husband.

Before David could respond, Eleanor's mum was already moving away, then followed by her husband. Eleanor looked bewildered.

"I think they meant you as well," David said to Eleanor, who then turned and followed them.

"Was it something I said?" Nicola asked David when they were alone.

"No, I don't think so," David said slowly.

"Odd," Nicola said.

"Forget it," David said. Then, "Bother."

"What is it?"

"I wanted to ask Eleanor's help in choosing a present for my daughter. Ah well."

"Can I help?" Nicola asked.

"Oh. I don't know?"

"Okay, tell me about your daughter," Nicola said.

In the end, since it wasn't just his daughter, Nicola suggested that they meet up in town the following morning. She said that she had already planned on going in anyway, and it might be easier to suggest something if she could browse.

"You didn't tell me that David was a single man, Eleanor," Eleanor's mum said, as Len drove them away.
"A single man? What do you mean by that?" Eleanor said.
"Nothing," Len said, interrupting. "So when did he lose his wife, Elly?"
"Last Feb, I think. I remember the pastor talking about it. She wasn't ill for long, if I remember."
"Did he have a family?" Len asked.
"Yes, a son and daughter, oh, and a grandchild."
"So he's not young then," Mrs Jenkins said.
"He's …" Eleanor paused. She was about to tell them how old he was, but something in the tone of her mother's voice warned her. "Somewhere between old and young, I suppose. But he has been very helpful. I know Tom really appreciated his help."
"Yes, it's a pity Tom had to go off to university," her mother said. "Didn't I see him around? Couldn't he have sung with you?"
"Mum! And when would we have practised?"
"Exactly," Len Jenkins said. "Let's change the subject. I think your church put on a good show tonight."
"Thank you, Dad," Eleanor said. It wasn't meant to be a show, but if it got her father to go to church, she was pleased.

Eleanor's parents discussed the matter later that evening, but after Eleanor had gone to her room.
"I'm not happy, Len," Sheila Jenkins said.
"I can understand that, but now is not the time to make a fuss. If we stopped her now, well, how would you explain it to start with?" Len said.

"What do you mean?"

"Okay, give me a reason?"

"We are not happy that she's been with a ..." she hesitated.

"That's just it, we didn't know. It makes us look bad."

"But I assumed that she, I mean that he had a wife with him."

"Sheila, it would have been worse if he did have a wife, and she, I mean the wife wasn't around."

Sheila thought. "Okay. We let her sing, but then I think no more."

"But how, I mean, without causing a big upset. She's a good girl, Sheila. I think she sees this as part of her good deeds. We have no reason to think that there's been any, you know," Len said. "No, we must be very careful. Let's not rush. And we don't want to spoil Christmas, do we?"

David met Nicola as arranged in one of the well known coffee houses. This was Nicola's idea, and David had not been very enthusiastic about shopping with a young woman, barely out of her teens, but Nicola seemed very sure of herself. After coffee, she took David to a well known store and chose a silk scarf. But along with the scarf, David had to purchase a gift voucher. Next, it was a present for his grandson. Nicola seemed to know what was appropriate, having been told his age. Keith and Daniel were more of a problem since David was sure that Keith didn't need anything, and all Daniel wanted was money.

"David, it's the thought that counts," she said. "Do they smoke, drink, read, or listen to music? Do they wear clothes?"

"Oh. Keith does like whiskey."

"Any whiskey?"

"Ah! Okay, Sorted!"

"That leaves Daniel," Nicola said. "How about a book token? And wrap it in a pair of socks."

"Nicola, you're brilliant," David said. "Well worth the price of a coffee. Thank you very, very much."

Nicola laughed. "No problem, David. Okay, I'll be off now. Happy Christmas, oh, and I hope the singing goes well!"

David watched her walk away. It hadn't been as bad as he had expected. In fact, it had been similar to being with Eleanor. He had soon been unaware of Nicola's age, in fact, it could have been as if he was with Jenny. Very odd, David thought to himself, But it had been a very successful morning as far as he was concerned.

Christmas Day itself was a bittersweet time for David, and for Jill, although David did not realise it. It was not in his own home, and it was their first Christmas without Jenny. Present wise, Jill seemed to like the scarf, but maybe she liked the voucher better, David thought. Keith did like his bottle of whiskey, and his grandson did like his picture book and wooden toy. And David did like the sweater that Jill had knitted him, but he wasn't sorry when it was time to drive home. Christmas without Jenny was harder than he had expected. On top of that, it reminded him of the days of her suffering, and of course, the anniversary of her death was approaching. He was so grateful that he had the performance with Eleanor to think about, and wondered if he should contact her for a final practice. The only other thing on his mind was the impending visit of Daniel and his girl friend. He had already made up their beds. Daniel in his old room, and, Stephanie – or was it just Steph – in Jill's old room.

Boxing Day was hard. He had been invited to stay over at Jill's and now began to wish he had done. Instead, he went for a cycle ride. Without thinking, he followed the route to the swans. On reaching the bridge, he paused to look over. Yes, there were swans, further upstream. Suddenly he found himself thinking of Eleanor, and wishing that she was with him. Wow, was it all that time ago, he thought. His mind moved on as he wondered what she was doing right then. Should he have suggested that they came together? Then he remembered Eleanor's mother's reaction. Something had been odd – was it she didn't approve of him helping Eleanor? She had been fine that time they had sung to her and her husband. He finally moved on – it was too cold to remain standing looking at the swans. The tea shop was closed, as he had expected, but he did find a pub open. And they could serve him a sandwich and hot chocolate. Once back home, he pottered around, and then watched three films in succession on his television, going to bed well past midnight. Fortunately, the exercise and then the lateness combined to ensure that he passed into dreamland immediately. He dreamed of swans – and Eleanor!

Len raised the subject of the performance with his daughter on Boxing Day. He heard Eleanor singing to herself in her bedroom, and knocked on the door.
"How's it going, Darling? Is that one of your songs?" he said, when invited in and saw her sitting on her bed with her guitar.
"Yes, Dad," she replied.
"Sounds good to me."
"Thanks, Dad."
"So when is it, remind me."
"Next Monday – in the afternoon."
"Can we come?" Len said. "Do you think anyone would notice?"
"Dad!"

"Could we come to your practice on Sunday? Would Mr Anderson mind?"

"I don't know. Do you want me to ask him?"

"Or could you do it here? We really would like to hear you sing."

"I'll phone him and see what he says."

"Unless you don't want us to hear you sing," Len added.

"No, actually, it's probably a good idea – so long as you don't find fault. It's too late to change things now."

"Don't worry, I'll keep Mum in check, dear." Len bent over and kissed his daughter's head. "Love you, Eleanor," he added, using her full name.

"And you, Dad," she said, with a smile. "I'll phone David, I mean Mr Anderson, tomorrow."

Len went downstairs to Sheila. "I've been chatting to Elly."

"Yes, dear?"

"Yes, I do wonder if we've over reacted."

"Better safe than sorry," she said.

"Anyway, I've suggested that we see their final practice. In fact, I suggested that it's here."

"Oh."

"Yes, and either way, we do not criticise her."

"Them, Len. Don't they both sing?"

"Okay, them. Agree?"

"And then they stop!" Sheila Jenkins said.

"And who is going to tell them?"

"I'll think of something."

David had two important phone calls the next day. The first was from Eleanor, and actually woke him up. It was the morning after the three late films.

"Hello," he said rather groggily.

"Are you all right?" Eleanor asked.

"Eleanor? Oh Eleanor. Are you all right?" David asked, stressing the word you. In his dream, she had been with the swans – swans – river – danger?

"Of course I'm all right."

"But it's not yet eight o'clock," David said.

"I'm about to go to work. Have I woken you up?"

"Yes – a late night," he said.

"With your family?"

"No, late film on T.V."

"Was it good?"

"No."

"So why did you watch it," Eleanor asked, with a laugh.

"Because ..." he began. Bother the girl, he thought. It's none of her business.

"David." This time Eleanor wasn't laughing. Only recently she had heard a discussion about Christmas being both a time of happiness and a time of misery – depending on one's circumstances. "I'm sorry, I wasn't thinking. I'll phone later."

"No, no. I'm fine. So, what is the matter? Are you ill?"

"David, I'm just going to work. No, it's Mum and Dad." (David felt a cold chill – so maybe there was something?) Eleanor continued, "They would like to hear us sing and Dad joked about coming on Monday, but he settled for listening to our final run-through. The thing is, they suggested that we do it here. What do you think?"

"Is that all?" David asked. At the mention of their names, he had wondered if they were going to stop Eleanor singing.

"So you don't mind, then?"

"No, that will be fine. In fact, it will be good for us to have an audience," David said.

"That's true. Right, must be off. Bye. See you Sunday."

"Bye."

David's second call was about mid-afternoon. It was his son, Daniel.

"Hi, Dad. I've got a problem," he said.

"Yes," David replied, guessing that Daniel was about to change the arrangements.

"Yes, Steph has some relatives dropping in on Saturday evening, and we're kind of expected to be here."

"Oh, so what do you want to do?"

"Could we come on Sunday, Dad? There's a train that gets in at five past one."

"Just in time for Sunday lunch. Good timing, Daniel."

"Dad!" Daniel said.

David laughed. "Sorry, but isn't that what students do? I was hoping that you were going to cook for me."

"Sorry, Dad, I wasn't thinking. Look, we could come on Saturday," Daniel said.

"No, Sunday is fine."

"Dad, I'm sure Steph would understand."

"Daniel. Five past one on Sunday. At the station. Okay?"

"Thanks, Dad."

Daniel didn't phone so regularly as Jill, but it still had the same effect. To David, the phone was a tool for conveying information. To Jenny, the phone was for talking. The calls to and from his children were much shorter than they used to be, and as a consequence, they reminded him that there was no Jenny. It was mid-afternoon, and the house was empty, and suddenly he felt very low. He picked up the television controller, but then put it down again. Sunday lunch. He really had been expecting Daniel to organise it, not that they had talked about it. Daniel had learned how to cook at university, but David had not benefited greatly as Daniel had spent most of the summer travelling. Well, it would have to be pasta.

Probably spaghetti, the good old standby. Or maybe rice. Perhaps he should learn to cook – properly.

He was disturbed from his thoughts by the doorbell. "No I don't want double glazing," he muttered, as he walked to his front door. "And I don't want to read the 'Watchtower!'" he added, as he opened the door. "Eleanor!"

"Hello, David," Eleanor said brightly. "What's that about a tower?"

"Tower? Oh, no, the Watchtower magazine. I thought you were JWs, or a double-glazing salesman."

"You already have double glazing," she said laughing.

"So why should a double-glazing salesman come here?"

"I wasn't thinking," David said. "Come in."

"Were you asleep?"

"No, of course not!"

"So you were awake, but not thinking," Eleanor said.

"No, I was thinking – I was thinking about something else."

"Something private?"

"No. No, Daniel just phoned to say he would be arriving midday on Sunday," David said.

"That's nice."

"Except that I was hoping he would cook Sunday lunch."

"David!" she exclaimed. "That's a terrible thing to say." They were still standing in his hallway, Eleanor with her hands behind her back. David hung his head.

"It is. Sorry. Anyway, why do I have the honour of your company? Is it about Sunday?"

"No." She brought her hands round to her front and handed David a parcel. "Happy Christmas."

"Eleanor!" he gasped. "You shouldn't have."

She laughed. "Wait until you see what it is. I saw it and thought of you."

David took her into his lounge and then unwrapped his present.

"Eleanor! You cheeky woman," he said, and laughed. It was a book about cooking, but it was the title that amused him. 'Simple Cooking for the Simple Man.' But it wasn't just the title. The front cover showed a before and after title. The second word 'Simple' had been added above a crossed out 'Single'.

"That's sexist! Was there one for the simple woman?"

"Of course not. Actually, I imagine you can already cook some, if not most of the meals in the book, but it does include simple cakes."

"So will it cover me for Sunday?"

"Not if you want the traditional dinner with bells and whistles."

"Oh!"

"But I could help you," she added.

"Really?" David gasped. "How?"

"Have you got some paper?"

Eleanor left about twenty minutes later. First, she had made David decide on the meat. Then she told him exactly what to buy. Next, she added a shopping list of vegetables. Then it was to the kitchen to check the cupboards, and more things were added.

"When did you last use, no, when was the blender last used?" Eleanor asked.

"Daniel used it in the summer, oh, and Jill has used it recently – I think."

"So it still works?"

"Try it," David said.

It worked.

"Okay. So how about crumble – apple? Rhubarb?"

"Can you get apples and rhubarb at this time of the year?"

"Good point. What's in your freezer?"

"Not a lot. Ice cream of course. There is some frozen fruit, I think."

"Don't you use it at all?"

"Oh yes, I cook dollops of rice and freeze them. Sometimes I cook a batch of mince, and then freeze separate portions."

"Okay, let's investigate the freezer."

To the list was added instructions of when to remove the frozen gooseberries they had found and when to prepare the vegetables.

"And I will come round before church on Sunday morning to supervise you. You can take me to church leaving the roast in the oven, then pop the crumble in before you collect Daniel."

"But what about cooking the vegetables?"

"The roast pots and parsnip will go in after the service, that is, with the crumble. Look, I've written it down. You can cook the carrots after you have collected Daniel. And you already eat frozen peas."

"And you will be here on Sunday?"

"Yes. Bye."

Eleanor's visit had raised David's spirits, and he spent the rest of the afternoon reading his new cookbook. Eleanor was correct in her assumption that many of the simple meals were already known to him. He had cooked omelettes, but not with so many different fillings. The book included some frozen ingredients, but purposely omitted anything that came in a can. David already knew about tinned rice pudding anyway, but a quick sweet based on custard, drinking chocolate, sultanas and desiccated coconut caught his eye. The other section that interested him was the cake section. No fruitcake, but there were instructions to make Parkin, meringue, and to

David's surprise, Victoria sponge cake. It also said that he could use the same mixture to make cup cakes.

Even though it was school holiday time, he followed his usual Saturday routine, except that the shopping aspect was expanded. He had added a few extra things to Eleanor's list based on his new book. He also tried to plan for having two extra mouths and so bought extra milk, extra potatoes, extra bread, and extra cereals. Then he added mushrooms, eggs, and bacon. In fact, he felt quite pleased with himself as he approached the checkout. However, before he reached it, another thought popped into his head – flowers. Women liked flowers, and Stephanie was a woman. The vase that Eleanor had needed had not been used again. It would be.

After dinner – he still called a cooked midday meal dinner – he was ready for his first project. Victoria sponge. A proper round one. With a filling. He knew where the kitchen balance was, he had the ingredients, and his book even told him how much to use for different outcomes. He decided not to be too ambitious, and found the appropriate but moderate sized cake trays in the kitchen. It went better than he had expected, and by tea time he had two discus sized cakes on the cooling grid. It was at this stage that he realised that he did not have a clue about a filling, or a surface topping. His first thought was to phone Jill, but then he hesitated. He wanted it to be a complete surprise to Daniel, and therefore to Jill. He could phone Eleanor. Of course.

Eleanor's mother answered the phone.
"Hello, Mrs Jenkins," David said. "Is Eleanor available?"
"Yes. Is this about Sunday or Monday?"
"Well," David began.

"Because you're still coming here on Sunday, right?"

"Yes, thank you, Mrs Jenkins."

"We're looking forward to hearing her."

"Yes, I expect you are," David said. "So, may I have a quick word, please?"

David had to wait, and when Eleanor came to the phone, she was breathless.

"David, is there a problem about Sunday?" she asked.

"No, not at all, why?"

"Mum seemed to think there was."

"No, it's something quite different. I've made a cake."

"You've what?"

"I've made a Victoria sponge cake, and I want to know about fillings. The book mentioned jam, but it also talked about butter icing. What's butter icing?"

"Oh, David," Eleanor laughed. "It's a mixture of icing sugar and butter, but we use margarine."

"Icing sugar. Oh. You just mix them?"

"Yes. In a bowl, preferably using a mixer. One part butter or margarine, two parts icing sugar. It's easier with margarine cos it's softer. If you use butter, you may need to warm it and beat it up first. Is that it?"

"Yes. Sorry."

"I look forward to seeing it. Don't eat it all tonight," Eleanor said.

"It's for Daniel."

"Then I hope he appreciates the help I've given you. You could flavour the icing with cocoa or coffee by the way."

"Oh, thanks. Yes, I could."

"See you tomorrow, then, bye."

David woke early on the Sunday morning. It had been a long night, with several periods of wakefulness as his brain went over his new role – that of being a cook. He had already experimented with making butter-icing, using margarine, after having to go to the supermarket to buy icing sugar, and his Victoria sponge now had a drinking chocolate flavoured filling and topping. However, it was the prospect of attempting a complete meal that worried him. In the end, he decided to get up and make a start before breakfast.

Eleanor was later than she had hoped, and later than David had expected. She apologised, handed David her coat and followed him into his kitchen. The meat sat all by itself in a roasting tray. Some peeled and crossed sprouts sat in a dish of water. Another bowl had peeled whole carrots. Some potatoes had been brought up to the boil, and then drained. A parsnip had been cleaned, and was on a plate. There was a bowl of gooseberries, taken from the freezer the night before.

"Wow!" she said, inspecting the layout.

"Do you need an apron?" David asked, seeing that Eleanor was wearing a dress.

"No, I'm not doing anything," she said, smiling. "I'm here to organise you. So I'll just sit here."

Under her direction, David cut the parsnip into pieces, and parboiled them. Then he had to prepare the meat for roasting, surround it with the potatoes and parsnip pieces, and put it into the oven. While the gooseberries were cooking in the micro-wave oven, he had to prepare the crumble topping. By the time he had washed up, tidied up, and laid the table, time was running out.

"Right, after the service, come home, put the crumble in, then go to the station. As soon as you get back, cook the carrots and sprouts," Eleanor reminded David.

"Okay. Hey, look at the time. We're going to be late."

"I assume you can manage the frozen peas and custard?" Eleanor said, as David drove them to the church.

"Custard?" David said.

"To go with the crumble."

"Oh! Yes. I didn't think of custard."

"Can you make custard?"

David laughed. "Of course. Haven't you heard of cornflakes and custard?"

"Are you serious?"

"Yes."

Eleanor laughed. "I wish I could be at this meal."

"Really? Okay, you're invited," David said, without thinking.

"David! Mum's expecting me."

"Another time?" David said.

Eleanor looked at him. "Are you serious," she asked quietly.

"I owe you, Eleanor."

"No you don't."

David shrugged. "Okay," he said.

"But if you invited me without thinking you owed me, then I might consider it," she said.

"Right, I'll bear that in mind," he answered.

The service had started, and they had to slip in and sit together. Then, at the end, because Eleanor had left her bicycle at David's house, they had to leave together. Eleanor stayed long enough to check the oven, and make David baste the roasting vegetables. Then he went off to the station and she went home.

Chapter 16

An Engagement

The train was on time, which was good because not only was the dinner not over cooked, it meant there was also some time available to chat with Daniel and Stephanie before the rehearsal. This was the first time that he had met Stephanie, and he soon found that he liked her. This didn't really surprise him, because he had a high opinion of his son, and his son's tastes, that is, apart from music. Jill had already expressed a favourable opinion of her, and had also expressed the view that this might be the 'real thing.' With this in mind, David found himself looking at her as a prospective daughter-in-law. When David informed them after dinner that he had to leave them later in order to go to a singing practice, Stephanie was interested. Daniel had been told about David's singing by his sister, but of course it was new to Stephanie. Daniel also knew that a young woman was involved, and was slightly embarrassed by it.

"Did you know that your dad was in a choir?" Stephanie asked Daniel.

"It's not a choir," David interjected quickly.

"You mean it's a boy band?" she said as a joke.

"Very funny," Daniel said.

"So what is it? A quartet?" Stephanie asked.

"There are just two of us, I've replaced somebody who left," David said.

"Oh, did they fall out?" Stephanie asked.

"Oh, no. I had actually been helping them, but he's at university now. Eleanor didn't want to continue on her own, so," David shrugged, "I stepped in. Our church does meetings in old people's homes, and Eleanor and I sang.

Then, this particular home asked us to do a session on our own."

"Did you know that, Daniel?" Stephanie asked.

"Yes, Jill told me," he answered rather sheepishly.

"When is it?" she asked, turning back to David.

"Tomorrow afternoon. Sorry, but it had to be fitted into the holiday," David said.

"Tomorrow. So this is your final practice?"

"Yes."

"Where? At your church?" Stephanie asked.

"No, it's at Eleanor's, why?"

"Can we come? Is that okay, Daniel?"

"Ah," David said.

"Well, Dad?"

"I ought to check with her parents first," David said.

"Oh, so she still lives at home?"

"Yes, I'm afraid so," David said.

"What about tomorrow? Do you think that would be allowed?" Stephanie persisted.

"Well, if you really want to, I can't see why not. What about you Dan, will you want to come too?"

"Yes, yes, I think I would," Daniel said.

David was pleased with their final session. Eleanor had also scripted the introductions to the songs, and David was happy to go along with them. They were going to sing their songs in an approximately historic order, with a break in the middle. This was when David was going to show the pictures of his trip across the USA. It would also allow them a break from singing. Eleanor's parents sat in for the whole session, apart from making them a drink half way through. David found this slightly unnerving, but as Eleanor thought it was helpful having an audience, albeit of only two, he accepted it as being useful. During their break, he told them about Daniel and

Stephanie's visit, adding that he might bring them with him because they would also like to hear them sing,. As he was leaving, he asked Eleanor about picking her up the next day, but Eleanor's mother immediately said that she would be taking Eleanor, adding that she might also stay on to bring her home afterwards.

"You don't have to, Mum. I'm sure David wouldn't mind bringing me back afterwards," Eleanor said.

"Eleanor, dear, he has his son to see," Sheila Jenkins said.

"Thank you, Mrs Jenkins," David said. "Of course I wouldn't have minded, but I appreciate your offer. So, see you tonight, Eleanor?"

"Yes, of course."

"And you too, both?" David said addressing himself to her parents.

Len Jenkins looked embarrassed, but Sheila immediately replied. "Yes, I'll come with you," she said to Eleanor.

"Good. Bye then."

David was accompanied to church by Daniel and Stephanie. After the service, there was coffee, which gave opportunity to the various students home from university, and others who were back visiting families, to catch up with each other's news. There were contemporaries of Daniel who wanted to speak to him and meet the girl with him. There were friends of David who had the same idea. However, Stephanie wanted to meet Eleanor. While David was at Eleanor's house earlier that afternoon, Jill had phoned, expecting to speak to Daniel as well as David. When Daniel put her onto Stephanie, Stephanie took the opportunity to ask Jill about the woman who David had helped.

"What do you know already?" Jill asked, ignoring the reference to Eleanor as a woman.

"Virtually nothing. Daniel doesn't seem interested in

talking about her. Have you met her?"

"Yes, she came round for a practice when I was there."

"So what is she like?"

"She's very nice. And she has a lovely voice."

"What about, you know? Is there something else?"

Jill laughed. "Stephanie! What made you ask that? Did Dad say something?"

"No, not at all. It's just that Daniel seems secretive about it – as though there's a relationship that he doesn't approve of."

"Ignore him – he 's a man. Will you be able to meet her yourself?" Jill asked.

"Hopefully. Your dad thinks we can go to the old people's home tomorrow."

"Are you going to church tonight? I think you may meet her there."

"Oh, of course. Yes, perhaps I will," Stephanie had said.

Now, standing with Daniel, she kept glancing around. She noticed that David was talking to two women. She had already noticed that two other women had spoken to him, but they were young. One of these two, the older one could be the singing partner, she thought. As Daniel's friends were not interested in her, she excused herself and walked over. David saw her immediately.

"Hello, Stephanie, this is Eleanor," he said, indicating the younger woman, "and this is her mother, Mrs Jenkins. This is my son's girlfriend, Stephanie," he added, talking to Eleanor and her mother.

Stephanie was too surprised to speak, but Eleanor reacted immediately by giving her a hug.

"David told us you had come. How was your journey?" Eleanor said.

"Fine."

"David said you wanted to come tomorrow," Eleanor said.

"We are talking about singing, aren't we?" Stephanie asked, still feeling unsure. "I mean, who sings? Is it you or your mother?"

Mrs Jenkins laughed. "It's Eleanor of course."

"I'm sorry. You see, I didn't even know that Daniel's dad was singing until this afternoon."

"So you may come?" Eleanor suggested.

"Well, yes. I hope you don't mind."

"I don't mind at all, and I don't expect George will object," Eleanor said.

"George?"

"Yes, the chap organising it. I think Mum wants to stay as well."

"No, dear. It's just that it's easier to stay than go home and then come back for you," Mrs Jenkins said.

"We could bring her back, Mrs Jenkins," David said.

"I don't want to bother you, Mr Anderson," Sheila Jenkins said.

David didn't know what to say, so he looked at Eleanor.

"Mum, let David bring me home, okay?" Eleanor said. "It will also give us a chance to go over it afterwards, you know, maybe get some feedback from Stephanie."

"Well, if you don't mind," Sheila Jenkins said.

"It will be a pleasure," David said. "Now if you could excuse me, I need to go and put something into the church office. Can you look after Stephanie for me, Eleanor, please?"

As David left, James, the church Pastor joined them.

"You must be Eleanor's mother," he said to Sheila Jenkins. "I saw you with Eleanor last week, didn't I?"

"Yes, it was a lovely carol service," she answered.

"And are you another relation?" James said to Stephanie.

"No, I'm with Daniel, David's son," Stephanie replied, looking around.

"Oh yes, silly me? Sorry," James said, also looking around.

"Let's go and find him. I'll see you at home, Mum?" Eleanor suggested. It was a rhetorical question, and Eleanor did not wait for the answer, but left her mother with the Pastor.

"You must be very proud of your daughter, Mrs Jenkins. She has a lovely voice. I would have liked her to sing tonight, but she said she was working on something for the old folk."

"Yes, I would like to ask you about that."

"Yes?"

"What do you think about it?"

"Well, she has a gift," James said, uncertain about the question.

"I don't mean that."

"Sorry?"

Sheila Jenkins looked around. It was still quite crowded. "Is there anywhere more private?"

James thought hard. His vestry? Or outside?

"Let's step out side," he said.

"What's on your mind," James asked, having checked they could not be overheard.

"I assume you know that Eleanor does not sing on her own?"

"Yes," James said slowly, "David Anderson helped her."

"Did you know that they were asked to sing again at the old people's home?" Sheila Jenkins said.

"Go on," James said.

"Well we, that is my husband and I, didn't realise that it had involved them spending a lot of time together."

"Are you saying that there is an improper relationship?"

James asked. "Do you have evidence? David is a teacher and a respected member of the community."

"No, not at all," Sheila Jenkins answered quickly.

"But you have concerns?" he said quietly. He knew that improper relationships, as he put it, did occur, both in the church, as well as in schools. Only that morning he had noticed that David and Eleanor had arrived late, and together. And he suddenly remembered a comment that his wife had made.

"Reverend, Eleanor is seventeen. Mr Anderson is the father of adult children."

"You know he lost his wife, oh, nearly a year ago?" James said.

"So maybe they are both vulnerable?"

"Have you spoken to Eleanor about it?" James asked.

"Goodness me, no."

"I don't see how we can stop them singing tomorrow," James said.

"I agree. No, it's whether they should be encouraged to continue. It's a pity that there isn't another boy – or girl – of her age. There was a nice boy, but he's gone to university."

"Yes, that's how David got involved. Tom had hurt his hand, so David played for them."

"Maybe it's time for them both to move on. I mean, suppose it did develop into something, er, unpleasant. It wouldn't do your church's reputation any good. And even if it didn't, wouldn't people start to gossip?"

"So what do you suggest?" James asked.

"Don't ask them to sing again."

"Okay. But suppose they are asked again by the home?"

"Well, Reverend, I assume that you have some influence there." She paused. "But really, Reverend, I would have thought that a quiet word with Mr Anderson might be in order. Point out how unseemly it looks, him and a mere

seventeen year old doing things like singing together. I'm
surprised that nobody else has mentioned it."

"I think we all have such high opinions of them both, Mrs
Jenkins, and I am sure that you have nothing to worry
about."

"Now or in the future?"

"Both."

"So you won't say anything?"

"I didn't say that. I do appreciate your concerns, Mrs
Jenkins, but I need to think about it." He put out his hand.
"Thank you for being so frank, Mrs Jenkins, and thank
you for coming tonight."

Stephanie was very happy to be assigned to Eleanor, and
was in no hurry to find Daniel.

"Can I ask you something?" she said.

"Yes, of course," Eleanor replied.

"How well do you know Daniel's dad?"

Eleanor stopped and faced Stephanie. "Pretty well. Why
are you asking?"

"Are you his girlfriend?"

"What?" Eleanor gasped. "Of course not. What ever
made you think that?"

"I didn't think it. I was just asking," Stephanie said.

"But why? Has anybody said something?"

"No, just the opposite. Daniel knew about you, but he
didn't say that you were my age."

"How old are you, Stephanie?" Eleanor asked.

"Twenty one."

"Then I'm four years younger than you."

This time it was Stephanie who was stunned.

"Have I shocked you?" Eleanor added. "Let me explain."

Eleanor described how she had originally sung with Tom.
"He's here tonight actually," she said, and went on to

explain how Tom's injury led them to asking David to help, and how that when Tom had gone away, she still needed David to play his guitar for her. "I was asked to sing at a youth meeting, so he helped me there, then at an afternoon session at an old people's home. He refused to sing with me at the youth meeting – said he was too old – but he did sing on the Sunday afternoon. Then we were asked to do a session, just on our own." She added that it meant spending a lot of time together finding and putting together over a dozen songs. "George, the man organising it asked us specifically not to sing hymns. I said to David that it was an opportunity to show them that Christians can sing more than hymns. But I'm slipping one gospel song in," she added, with a grin.

"Oh," Stephanie said.

"So, no romance, okay?"

"Sorry."

Eleanor smiled. "So what about you? Is it serious?" she then said to Stephanie.

Stephanie didn't answer.

"Oh, sorry. Shouldn't I ask?"

"I don't know. I think I'm the first girl he has brought home."

"How long have you known each other?"

"Since going to university."

"Oh."

"But we've only been going out together for about a year. Just before his mum died."

"But you like him?"

Stephanie smiled. "Very much," she said

"Well, if he takes after his dad, I can understand that."

"Pardon?"

Eleanor felt herself blushing. "I mean, his dad is a very nice person. Come on, let's find Daniel."

By the time they found Daniel, David had finished his task in the church office, and was with Daniel.

"Right," David said, looking at his watch, "I think we should be going." He turned to Eleanor. "How are you getting home, Eleanor? Do you need a lift?"

"I'm okay, thank you. Lizzie's mum is coming to pick us up."

"Good," David said. "See you tomorrow then, bye."

The two girls hugged and said goodbye.

"She seems a nice girl," Stephanie said casually from the back seat of David's car.

"She is," David said.

"Have you known her long?"

"I've known who she was for a while, I suppose, but not to speak to until nearly a year ago – no, less than that. I was having a bad morning and she brought me a cup of tea."

"Sorry, she brought you a cup of tea?" Daniel said.

"Yes, one of the old ladies asked where your mum was. Three or four months after the funeral. I didn't cope, and went off to have a quiet moment on my own. Eleanor had noticed what had happened, and very quietly, just brought me a cup of tea."

"But you don't drink tea, Dad."

David turned to Daniel. "Daniel, it helped, I can assure you. Anyway, some time later I met her on the bus, and we spoke, and then again later she helped me with flowers for your mum's grave. When her singing partner, Tom, sprained his wrist, they asked me to play for them. When Tom went off to uni, she asked me to play. And the rest is history, as they say."

"And her boyfriend doesn't mind?" Stephanie asked, quite deliberately.

"Mind what?" David said.

"Her spending all this time with you, I mean, it must have

taken a lot of time preparing for tomorrow."

"Actually, I don't think there is one. I thought Tom and her were, you know, going out, but apparently not. She's never mentioned a boyfriend, but it's not my business anyway."

"No, I suppose not," Stephanie said, while making a mental note to find out.

Nothing more along those lines was said, and after spending a pleasant evening together, David retired, leaving the young couple in the lounge. After a certain time interval, Daniel asked Stephanie what she thought of his father.

"He's okay, nearly as nice as you," she said, and kissed him. "Mind you, I think Eleanor would rate him better than you."

"What do you mean?"

"Didn't you notice?" Stephanie said.

"Notice what?"

Stephanie pulled away and looked at him directly. "You knew she was at school, didn't you?"

Daniel nodded. "Jill told me."

"And you didn't tell me."

"Jill said not to. She said to let you form your own opinion."

"Of her, or of their relationship?"

"I don't think there is a relationship, Steph. I think Dad would have told me."

"Well, I think Eleanor would like there to be a relationship."

"Stephanie! You're not serious!" Daniel gasped.

"It was something she said – then she went very red. Oh, and didn't you notice the way she looks at him."

"Sorry, Sweetheart," Daniel said.

"You watch her tomorrow, and see what you think."

"When I'm not looking at you?"

Stephanie gave him a gentle punch. "Silly man."

"Which brings me back to my first question – my dad."

"I told you, I like him."

"Enough to be your father-in-law?"

"Pardon?" Stephanie looked at him. "If you said what I think you said, you didn't get it right."

"Oh! Okay, Stephanie Jordan, would you marry me?"

"Wow!" Stephanie exclaimed.

"And that's not the right answer."

"No, it's just that Eleanor asked me how serious it was, I mean, we were, are."

"What did you say?"

"I said that I thought I was the first girl you brought home."

"You are," Daniel said.

"Then I hope I'm the last."

"So the answer is?"

"Yes, of course."

"Shall we go and tell Dad?" Daniel asked, after another kissing session.

"Won't he be asleep?"

"I don't know."

"Tomorrow," Stephanie said.

"Busy day, tomorrow. Tell Dad. Go to grave. Go to their performance."

"And look for a ring?" Stephanie added.

David's normal breakfast was cereal and coffee on his lap, however, he had suggested a sit-down-together cooked breakfast.

"Dad, Steph and I need to pop into town this morning," Daniel said, as they sat down.

"Okay."

"But I, er, we would still like to go to the grave with you."

"Both of you? Don't feel obliged, Stephanie," David said.

"I'd like to come too, Mr Anderson," Stephanie said quietly.

"It seems funny you calling me Mr Anderson," David said. "Please call me David. The young people at church do."

Stephanie looked at Daniel, who shook his head slightly.

"So shall we go straight after breakfast?" Daniel said.

The gravestone was now in place, and they placed the flowers into the vase. David found it hard standing by the grave. He had been accompanied by Jill the first time he came after the stone had been erected. This time he was with a young couple holding hands, and it emphasised his own singleness. He looked at them, wondering. Was this girl his future daughter-in-law? Jenny would have approved of her, he knew.

"Thank you for coming, Daniel, and you too, Stephanie," he said. "I'll drop you off near the centre now. Don't be too late back. We'll eat tonight, if you don't mind, but I don't want to be late this afternoon."

"Of course," Daniel said.

"Do you have much to buy?" David asked, conversationally, as they walked back to his car.

"Not really," Daniel replied, casually.

Once he reached home, David felt lonely. If it hadn't been that Daniel and Stephanie were expected for lunch he would have been tempted to go for a cycle ride. Instead, he picked up his guitar and practised the songs. The most difficult one was Eleanor's jazz number, and for that, he played the record. He was going to play some chords, and some riffs, using his guitar plugged into his amplifier. Daniel and Stephanie arrived well before lunchtime, and let themselves in.

"Hello, had a good morning? Get want you wanted?" David asked. He was still sitting in the lounge with his guitar.

"Yes," Daniel answered.

"Coffee?" David said, getting up.

"We had some in town, Dad." Daniel replied. "Dad, Steph wants to ask you something."

"Yes," David said.

"I don't want to call you David." She paused. "Can I call you Dad?"

David looked her, then at Daniel, then back to Stephanie. "Well, yes. Okay," he said slowly. Then she brought her left hand round and held it out towards him. Suddenly it dawned on David. "Oh," he exclaimed. "So that's why you went to town."

David kissed her, but suddenly the joy was replaced with a feeling of sadness. "If only your mother could see you now, Daniel. She would have been so proud of you," he said, feeling himself welling up. Suddenly Daniel hugged him. "I still miss her too, Dad. And I wish she could have met," he paused, "the future Mrs Anderson, junior."

"The future Mrs Anderson, Daniel." David said quietly.

Lunchtime was a quiet affair. It wasn't just that Jenny was missed, David was also thinking of the afternoon's performance.

"Are you nervous, Dad," Daniel asked.

"Yes, of course."

"But you've done it before – you used to sing with Mum, didn't you?"

"Yes, but I was much younger then."

"Why did you stop?" Stephanie asked.

"I don't know. We had a family, moved around a bit, pressure of work. Do you tell people that you used to sing

– or wait to be asked. No one asked."

"Mum and Dad used to sing at home," Daniel said. "I remember being embarrassed when my friends heard them."

"Why?" Stephanie asked.

"Wrong kind of music," Daniel said.

"Then you'll be embarrassed this afternoon, Danny boy. Ours songs are not just golden oldies, they're from Noah's top ten. Perhaps you'd better not come."

"We're coming," Stephanie said.

Although they were not expected until two thirty, David arrived half an hour early. He was going to use his guitar and amplifier, so wanted to test the sound. Also, he wanted to make sure that his scanned slides were all right. They were on a memory stick and a CD, just in case, with George doing the technology part. They had been named numerically so that they would show in a predetermined order, leaving David free to talk about them. At home, this part had lasted twenty five minutes. Eleanor and her mother arrived ten minutes early, which was later than David had hoped. They were shown through to the resident's lounge, to meet with the other three.

"Are you sure that you don't want me to pick you up after?" Sheila Jenkins said to Eleanor.

"Mrs Jenkins, I don't know what time we'll finish," David said.

"Especially if they get asked for autographs afterwards," Daniel said.

Sheila Jenkins looked at Daniel.

"Please excuse him, he's my son," David said quickly. Then he turned to Eleanor. "Let's go and work out where we will stand, and check our guitars, look, the audience is already arriving."

The performance was very successful. After a nervous start, David and Eleanor quickly found their feet. After the first seven songs, all of which they sung together, David announced that he was going to show pictures from his trip across the USA. This had been in his first year of marriage, and had been done on a budget. Even the flights had been standby tickets, and the journey had been by bus. They had been lucky in that by using a posh English accent, they had sometimes been invited to stay with people, as apart from cheap motels. It was the accounts of such invitations that made the commentary more interesting. Although David had obviously seen the pictures when he had selected them, there was a certain poignancy following that mornings events. It was the same for Daniel, since many of the slides included pictures of his late mother. For both Eleanor and Stephanie, it was seeing pictures of Jenny as a young woman that were of interest, rather than the mountains, bridges, and building in front of which she was standing.

The second part of the performance began with Eleanor's jazz number. This was Eleanor's first solo number, and she hoped that nobody knew the Ella Fitzgerald version. David used his amplifier for this, either playing a single note riff in harmony, or occasional chords. Then they sang a few more songs together, where David sang harmony to Eleanor's melody. Eleanor's penultimate song was a more recent folk song – 'The Streets Of London,' before she announced her final song.
"Some of you may remember that David and I sang to you on a Sunday afternoon. When George asked us to sing this afternoon, he suggested that we left our Sunday songs out. However, what George called a Sunday song is part of my everyday life, and it expresses what I believe. It's an old song, and I would like to end with it."

David had practised with her, and he expected her to
show some nervousness, as she had with her jazz number.
But she blossomed as she sang, with no sign of nerves,
and David almost lost his concentration as he
accompanied her. As she finished, some applause began.
Not strong, after all, they were old people. Eleanor stood
still, and waited until it died down.

"Thank you for listening," she said. "David and I feel
privileged to be of service." Then she turned away, and
walked to the side.

"So, that's over," David said, as they drove away. "How
are you feeling, Eleanor," he said, speaking to Eleanor
who was in the back seat.

"I'm still feeling high," she said.

"Do you have to go straight home," Stephanie asked.

"Why, what do you suggest?"

"Dad," Stephanie asked rather nervously, "could we stop
off for coffee somewhere?"

"Yes, of course. Or we could go home – that would be
easier."

Stephanie turned to Eleanor. "Would that be okay?"

"I don't want to intrude. Isn't it family time?"

"Well, I don't mind. In fact I'd like to have a woman to
talk to," Stephanie said.

"Is that okay with you, Eleanor," David asked. "You
could phone your mum to explain where you are," he
added.

"Yes, all right," she said, but slowly. Something was
bothering her. It was Stephanie. She had just called
David, Dad. Odd.

Once home, David and Daniel carried in David's guitar
and amplifier, and Eleanor followed Stephanie into the
kitchen. This evoked further feelings, but this time she

knew why. She knew this kitchen as well as David, but it wasn't hers, so she held back. However, since the kettle was in it's usual place, and very obvious, she felt free to offer help.

"Shall I put the kettle on," she asked. Then as Stephanie looked around, she added. "The coffee is in that cupboard, and there are mugs in there."

With the kettle on, and the mugs and coffee on the bench, they faced each other. Stephanie was a little surprised that Eleanor knew her way around the kitchen. Eleanor was still thinking about the way Stephanie had addressed David. Stephanie had removed her gloves and so Eleanor looked at Stephanie's left hand.

"Is that what I think it is," she said, indicating the ring. Stephanie smiled, lifted her hand towards Eleanor, and nodded. Eleanor squealed and hugged her.

"When?" she said from somewhere around Stephanie's neck.

"Last night and this morning. We bought the ring this morning, and luckily, it fitted," Stephanie said, as they released each other.

"Any date yet?"

"No, we haven't had much time to talk about things. Oh, we haven't even told my parents."

"Will they be surprised?" Eleanor asked.

"I don't think so – I know they quite like Daniel."

"And so they should," Eleanor said. "After all, he has a good pedigree."

Stephanie looked at her.

"I mean, both David's children seem well brought up," Eleanor said, and blushing again.

She left Stephanie and went through to the lounge.

"I hear congratulations are in order," she said, going up to Daniel, who beamed.

"Yes, thank you," he said, shaking her hand.

Eleanor turned to David. "David, I feel I'm intruding. Shouldn't you be celebrating?"

"You're right," David said. "We should go out. How about we eat out tonight? Ah, Stephanie," he added, as Stephanie entered the lounge, "Eleanor suggested we should celebrate your engagement. I should have thought of it, but what with the singing, well, sorry. So, let me take you out. Thanks, Eleanor." He turned back to Daniel. "This girl is amazing. What did you think of dinner yesterday?"

"Well, I was surprised, Dad."

"Eleanor organised it. She told me what to do, and even came round on Sunday morning to supervise me." David explained.

"So that's how you know your way around the kitchen," Stephanie said.

"Oh, no, Eleanor's been coming here on Sunday afternoons to prepare for today. Anyway, let me go and book up."

"Dan," Stephanie whispered urgently. "Shouldn't Eleanor come too?"

"No!" Eleanor exclaimed. "You don't need me."

"Dan!" Stephanie said, looking at him. "Please?"

"Eleanor, we would like it if you could come."

"But what about your dad. And my mum?"

"Dad won't mind, and why should your mum mind?"

"Just a feeling."

"Dan, go and tell your Dad to book four people, just in case," Stephanie said. "Then she can say that you and I have asked her."

When Daniel returned, Stephanie voiced her other concern

"Dan, we haven't told my parents yet. What are we going to do?"

Daniel grinned. "Sorry, but I was talking to Dad about that, and he said I could borrow the car and drive us down to tell them personally."

"When," Stephanie exclaimed.

"Tonight."

"But what about the meal out?"

"We've booked an early meal. Then we'll drive on down."

"But they could be out!"

"Ah, okay. We'll phone just for a chat, and you can casually ask them what they are doing tonight. How about that? If they are going out, then maybe tomorrow morning."

Eleanor made her phone call first. Her mother wasn't enamoured with the idea, but Eleanor stressed that Stephanie wanted to include her, and that she wouldn't be late back. Stephanie made her call, and in the course of the conversation discovered that her parents were not going out that evening. Because Eleanor had worn a dress for the afternoon performance, she had no need to go home to change, and so remained at David's house for the rest of the afternoon. This suited Stephanie because as Daniel and his dad had some things to do involving them both, she then had Eleanor for company. Even though there was an age difference of four years, it was not obvious, and the two girls seemed to bond. Stephanie managed to hide her surprise as she learnt about the jazz evenings and the afternoons spent practising.

"So how did you discover that Dad played the guitar?" she asked, after learning about Tom and his injured wrist. She noticed that Eleanor hesitated, and possibly coloured up.

"It's complicated," she said.

Stephanie waited.

"I'd been to the cemetery with my mum, and we happened to go past Jenny's grave, and we noticed that the flowers needed changing, so I told David on the Sunday morning. He said there weren't any flowers at all. Anyway, he suggested that I showed him, so we went. When we came back I saw his guitar."

"Oh," said Stephanie, but wondering why Eleanor had been inside David's house. Perhaps she needed to use the little room. Best not to ask. On the other hand, Eleanor didn't think it was necessary to mention the times she had listened to David's music, or the cycle rides to see the swans. It had slowly dawned on her that she was being pumped for information about her and David.

"Anyway, that's enough about me," she said. "How did you meet Daniel? No, no. What about the engagement? Last night when I asked if you two were serious, you were vague. Then the next day I find out that you are engaged. Come on, tell me!"

Eleanor would have been very surprised to learn that she was being discussed in the manse. James was sitting with his wife.

"You're looking very pensive dear? Penny for them, or is it confidential?"

"Lucy, dear, do you remember telling me that you'd seen David Anderson and Eleanor Jenkins together out in the country?"

"Yes, cos you were sure I was mistaken."

"Hm," he said.

"Go on. Are you going to admit I was right?"

"And you still feel certain?"

"Oh yes. It struck me as odd at the time – you see, at first I assumed it was Jenny. But then I realised that Jenny was dead. Why, do you think something was going on?"

"I think her mother does," James said. "Her mother spoke to me last night."

"And she told you that there is something going on?"

"No, she didn't say that. She merely pointed out that they had been spending a lot of time together over this singing – did you know they had been invited back to the home to entertain the residents?"

"No, I didn't. I take it that George arranged it."

"They were there this morning, and I phoned George to see how it went. Apparently it was good."

"And is that it?"

"Do you remember how David played with Tom and Eleanor?"

"Yes, and he played for her after Tom had gone to university," Lucy added.

"Well, they did something together at a youth meeting, then again for the Sunday at the home, and then this morning. This morning they actually sang together, old folk songs mainly, but Eleanor did sing one gospel song."

"And Mrs Jenkins isn't happy. Why doesn't she deal with it? What did she actually say?" Lucy asked.

"She's passing the buck, Lucy. She wants me to talk to David. She was careful not to say that there was something, only that if something did develop, then we, that is, the church would be responsible. And even if it is all innocent, how does it look?"

"She has a point, James."

"But just supposing there was something? It's not illegal, not even immoral. David is single. Eleanor is single."

"She's seventeen – I remember her birthday weekend – so it's unwise. I understand how she feels."

"Who, Eleanor?"

"No, her mother, silly."

James sighed. "You're right. I'll speak to David."

Chapter 17

The New Year Social

The meal out had been a success. After the meal, Daniel
and Stephanie had driven back to her parents in David's
car, having dropped Eleanor and then David back at their
homes. They planned to return the next morning since
they were officially with David, and assumed that they
would all go to the New Year's Eve social together.
Daniel was also going to cook lunch for them. Maybe it
was his work, or the forthcoming singing with Eleanor,
but not only had David been unprepared for Christmas
itself, he had been unprepared for the sadness he then
experienced. With this in mind, and now that the singing
was over, he decided not to go to the New Year's Eve
social at the church. Both he and Jenny had gone last
year, even though she was ill, and he knew it would bring
back memories. He had just finished his breakfast when
Jill rang, primarily to ask about the afternoon before.
David had to admit that it had gone well, and told Jill
what songs they had sung.

"Is this the start of a new career then, Dad?" Jill asked,
and laughed.

"Why, are you worried about being embarrassed?" David
replied.

"Embarrassed?"

"Old man and teenager top the charts."

Jill howled with laughter. "No, I don't think I have to
worry about that," she said.

David feigned mock indignation. "I don't know how to
take that. Are you saying we're not good enough – or that
you wouldn't be embarrassed?"

"Dad, it's not the teenager bit. I'd have been embarrassed if you and Mum had topped the charts."

"Did we embarrass you when you were kids?"

"Dad! Of course you did. All kids are embarrassed by their parents at times. Anyway, what did Dan and Steph do when you went?"

"They came too."

"What? Was that your idea?"

"No, of course not. It was Stephanie's."

"Oh. Can I speak to them?"

"Ah, no. They have popped back to see Stephanie's parents. They went last night."

"What? I will have something to say about that to Dan when I speak to him. They are supposed to be with you."

"They are. They'll be back soon. I'll get Dan to phone you as soon as he arrives."

"Why did they go?"

"I'll let Dan tell you," David said.

"Sounds very off. Anyway, how are you, in yourself? Are you going to the social tonight?"

David hesitated. "Probably not," he said slowly.

"Feeling down, Dad?"

"Yes. Maybe after all the preparation for the singing."

"I think you should go," Jill said. "You won't be on your own."

"What do you mean?" David said quickly. Was Jill referring to Eleanor?

"I assumed Dan and Steph will go, or am I wrong?"

"No, you're right. Sorry. I'll think about it."

"Please go, Dad. I don't want to think that you are at home on your own tonight, okay?"

"We'll see," David said.

"Okay," Jill said. There was no point in pushing him, she knew, but she would have a word about it with Dan when he phoned. "You will get Dan to phone, won't you, Dad?" she added.

"Yes, of course, Dear."

"Sure?"

"Yes, I know he'll want to speak to you anyway."

"Oh? What about? Is he applying for a job?"

"I'll leave that to him."

"Dad! Oh. I forgot. How did you get on with Steph?" David laughed. "I assumed that was what you were phoning about."

"Well?"

"She's very nice."

"Is that all you can say? Didn't you wonder about, you know?"

"Really?" David said, putting surprise into his voice. "Is that on the cards?"

"That's what I'm asking you, Dad."

"Look, I'm a man. You don't expect me to read people's minds, do you."

"Not minds, Dad. How do they behave towards each other? I thought Dan sounded serious about her when we last spoke."

"I'll watch carefully and tell you, Jill." David said. "Or should I ask him?"

"Dad!"

David felt quite elated when he put the phone down, thinking about what Jill's reaction would be when Daniel did phone her later. He knew he had an hour before Daniel would arrive back, so he picked up Eleanor's present to him. The Victoria sponge cake had been appreciated, and he felt quite proud of himself. He knew that people took food to share at the social, usually finger food and home made cakes. He hadn't been asked, and hadn't been offended. If he had been asked, he would have picked up some bites at the supermarket. But now he had a cook book – of his own. He flicked through the book. Another cake? Or what? Quiche? Quiche Lorraine. He read through ingredients, and the timing. Got that, that and that, he said. And just over an hour.

Actually, it took well over the hour. It was the preparation, not the cooking. It was still in the oven when Daniel and Stephanie arrived back. Daniel noticed it first. "Dad, are you cooking something?" he said.
David tried to act nonchalantly. "Yes. Doing a quiche. Thought I'd use the kitchen before you got back, but I've overrun slightly, sorry."
"You're cooking a quiche?" Daniel repeated.
"Uh-huh," David said.
"What so strange about that?" Stephanie asked.
"Dad's never cooked a thing in his life," Daniel said.
"Oh yes I have. I can cook spaghetti," David said. "And rice."
"And baked beans," Daniel added. "So what's brought this on?"
"I bet it was this," Stephanie said, picking up the book. "Right?"
They knew about his present from Eleanor because of the Victoria sponge. Stephanie then opened it and looked inside the front cover. "Oh!"
"What?" Daniel said.
Stephanie passed him the book. Daniel read what was written inside the cover, and looked at his Dad.
"What?" David said.
Daniel handed him the book. David had not looked inside the cover, and didn't realise that Eleanor had written there. "Oh," he said. "But it doesn't mean anything, does it?" he added quickly.
"Probably not," Stephanie said. "Anyway, it was very

thoughtful of her. Is the quiche for lunch?"

"No, it's for the social tonight. But we could eat it now if you like."

"Let's wait and see what it looks like," Dan said.

"Yes, okay. Oh, Daniel, could you phone your sister?" David said, suddenly remembering.

David was left alone with Stephanie. He should have asked about how her parents had reacted. Instead he asked about the words in his book.

"It doesn't really mean anything, does it?"

"No, we used to write with love on our cards to our teachers," Stephanie said.

"To male teachers, and at secondary school?"

Stephanie giggled. "Yes."

"But were you serious?"

"Some of us were."

"Stephanie, don't say that."

"Sorry Dad. No, I agree, it's just a way of saying things. I'm going to tell her how much you appreciate it."

"Only if the quiche turns out all right," David said.

"Well, the Victoria sponge was all right. No, it was more than all right. It was brilliant."

"Thanks, Stephanie."

Eleanor phoned David towards the end of the afternoon.

"David, my guitar's at your house," she said.

"Yes, I thought about bringing it round on the way to church. Would you like a lift?"

"No, don't do that. Could you bring it to the church for me?"

"Yes, okay. Are you singing tonight then?"

"No, of course not."

"I could bring it on the way."

"No, at the church. Got to go. Bye."

"That was odd," David said, as he returned to the lounge.
"What was?"
"That was Eleanor. Could we take her guitar tonight?"
"Is she singing, I mean, are you both singing then?"
"No. I offered to drop it round on the way, but she was adamant. She sounded odd."
"In what way?"
"Not sure. Almost as if she didn't want to speak, but had to."
"I'm sure it's nothing," Stephanie said. "Anyway, ask her tonight."

Eleanor was already at the church and waiting in the entrance hall when David and his family arrived. Daniel was carrying her guitar, so Eleanor came across to collect it.
"Eleanor, can you look after Stephanie for me, I want to show Daniel something in the office for a few minutes," David asked her.
"Where do I take this?" Stephanie, who was carrying the quiche, asked Eleanor.
"Did you make that?" Eleanor asked, as she led the way to the kitchen.
"No, David did," Stephanie replied. "He did it this morning using your book." She paused. "The one you wrote in," she added quietly. "He is very pleased with it." Eleanor did not react, so Stephanie continued. "What made you buy it, Eleanor?"
"Oh, it was something he said about not having a cake, and I said he should learn, that's all."
"Well, Daniel was very impressed. So, it was a good idea, well thought of."
As they returned from the kitchen, Stephanie asked if Eleanor was with friends.
"There's a group of us, why?" Eleanor replied.

"Oh. I was hoping you would join me. At least until Daniel comes back."

"Why don't you come and meet my friends first then?" Eleanor said.

Stephanie was introduced to Eleanor's friends, including Tom, Ali, Nicola and Lizzie, and stayed talking until she saw Daniel. He recognised Tom and Nicola and came across, and also chatted with them. Then Eleanor spotted David.

"David's back," she whispered to Stephanie.

"Daniel, your Dad's back," Stephanie said to Daniel, as she stood up.

"Okay. Right, see you all," Daniel said, standing up as well.

"Are you coming, Eleanor," Stephanie asked. Eleanor looked uncertain. "Please? I need a female to talk to," Stephanie added, giving Eleanor an imploring look, and then smiling as Eleanor got up too.

David's little party then remained together, with various people coming across and chatting to Daniel and being introduced to Stephanie. Apart from food and drink, there were fun items and quizzes. Someone gave a humorous recitation. Another couple sang a humorous song. Then the organiser approached Eleanor.

"I've been told that you were invited to sing at an old people's home on Monday," he said.

"Yes," she said warily.

"I see you have your guitar. Any possibility that you could sing now, please?"

"No," Eleanor replied, shaking her head.

"Yes, go on," Stephanie said. "Please."

"There were two of us," Eleanor said.

"Dad?" Stephanie said, looking at David.

Eleanor looked at David. "What do you think? And which

one?"

"Ella," David said, getting up. "Come on."

James had heard Eleanor sing several times, but he was
surprised by her rendering. When she finished, everyone
clapped. Eleanor waited until they had finished.

"I also sang this song," she said, looking at David. "The
last one, David. Remember?" She turned back to the
people. "We were asked to sing secular songs, but I added
this one Christian song because I wanted to tell them
what I believed. Please don't clap at the end."

At the end, one or two people clapped, but most did not,
as requested by Eleanor, and she walked quickly back to
her seat. Because of Eleanor's mother's request, James
had been watching Eleanor and David to see he if could
notice any inter-reaction between them. He was not the
kind of man who put off doing things, however, because
of the situation he felt that he still needed to ponder. In
his own mind, he was certain that David had no ulterior
motives in his dealings with Eleanor. If anyone did have
unwarranted feelings, it would be Eleanor, after all, she
was just a teenage girl while David was a mature and
respected man. He did feel a degree of resentment against
Sheila Jenkins, even though he knew he should not. He
was glad that he had decided to wait until the new year
itself before he spent some time with David because it
seemed to him that there was more inter-reaction between
Eleanor and Stephanie, two girls that had only just met.
However, for the two or three minutes that Eleanor had
been singing, there had been a connection between her
and David. But that was how it should have been then.
Maybe he didn't need to speak to David after all, but, and
this is where he did have a twinge of uncertainty – why
were David and Eleanor together when Lucy saw them.

Odd. He would have to inform David that their friendship had been noticed, and ask about it. The only real point he could make was about all the time they had spent alone. Maybe he would suggest that they stopped singing, at least for the time being.

The evening was timed to go on until just after midnight, that is, for those who liked to see in the new year. David had long given up that idea, but he assumed that Daniel and Stephanie would want to stay. He knew that the youth group were staying, and that there were already arrangements in hand about getting them home. However, he had noticed that a few people were already leaving. So at half past ten, he whispered to Daniel that he was also about to leave.

"Here, take the car keys, Daniel," he added.

"How will you get home, Dad?"

"I'll walk. It's okay."

"Let me run you home, and then come back," Daniel said.

"No, it's a fine night. I'll leave the front door unlocked for you. Can you look after Eleanor?"

"Yes, of course."

As David stood up, Stephanie and Eleanor both looked at him. "Will you excuse me, ladies, I think I'll wait until tomorrow to see the new year," David said.

"You're not staying?" Stephanie asked.

"No. Don't wake me up when you come in," he said, smiling at Stephanie. "See you on Sunday, Eleanor," he added.

A few minutes later, Eleanor stood up. "I think I'll go too," she said to Stephanie. "I'll see the new year in with Mum and Dad."

"Let Daniel run you home, he's got his dad's car," Stephanie said.

"No, I'll be okay."

"Daniel, take Eleanor home," Stephanie said to Daniel.

"No, Daniel. You stay with Stephanie," Eleanor said.

"But I've got Dad's car, Eleanor," Daniel said.

Eleanor smiled at him. "That may be the case, but I won't get into it. So, see you both on Sunday?"

"No, we're going on Friday," Stephanie said, standing up. "So ..." She held out her arms and they hugged.

Eleanor finally managed to extricate herself, and left the hall carrying her guitar. She collected her coat and scarf, and walked toward the door.

"Eleanor, what are you doing?" David's voice called.

Eleanor turned round. "What are you doing? I thought you had gone."

"I had to pop up to the office first. Anyway, where are you going? I thought the young people were staying 'til midnight."

"Yes, most are. I fancy going home."

"But I asked Daniel to look after you," David added.

"He's got Stephanie to look after, David," she said. "It's okay, I'll walk on my own."

"Don't be silly, Eleanor, I'll get the car keys back from Daniel."

"No!"

"Eleanor?"

"David, you should be with Daniel and Stephanie – they're going in a couple of days."

"And you are not walking home on your own!"

"You can't stop me."

"Then I'll come with you!"

"Daniel, we should be with your Dad," Stephanie said a few minutes later. "He shouldn't be at home on his own – we should be with him."

"You're right," Daniel said without hesitation. "Just let me say a few goodbyes." It took a few minutes, and his last stop was with James and his wife. Having explained why they were going, James asked if they were taking Eleanor.

"No, she's already gone too," Daniel said. He didn't understand the significance of the look that James gave Lucy, and then went back to collect Stephanie.

"Dad will be surprised to see us," Daniel said, as they drove out. "I wonder how far he's got?"

But it was Daniel who was surprised – firstly because they didn't catch him up, and then, secondly, because the door was locked when they did get home.

"He's not home," Daniel exclaimed.

"Or he's locked us out," Stephanie replied.

"No. But where is he?"

"Shortcut?" Stephanie asked.

"No, I don't think so. We'll have to go back, Steph, we don't have a key. Maybe he didn't leave."

"Unless he waited for Eleanor."

"Steph, what are you suggesting," Daniel said quietly.

Stephanie hesitated. "You must have noticed, Dan."

"Noticed what?"

"I'll tell you in the car, come on. Let's go and find your dad. There's no point in waiting here."

"Dan, you knew about Eleanor, didn't you, yet you didn't tell me," Stephanie said as they drove back to the church.

"I didn't know her name."

"You knew he was singing with a young girl, right?"

"Yes, Jill told me."

"And it bothered you?" Stephanie asked.

"Well, yes. I was embarrassed. You must agree that it is an unusual combination."

"Do you think something is going on?"

"I don't think Dad is that silly, apart from the fact that Mum hasn't been dead a year."

"Are you still bothered?"

"I don't know," Daniel said. "What do you think?"

"It seems that it all started innocently. First your dad helped her and another boy, then when he left, she felt she couldn't perform on her own."

"Are you saying that she engineered it?"

"No. But I'm pretty certain that she has feelings for him," Stephanie said.

"Feelings?" Daniel said, and laughed. "Are you thinking about what she wrote in the book?"

"It's not just that. Didn't you notice the way she looks at him? The thing is, has your dad noticed – or, dare I say it, does he feel the same way?"

"Oh, Steph, what do we do?"

"We can't do anything, Dan. It's only a feeling on my part."

Daniel laughed again. "You and your feelings, Steph! Let's hope you're wrong."

David and Eleanor were deep in conversation. It started by Eleanor apologising for her abrupt manner on the phone earlier that day.

"Mum was listening," she said, by way of explanation.

"So?"

"She had already had a go at me for last night. I told her it was Stephanie and Daniel who invited me. She thought I should have come straight home and not intrude on your family time."

"Was she really cross?"

"Yes."

"I'm sorry, Eleanor. I didn't mean to cause trouble."

Eleanor shrugged. "I'm seventeen. Goodness, some of my friends go clubbing until the small hours."

"They're only thinking of you, Eleanor."

"They said they were thinking of you."

"Well, apart from getting you into trouble, I enjoyed your company last night, so don't worry on my behalf. Anyway, why haven't you remained at the church? I asked Daniel to look after you," David added. "Did they ignore you?"

"No, Steph was great. I really like her."

"Well?"

"Things suddenly felt flat. I suppose it was after all the work we did for yesterday. I just felt like going home."

"I know what you mean. At least I've had the visit of Daniel and Stephanie."

"And the engagement. Are you pleased?"

"Yes, apparently Jill's met her and liked her."

"Have they set a date?"

"I don't know. What with them going back to Stephanie's home, and then tonight, we haven't talked about the future. And talking about the future, what about yours?"

"Mine?"

"Eleanor, you're in the sixth form. Are you thinking about university?"

"I don't know. Is it really worth it, what do you think?"

Daniel and Stephanie arrived back at the church without seeing David on the way. After Daniel had checked that David had really gone, and was not even in the office, he bumped into Lucy, the Pastor's wife.

"Hello Daniel, lost?" she asked.

"I'm looking for my Dad."

"He left with Eleanor, didn't you know?"

"But he left first."

"Maybe he waited."

Daniel drove toward the direction that he thought Eleanor came from. Even though he had dropped her off the night before, Daniel wasn't sure of the exact road, but since they had no key, there was no point in going back home without making some effort.

"I know it's round here somewhere," Daniel said, as they turned another corner.

"Look, is that them?" Stephanie suddenly exclaimed, pointing at two figures in the distance. "Yes, it is," she added as they drew nearer.

"At least they're not holding hands," Daniel muttered. They were on Daniel's side, so he lowered the window as he drew level. "Taxi, Sir?" he called.

"Daniel? What are you doing here?" David said.

"Looking for you. We decided to go home, but we were locked out, so we're looking for the key."

"Oh." David began to fumble in his pocket.

"Dad!" Daniel said. "We were looking for you. Or would you rather walk home on your own. Come on, get in, both of you."

They were close to Eleanor's house, and after dropping her off, Daniel drove them home.

"You were deep in conversation, Dad," Stephanie said, twisting in her seat. "You didn't hear the car, did you?"

"No. We were talking about university, pros and cons, and whether the expense was worthwhile. Then she was telling me about the trip to Romania."

"Romania?"

"Yes, we have links with a church and orphanage, and some of the young people visit there."

"Oh. Like our church has a link with Bulgaria," Stephanie said.

"I get confused between the two countries," Daniel said.

"Bulgaria is at the bottom, Daniel, get it, bb," David pointed out.

"Hello, Eleanor, didn't expect to see you yet. Problem?" Mrs Jenkins said, as Eleanor let herself in.

"No, I just felt like coming home."

"You haven't fallen out with Lizzie?"

"No, Mum," Eleanor replied, laughing.

"Then how did you get home? You haven't walked on your own, have you?"

"No," Eleanor said.

"So how did you get home?" Sheila Jenkins said, folding her arms.

"Didn't you hear the car? Daniel and Stephanie picked me up."

"Oh! Then you were walking."

"Okay, yes, I was, but they picked me up."

"I'm not pleased. You shouldn't have walked on your own."

Eleanor hesitated. She hadn't been on her own, she had been with David, but she had a feeling that that would also have been wrong. "Sorry, Mum."

Daniel and Stephanie spent New Year's day with Daniel's father. Daniel asked David about the American trip. David found out more about Stephanie. Daniel asked about David's two jobs, school and church work. They talked vaguely about wedding dates, with David broaching the subject of finance. Not just about the cost of weddings, but the money needed to set up a home. After lunch, supervised by Daniel, they went for a walk.

"Will you be singing with Eleanor again?" Daniel asked, casually.

"We haven't been asked, but I expect we could be."

"Did you enjoy it, Dad?" Stephanie asked.

"I did. At first, I found it mildly embarrassing, being with two younger folk."

"So how was it with one young person?" Daniel asked.

"I didn't sing at first – I was the accompanist. She sang at a youth meeting, and I said it wasn't right for me to take part. Eleanor agreed, but only on condition that I sang with her at the old people's home. Then we were invited back, just the two of us."

"And you were pretty good, Dad," Daniel said.

"Thanks, Dan, but Eleanor was the star."

"Where did you get the songs from?" Stephanie asked.

David laughed. "That was the hard part – what to sing? I bought a book of traditional folk songs."

"But what about that jazz number?" Stephanie asked.

"Ella Fitzgerald – album in my loft."

"What about embarrassment – are you still embarrassed?"

"Not when I'm with her. Look, I teach girls, and compared to them, Eleanor is an adult. But then I remember that she isn't. What do you think of her?"

"I think she's lovely," Stephanie said quickly.

"So do I, but I mean in terms of her character. She will make someone a fantastic wife."

"But, Dad, is it wise to spend so much time with her?"

David paused. "I take your point, Daniel. I was concerned to start with, but I supposed I just got used to being with her."

"How many people know just how much time you put into practising?"

"Hardly any. I have tried to be discreet."

"For whose sake, Dad?" Daniel said.

"What do you mean?"

"Well, could Eleanor have misread your motives?"

"Daniel!"

"It's got to be considered, Dad," Stephanie said very quietly.

"No. She's not stupid. Let's leave it."

The subject was dropped, and nothing more was said. David used his cookery book again, with Daniel helping him, although David did ask Daniel to take charge of the main meals for them. David took them to the station, but then, as the train pulled away he felt very down. Part of him wished he had a music practice with Eleanor to look forward to. Then he remembered Daniel's comment. But what were his own motives? Did he have any motives? Loneliness? Was he using her just for her company? In which case he was being selfish. He thought back to the cycle rides – yes, they were more enjoyable because she was with him, but he hadn't been using her. And the singing, well that had just happened, like Topsy in Uncle Tom's Cabin, it had just 'growed'. But he had enjoyed both the time spent in practising the songs as well as the time spent in not actually singing. He went out to his car and drove to the church. Because of family and the public holiday, he was slightly behind on his work.

Chapter 18

A Quiet Word

David let himself into the church office, but it was hard to concentrate. He was quite pleased when after an hour, James came and joined him.

"Have you had coffee yet, David?"

"No – are you making it then?" David replied.

James returned a few minutes later with two mugs of coffee.

"It was good to see Daniel," he said, as he handed David a mug, and then sat down opposite him.

"Thanks. Yes, it was."

"And I hear you will have a daughter in law. Was that expected?"

"Not by me," James replied.

"Are you pleased?"

"Yes, she's a lovely girl."

"Have they named the day?"

"Not definitely, but they have ideas."

James paused. "I know it's not a year yet, but do you think you might eventually remarry?"

"No," David said.

"Oh?" James said.

"We talked about it in general terms, you know, the way one does. I wouldn't have wanted Jenny to live the rest of her life alone if it had been me."

"And did she feel the same?"

"Oh, yes."

"But you don't see it happening to you."

"James, I wouldn't know how to go about it. I mean, it's not like buying a loaf of bread – or even a new car."

"There are agencies, David. Even Christian ones," James said quietly. "I know a couple who met like that." He paused. "So how has this job been going?"

"Is this my half yearly review?" David replied, with a grin.

"No, of course not," James answered quickly. "Mind you, I must say that I have appreciated you stepping in."

"It helped me too," David said. "That and helping Eleanor with her singing."

James hesitated. David had brought up the subject for him. "Yes, the singing," he repeated. "I heard from George that it went very well."

"Yes, Eleanor is very talented," David said.

"Who decided what to sing?"

"We both did, I suppose. Given that George said it was to be secular, and that they were older people, I bought a bought a book of old folk songs. We also looked though my old record collection."

"So it took up quite a bit of time?"

"Yes, I suppose it did, but that was okay."

James hesitated again. He decided to take the bull by the horns. "David," he said quietly, and looking directly at him, "is there anything going on between you and Eleanor, apart from the singing?"

"What?" David exclaimed. "Whatever made you say that?"

James didn't answer, but just looked steadily at David.

"No, of course there isn't!" David said, raising his voice. "Now tell me why you asked me."

James didn't answer directly. "David, would you like to be a church minister?" he asked.

"No, of course not."

"Why not?" James asked.

"You know why not. I don't have a gift for it to start with."

"And you wouldn't want to ask difficult questions?"

David saw the connection immediately. "Sorry, James. But you must have a reason to ask."

"Okay, but you will appreciate I can't mention names, but your times together have been noticed."

"Oh, like me walking Eleanor home after the social?" James kept his face steady – he was glad Lucy had seen them and told him. "Not just that," he said.

"Well, I can assure you, James, there is nothing happening between us."

"But you have spent a lot of time together, and not all in public."

"What's that got to do with it?" David felt annoyed again, and his voice betrayed his feelings.

"David, Eleanor is only seventeen. Do you think it is wise to spend so much time alone together? I mean, she is rather attractive."

"James. That's got nothing to do with it," David said.

James waited for David to calm down. Then he continued. "David, you read the papers. It happens – sometimes before you realise. And even if you are totally unaware of her feminine charms, should she be spending so much time with a mature man, an eligible man, if you will forgive me saying so?"

David didn't answer.

"Have my questions come as a complete shock to you, David?"

David shook his head. "I think my son was trying to say the same thing."

"Nobody else?"

"No. Not that I'm aware of."

"And it's not just the time you are together, it's also being seen together. People jump to the wrong idea; you know that."

"Like you?"

"No, not like me. I didn't want this conversation."

"So, what now?"

"As far as I'm concerned, I've had the conversation. You are not doing anything wrong, but I would question your wisdom."

"So no more singing?"

"If George asks you, then it's up to you, but I don't think he will."

"You've had a word?"

"We have talked. By the way, he didn't realise Eleanor was so young."

"And the church won't ask us?"

"David, put yourself in my shoes."

David sat and thought about it.

"So who will tell Eleanor?"

"What is there to tell? I mean, if the only reason for you to spend time together no longer exists, then problem solved," James said slowly, and looking deliberately at David.

"Quite so," David replied, equally slowly and deliberately.

David didn't sleep well that night. It was all very well for James to say the problem had been solved, but despite their age difference, David regarded Eleanor as a friend. In fact, it was Eleanor who had first used the word, months ago. Friends did not just ignore each other. The other problem was that of his feelings towards her. Did he have feelings that warranted James' concerns? He was very fond of her, yes, but in a fatherly kind of way, at least, that is what he hoped it was. However, he remembered that on one of their cycle rides she had said that she did not see him in that way. So how did she see him? He had, he was sure, given her no reason at all to think there could be a romantic future for them. Okay, she was only seventeen, but she was an intelligent, well-balanced and mature young lady. So that left what other people might think. He was tempted to ignore this, but he knew it was important – both for Eleanor's reputation, and the reputation of his church. He would speak to Eleanor, it was the least he could do.

Saturday was back to normal – housework, shopping and cooking. He also had some school preparation which needed finishing. There was one other thing on his mind now that January had arrived. It was the first anniversary of Jenny's death. It had been strange, but nothing at all had been said over the Christmas period. It was as if they wanted to have no shadow over this Christmas. A year ago, Christmas had been a sad time as everyone had known that Jenny had only days to live. With Stephanie staying with him over new year, Daniel and David had avoided the subject. He decided to talk to Jill about it on Sunday afternoon.

On Sunday morning David knew he had to speak to Eleanor – but when and where? Eleanor was sitting with her friends, and David had been seated in his usual position near the back. After the service David had a job to do in the church office, and he guessed that Eleanor would be gone when he finished. He walked over towards where Eleanor was standing with her friends, but then thought better of it. Eleanor just happened to turn and see him. For a moment, they just looked at each other, then David turned and walked away. He sat in his office, with his head in his hands, his work untouched, and didn't hear the knock. He heard the second, louder, knock.

"Come in," he called, without looking up.

"David?"

He looked up quickly. "Eleanor?"

"What's the matter? Are you thinking of Jenny?" she asked.

"Jenny? Jenny died a year ago."

"I know. It will be the first anniversary soon, won't it," she said quietly.

"Eleanor, my dear, I wasn't thinking of that. No, there's something else. Come in and sit down, I need to talk to you." David waited until Eleanor was seated. "Eleanor, we won't be asked to sing again," he said.

"Why? How do you know?"

"It's complicated, but basically, someone, or even some people think that we have been spending too much time together. And for the wrong reasons."

"Who told you that?" Eleanor asked.

"James talked to me."

"James talked to you? About us?"

"Yes. I think someone spoke to him about us."

"Who spoke to him?"

"He wouldn't go into details."

"So, what now?"

"Perhaps you could find another singing partner. Hopefully not one old enough to be your father?"

"Is that all you can say?"

"Eleanor, I think very highly of you. You've helped me to get through this year far more than you will ever realise, but, maybe James has a point. You should spend more time with people of your age, and maybe I should do the same."

For a moment they sat looking at each other, before Eleanor spoke.

"Thank you for telling me, David," she said in a whisper. Then she got up and left the room. David sat for a long time, feeling very miserable before getting up, and leaving. Eleanor had already gone home.

Jill phoned him in the afternoon, soon after dinner. "Hello, Dad. How are you?"

"I'm feeling pretty low, actually," he replied.

"Oh. Do you know why? Is it school?"

"Probably not."

"Is it," she hesitated, "the anniversary?"

"No," he said. "But maybe we should talk about it."

"Dad," she said suddenly. "School starts on Tuesday, doesn't it?"

"Yes, why?"

"Why not come here this afternoon?"

"Right now, Jill?" David asked.

"Yes. We didn't get a chance to talk properly at Christmas, did we? Bring your things, and stay over night." She paused. "Or are you expecting to meet anyone tonight at church?"

"No," he said. "No, I'm not."

"Then just throw some things into a bag, and come. You can have tea with us – oh, have you had dinner?"

"Yes."

"Right, see you in just over an hour."

David went to his bedroom in a daze. He was dressed rather formally, he always did dress formally on a Sunday, so he changed. Then he packed his night clothes, his wash things, and a change of undies into a bag, and left. All within eight minutes of the phone call. He had never behaved like this since, he thought hard – when he was a student. What had made him agree, but then he knew. It meant he wouldn't have to face Eleanor. The look on her face before she left haunted him. He'd seen the same look once before, on another girl's face. The girl he had been going out with when he had first met Jenny, and he had to tell her that he had met someone else. But Eleanor wasn't his girl friend, and their association was a business relationship. Except that he knew it wasn't. Singing together had only been part of the relationship. What about the time spent just talking, as apart from listening to his music, or even teaching how to cook? Or the cycle rides? Or the jazz nights?

Jill was waiting for him and came out as he pulled onto their drive.

"Hello, Dad." she said and hugged him. "I'm glad you came."

"Are you really sure, Jill?"

"Don't be silly, Dad. Of course I'm sure."

"What about Keith?"

"Dad! Keith has swapped with me tonight, so we can have some time together," Jill said.

"Right. Okay."

"Dad, we didn't talk about Mum over Christmas. Perhaps we should have."

"It's not just that, dear," David said.

"Oh?"

"It's complicated. Can we leave it for the moment?"

"Yes. Come on in. Keith has lit a log fire just for you."

David pulled himself together in the afternoon and played with his grandson. Then he enjoyed having tea-time with the family. After tea, there were the tea things to wash, and then bath-time for his grandson. Finally, he sat down with Jill in the lounge. Actually, Jill sat on the carpet next to him.

"Dad, how much do you miss Mum?" she said.

"It comes and goes, Jill," he said, after a pause.

"Is that why you became friendly with that girl?"

The question brought him up with a jolt. "Goodness, no, I don't think so," he said.

"You're not sure?"

"Jill, if your mum had been alive, I certainly would not have been as involved as I was."

"So how involved were you?" Jill asked.

"Well, to start with, there were three of us. The lad she sang with had hurt his wrist, and couldn't play his guitar, so I helped. Then when he went to university, Eleanor asked me to carry on."

"And is that all there was? Wasn't there something to do with swans?"

"There's more than that, Jill."

David told her the whole story, starting with how Eleanor had brought him the cup of tea, how she had spoken to him on the bus, and about the flowers at the cemetery. That's how she knew about his guitar, he explained, hence the singing. He also told Jill about the coffee house meeting, leading on to the jazz nights. He didn't go into details like treating Eleanor to the cream-tea or the sun cream incident. Jill listened in silence. In fact she knew most of it having talked to Daniel and Stephanie the night before. Then he told her about the meeting with his pastor and the subsequent meeting with Eleanor.

"I feel such a rat-bag, Jill," he said. "The look on her face. That's partly why I came here – I couldn't face her tonight."

"You're obviously very fond of her," Jill said carefully.

"I am fond of her – she's a lovely person."

"Is she like Mum?"

"What?" David exclaimed. "What made you say that? Is that what you think, that I'm just looking to replace your mum? Well, I'm not."

"But has it helped, the singing and going out to the jazz nights?"

"Yes, it has, Jill, and that's what is making it worse. I feel I used her, and what about your mum? Should I be doing things that make me forget her? I mean, how do you feel knowing that I've been friendly with another woman? Especially when that woman is a schoolgirl."

Jill looked up at David. "Dear Dad," she said. "I do love you. Keith and I have talked about what we would do in similar circumstances. He says I would need to remarry – that I need a man. And not because of that," she added quickly. "I'd be lost without Keith, and he says I would need to find someone to look after me – and to unblock the drain, and remember to get the car serviced."

"That's something that Eleanor said, it just slipped out. Well, it didn't but I made her tell me what she had nearly said."

"Pardon?"

"Quite early on, we were talking about food, and whether I had eaten. When I described my dinner, she laughed and said that I needed a woman. Well, she stopped herself, but I coaxed it out of her."

"I think you need a woman, Dad."

"Maybe, one day," David said. "but let's get Daniel married off first, shall we?"

"Dad, one more thing. Are you in love with Eleanor?"

David looked at his daughter. "Darling, would that be appropriate?" he asked quietly.

"Well?" Jill said.

"If I were Daniel's age, I would be. But I'm old enough to be her father, so my feelings must be strictly paternal."

"What about Eleanor, could she be in love with you?"

"Not if she has any sense."

"She's a woman, Dad, and I've heard your comments about women and logic."

"Jill!"

"So?"

"Okay, if she is that silly, then maybe my pastor has a point."

"That might have been his reason, Dad," Jill said quietly.

Eleanor didn't go to the evening service. She spent the time alone in her room, mainly doing nothing, but some of the time she listened to music on the record player. When she had borrowed the Ella album, she had borrowed two other albums. They would have to be returned some time, she knew, but not right then. She had also spent some time crying, but she had washed her face, and applied make-up, more make-up than she normally used. Her mother guessed something was wrong, and assumed that it was a falling out with a friend. There was no boyfriend that she knew of, for which she blamed David and the singing, so it must have been a girlfriend

"Eleanor, what's the matter, Darling?" she said, after knocking on her daughter's closed door.

"It doesn't matter?"

"So why haven't you gone to church?" her mother asked.

"I don't feel like it"

"Have you had a quarrel?"

"Quarrel? Who with?" Eleanor said.

"That's what I'm asking, dear?"

"No, I haven't had a quarrel."

"Okay, dear." Her mother turned to go.

"Mum?"

"Dear?"

"We've been told there's no more singing."

"No more singing?" her mother said, playing dumb.

"Why"

"Apparently because someone thinks we have been spending too much time on it."

"Well, you have spent quite a lot of time practising," Mrs Jenkins said.

"Not just rehearsing. Being with David."

"Oh," Mrs Jenkins said, her hopes rising.

"It wasn't you, was it, Mum?"

"Eleanor!" Her mum said, sounding shocked. "Of course not," she lied. "I know just how much the singing meant to you."

"I think someone suggested that we weren't just singing."

"I can understand that. I mean he's an eligible bachelor now, isn't he?"

"Mum!" Eleanor had raised her voice. "How can say such a thing? His wife hasn't been in the grave for a year." At this point, Eleanor burst into tears. Her mother hugged her and made sure she made no further inflammatory comments. She felt slightly sorry for her daughter, but not too sorry.

"Mum," Eleanor said, as she regained her composure. "I've decided to go to Romania, to the orphanage, at Easter."

"Yes dear. But what about school work?"

"It's in the holiday. But I'll need to find a better job to pay for it."

"No, dear. Your father and I will help."

Chapter 19

Life Without Eleanor

David was dreading the first Sunday after his meeting with Eleanor. He arrived late and wondered if he would be able to avoid meeting her completely. That was not to be. He did have an unfinished task in the office, and went to collect a cup of coffee first. That was where he met Eleanor. She was on coffee duty. He managed to gather his thoughts in time, so that as they came face to face at the hatch, he was ready. It was Eleanor who was unprepared.

"Hello, Eleanor. How was school this week?" he said.

"Er, er, fine, thank you. Sugar?"

"Yes, please. Just one."

"Stupid me," she muttered, as she added the sugar. "I knew that."

"Thank you," he said, and moved on.

Eleanor stared at him, or rather at his back. What was it about him, she thought. He had not been unfriendly – he had asked about her week. But she sensed that it was a formal enquiry. No smile! That was it – no smile. And he had been in a hurry to move on.

Eleanor felt herself welling up. She turned and walked across to Mrs Mayfield.

"Mrs Mayfield, I'm not feeling good, could you excuse me, please?"

Mrs Mayfield looked closely at Eleanor. "What's the matter, my dear?" she asked.

"I, I can't say," Eleanor uttered. She turned and rushed out of the kitchen. She managed to hold back her tears until she was well away from the church. Then the fountains opened and she made no attempt to hold them back. For a few minutes she did not care that people might notice, but then suddenly stopped. If she arrived home early, especially with red eyes, then her mother would ask questions. She turned to go back to the church, but then stopped. That was no good – she could meet David again. Instead, she turned and walked slowly towards home. There was a park where she could stop and pull herself together.

Back at the church, Mrs Mayfield had shrugged. She was surprised and yet not surprised. She had not expected behaviour like that from Eleanor, but then, well, she was a teenage girl. "Boyfriend troubles," she said to herself, and got on with her coffee duty. David sat in his office, thinking. "Well, that hadn't been too bad," he said, speaking to himself. "Thank goodness she's a mature and sensible girl." It made him feel a lot better. He took a deep breath, and pulled a file towards himself.

Eleanor sat on a seat in the park, and went over her conversation with David one week earlier.
"Eleanor, I think very highly of you," he had said. He had sounded sincere, so maybe he really did mean it. "You should spend more time with people of your age, and maybe I should do the same." Maybe he was right, she thought. But it was his comment that she had helped him get through the year that made her well up again. She knew that she should expect nothing in return, and she had coped. But his coldness just then – surely she could expect something? Friendliness? Was that wrong? Or was it that he was a man? She felt the cold seeping in and got up from her seat.

Eleanor confirmed her decision to join the Romania party.

Although her parents had agreed to cover her personal cost, there were general fund raising efforts, such as baking cakes and washing cars. Eleanor threw herself into all these activities with enthusiasm. However, she detached herself from some of the youth activities. This was because she considered some of lads to be very immature, while the main topic of conversation among the girls was about boys. She was soon asked to sing, and she quietly and firmly refused, giving no reason. Even schoolwork became a chore, and she even wondered if she should have left school. Not that she knew what to do instead.

It might be considered invidious to compare David's new term with that a year earlier. A year earlier, he had lost his wife soon into the term. This time he had only lost his best friend, but it was like kicking a man when he is down. His time with Jill had been a big help. First in just talking about the situation, but also in planning for the anniversary of her death. At Jill's suggestion, they had a family day where they remembered and celebrated Jenny's life. They visited the grave to leave more flowers. Then, at Daniel's suggestion, they used the old slide projector and looked at more of the old slides, especially those of Jenny as a young woman. One positive outcome was that Keith and Jill decided to buy David a slide copier, so that he could digitise his slides later, plus all the others that he had stored away in boxes.

David still had two months of church work, which along with his school teaching kept him busy.
Even so, he did find his thoughts turning to Eleanor. Following the initial conversation at the coffee serving hatch, he had various brief encounters with Eleanor. He usually said that he hoped school was going well, or that

he hoped her Romania preparations were going well. He did keep up with the Romania news, taking his car to be washed, and buying far more cakes than he needed. Part of the plan was to acquire a quantity of second hand clothing to be part of their luggage allowance, and which would then be left behind afterwards. David asked about her plans in this area, and as a result, he went to several charity shops and bought over half a dozen shirts. He wondered whether he should have bought women's clothes, but thought it might look odd if he was seen buying skirts or dresses. After another conversation with Eleanor he bought socks, that is new socks. He put these through his washing machine before giving them to Eleanor.

His conversations with Eleanor were brief, civil, and pragmatic – school or Romania. However, the most serious and lasting conversation between them occurred towards the end of February. It had been raining when David left home for the Sunday service, so he had used his car. Eleanor had again been on coffee duty which meant that she had been delayed. As David left, having been in the office, he found her by the entrance, looking out at the pouring rain. He was behind her, and for a moment, he hesitated. His car was in the car-park, and he had to use the same door. He coughed, and she turned.
"Is your mum or dad coming for you, Eleanor?" he asked.
"No, when they dropped me off, I said I'd get a lift."
"Oh, with the Mayfields," David said, referring to the couple who Eleanor had been with, and who were still in the kitchen.
"Yes, that's what I hoped, but they walked."
"Well, you're in luck. I've got my car today," he said, assuming that Eleanor would accept.
Eleanor waited under the porch as he went for his car.

She ran the few yards, and jumped in.

"Thank you, David," she said, turning and smiling.

"My pleasure," David replied.

Then they rode in silence for a few minutes.

"How are your family?" she asked, breaking the silence.

"They're very well, thank you."

"Have you seen them recently?"

"Yes, we met up for the anniversary," David said.

"Of Jenny's death?"

David told her what they had done as a family. Then he asked about her latest plans for Romania. Then they rode in silence. As he turned into her road, she suddenly asked him to stop.

"Right here? You'll get soaked," he said, but stopping the car as requested. Eleanor's house was a hundred metres further up the road.

Eleanor sat without moving. Finally, she turned towards him.

"David, what exactly did the pastor say?"

David hesitated. He had gone over the question many times, partly wondering what the outcome would have been if Eleanor had been in a relationship with him. "He asked if there was anything going on between us, apart from the singing?" he replied.

"What? Whatever made him think that?"

"I don't think he did. I asked him why he asked, and he as good as said that it was his job."

"But he must have had a reason!" Eleanor persisted.

"He said he couldn't mention names, but our times together had been noticed by someone, or was it some people. No, he just said noticed. So I don't know, but there again, he said names, plural. He pointed out that we have spent a lot of time together, just the two of us, but he also said that some of it was in public, and that people jump to the wrong conclusions. Remember, I walked you home, that is, until Daniel found us. Someone must have noticed, but he seemed to know about other times."

"The jazz nights, or the bike rides, David?"

"I don't know. Anyway, he then brought up our age difference, and also the fact that you are, and I quote, rather attractive."

"He said that?" she asked

"That was the only thing I couldn't argue with, but I said it was irrelevant," David said.

"Oh," she said.

"Eleanor, that's not the reason I liked being with you. I enjoyed singing with you, and just being with you."

"Did you?" she asked.

"Yes, I did, but then James pointed out that affairs do happen, and even when there is no affair, as I said, people jump to the wrong conclusions. He then said that even if I had not noticed, listen to this, your feminine charms, should you be spending your time with a mature man."

Eleanor didn't know what to say, so David continued. "I think my son felt the same way, Eleanor."

"What do you think, David?"

"I can see what they are getting at. Anyway, nobody has asked us to sing, so that has solved that problem," David said, thinking about George not asking them now.

"I've been asked, David," she whispered.

"Have you?"

She nodded. "Yes."

"Good. I like hearing you sing," David said, his voice not disguising his excitement.

"I said I wouldn't."

"But, Eleanor …"

"No. I will only sing with you."

"I wish you would sing, Eleanor. I like it, and you do have a gift," David said quietly.

"Maybe one day, but not at the moment." She paused. "I wonder who caused the trouble. I had half expected my mum to say something. Remember how she made us have the practice at my home. Do you think she thought something was happening? Would she have gone and visited the pastor? That's why I made you stop here. Look, the rain's stopped. I'll run from here." She pulled the door handle and got out quickly, then leaned back in. "David, thank you for saying what you said. We are still friends, aren't we?"

"I hope so, Eleanor, I do hope so," he said.

For the first time in weeks, David found himself humming as he drove home. Even Jill noticed that something was different when they spoke on the phone later that afternoon.

"Dad, what's happened?"

"What do you mean? Nothing's happened!"

"You sound different."

"Do I? In what way?"

"I don't know. Chirpy? And you seemed easier to talk to."

"Oh. Well – I know, the sun is shining."

"Well, I hope it stays shining!" Jill said, and laughed.

Once David's church duties ended, he was pleased with the extra time it gave him. He made a start on digitising his slides. However, he knew he had to make a decision about returning to full time teaching or remaining part time. Part time teaching would mean a reduced pension, but he could offset that by paying into an AVC. Or perhaps he could find a part time job outside of teaching – even a low skilled job. Or maybe study? But study what? He had learnt to look after the church accounts after a couple of days training, and with copious notes.

Meanwhile, he had his teaching. The beginning of the year had not been easy, for him or his pupils. It might have been the stress of Jenny's anniversary, or, and he recognised this, the result of James' discussion. Looking back, he knew he had been both upset and angry, and as a consequence, he knew he had not been patient or fair in many situations at school. However, as the term progressed, he felt that his attitude to people and pupils was improving. After the talk with Eleanor, he had one further question for James, but he didn't want to make a big issue of it. It meant he had to wait for an appropriate moment. It happened two weeks later. James called round to visit him.

David and James made small talk as David made coffee, and opened a packet of biscuits. Then James moved on to his reason for visiting.

"I just want to say thank you for looking after the church so well, David. Mark was very impressed, and grateful."

"No, thank you for asking me. It was just what I needed at the time – and I've learnt, well, started to learn, a new skill. I actually wondered whether to do a course in Sage"

"What else could you do? Go back to full time?" James asked

"Not until next September. I might study, if I can think of what to study, or I might find a little part-time job. I may just enjoy the spare time."

"Lucky you. There was something else, I forgot to ask how you were in January. I overlooked it until my wife pointed it out, I mean the anniversary of the funeral. I'm sorry."

"We had a family gathering – looked at pictures of Jenny, visited the grave. It was odd. We didn't refer to it at all over Christmas, but it was good to talk when we met up."

"And how are you now?"

David wanted to say that he was missing Eleanor. "I'm all right, thank you, James."

There was some more small talk. Then the pastor asked if he could pray for David. As James was leaving, David said he had another question.

"How many people know about our little chat in the church, James?"

"Only the two of us – oh, and Lucy. I talked it over with her."

"What about the person who spoke to you, did you tell him, or her?"

James looked at David. "Are you fishing?"

"Was it Eleanor's mother?"

"David, don't be naughty. But I can say this, I haven't spoken to Eleanor' mother since, oh, the Sunday after Christmas."

"What would you have said if I had confessed to having an affair with Eleanor?"

James stared at him. "Is this a confession," he asked.

"No, just suppose, that's all," David said.

"I don't know."

"Well, you pointed out that such things do happen."

"Not in my personal experience, David. And I hope they never do," he added, looking straight at David.

"I don't think you need to worry about it, James. Anyway, thanks for coming," David replied.

They shook hands goodbye.

The term finished. The Romanian party left. David saw his family, including his future daughter-in- law over Easter. Then he had the early morning phone call.

Chapter 20

The Airport Run – continued.

Having stopped for breakfast, David expected that
Eleanor would have remained awake. Her going back to
sleep meant that he had the opportunity to ponder on the
significance of their previous discussion. They were not
going to be just friends; they were going to be friends that
could enjoy doing things together from time to time. But
doing what? What did friends usually do? Meet at home.
Go to places such as the theatre, the cinema, concerts.
Visit mutual friends. Go for walks, rides – cycle rides. In
other words, do things in private and in public. Both areas
were frowned on by James. Meeting in private was
unwise from a personal perspective, while meeting in
public could lead to gossip. As he turned and looked at
her, he felt a surge of emotion, and his heart almost
missed a beat. He recognised the feeling – and it didn't
help. No, they were just friends, he told himself. Special
friends, true, but nothing more than just friends.

Eleanor slept for most of the way home. David stopped
the car two streets away, and touched her face gently.
"Sleeping beauty. Princess," he murmured. "Time to
wake up."
She stirred slightly, as David now studied her closely.
James was right, he told himself, she is, what was it,
rather attractive. No, she's beautiful, he thought.
"Come on beautiful princess, we're home," he said
slightly louder, and stroking her cheek gently. This time,
as she stirred, she opened her eyes, slowly. Then
suddenly.
"Where are we?" she exclaimed, looking around.

"Nearly home, Eleanor. We're in my car. I've just collected you from Heathrow."

"Oh," she said, then, "oh!" But this time louder.

"Where were you?" David asked, smiling at her.

"With you in a car," she replied quietly.

"Good, so are you awake now?"

"I was with you, and we were going on holiday," she said quietly.

"Pardon?"

"I was dreaming, David."

David turned and looked at her. "Oh, Eleanor," he said quietly, and then he started the engine.

Eleanor's mother was obviously looking out through her window, because even as David lifted Eleanor's case from his boot, she was down the path. Her first reaction was to embrace and kiss her daughter. Her second reaction was to ask where they had been.

"Nowhere, Mum," Eleanor replied. "Just coming home."

"But you're later than the others," she said accusingly, and looking at David.

"We stopped for breakfast, Mrs Jenkins. Apparently I should have taken breakfast with me."

"Oh. Yes, her father would have taken it," Sheila Jenkins said.

David put the case down. "Right, I'll be off now," he said, going back to the driving door.

"David." It was Eleanor. "Thank you for collecting me. And for breakfast," she added, walking round towards him. Then she hesitated. "I'll be seeing Lizzie tomorrow at the jazz night. Shall I say hello?" she said.

"Sorry?" David replied, non-plussed by the change of topic.

"I'll be at the jazz night," she repeated, but quieter, before turning and walking back. They watched him drive away, and then Eleanor turned to her mother.

"Mum! How could you be so rude? David was woken up early this morning just because Dad's car wouldn't start."

"But why him?"

"Pardon? What are you suggesting?" Eleanor gasped.

"Is there something going on?"

"What?" Eleanor shook her head in disbelief. "It was you, wasn't it?"

"What was me?"

Eleanor just stared at her, then she picked up her case and walked towards the front door.

As David drove away, he thought about the reception they had just received. Not a thank you for collecting their daughter, but a where have you been. Then he remembered his question to James, who had not actually denied that it was Eleanor's mother. So James hadn't spoken to her since the Sunday after Christmas. Which suggested that they had spoken then. He remembered leaving Eleanor, her mother and Stephanie together talking together. So she must have spoken to James then. Then there was Eleanor's comment about meeting Lizzie. It suddenly dawned on him. She was telling him where she would be. He would buy a ticket as soon as possible.

That was the beginning of their affair – as David thought of it. It was not an affair in the accepted sense; there was no physical relationship. It was just that they arranged to meet up on an irregular, but discreet, if not secret basis. David arrived at the jazz venue early. He didn't want to be seen by Eleanor's parents, assuming that they took her there, so he waited inside. He saw Eleanor and Lizzie before they saw him, and he walked to meet them. "Eleanor! Lizzie! Fancy meeting you here," he exclaimed, as they met.

"You know we always come, David," Lizzie replied. "More to the point, where have you been for the last couple of times?"

"You're right" David said, and not answering her question. "I have missed some, but I think I'll be regular again. So, going in?"

The seating was on a casual basis, so he ended up sitting between them. When he glanced at Eleanor, she smiled at him, but they didn't speak until Lizzie went to the cloakroom.

"So you made it?" Eleanor whispered.

"Yes, thanks to your comment. I didn't get it for a while. So who brought you tonight?"

"Lizzie's mum. Dad is picking us up."

"Okay. When's the next time we can just meet up accidentally?"

Eleanor thought. "I'm on coffee on Sunday morning. How about helping me?"

"But I'm not on the rota."

"So? Just ask Mrs Mayfield if she needs any help."

David was early at church on Sunday morning, and waited for Mrs Mayfield.

"Good morning, Mrs Mayfield," he said. "I was wondering, now that I don't have to rush off to the church office if you ever needed extra help."

"Why, yes, Mr Anderson, I do get let down sometimes."

"Well, I'm free this morning; shall I drop in to see how it goes?"

"That would be kind. I think we're all right this morning, but an extra pair of hands is always welcome," she said.

"Fine, see you later."

As he then went and found a seat, David felt mildly guilty that she would probably attribute his motives as altruistic. He made sure that he was already in the kitchen before

Eleanor. He was taking some instructions from Mrs Mayfield when Eleanor arrived.

"Hello, David," she said brightly. "Are you helping today?"

"Yes, I'm just receiving tuition from Mrs Mayfield," David replied.

"Would you like me to train him, Mrs Mayfield," Eleanor asked.

"Oh, Eleanor. Would you mind?"

"It's a woman's duty to train a man," Eleanor said, winking at David.

David waited until Mrs Mayfield was out of earshot.

"You cheeky wench," he whispered to Eleanor. Eleanor just smiled at him.

There was little time to talk once people began to queue at the coffee hatch, and David found he was just doing menial tasks like bringing cups to Eleanor when she asked. He was bringing another tray of cups as James took his turn at the hatch.

"Morning, Pastor," Eleanor said brightly.

"Morning, Eleanor," he replied. "You're very chirpy this morning. Oh." He paused as he saw David. "Hello, David. Found a new vocation then?" he said slowly, looking directly at David.

"Hello, James. Yes, I'm being trained," he replied, returning James' look.

James moved away, and there was a lull.

"I think it was Mum," Eleanor said to David.

"Mum?"

"Who spoke to the pastor. About us."

"I wondered that myself, so I asked James outright." James told her.

"What did he say?"

"He didn't deny it. Actually, he said he hadn't spoken to her since the Sunday after Christmas. She was with us when you met Stephanie, remember?"

"Yes, you went off. The Pastor joined us, and then I left him with Mum." Eleanor then had to give her attention back to the hatch. "Coffee or tea?" she said to her next 'customer'.

David and Eleanor were then kept busy serving for another seven or eight minutes, by which time people were handing in their empty cups. The cups needed to be washed, dried, and placed back into the cupboard, so it was not until they were finishing off that they had another chance to talk.

"It's young people's tea today," she said to David.

"Yes, I heard it announced."

"Well?" she asked.

"Well what?"

"Aren't you going to ask if I'm going?"

"Are you going?"

"Yes, unless someone invited me somewhere else," Eleanor said quietly.

Before he could answer, Mrs Mayfield came across.

"Mr Anderson," she began.

"Please call me David," he said, interrupting her.

Mrs Mayfield hesitated. "Er, David, thank you for helping today. I'm sure Eleanor appreciated it, but I think I can release you now."

"Right, okay then, I'll be off. Oh, Eleanor, that invitation you mentioned? Well, I think you should go," David said. "Bye."

Working with Mrs Mayfield, Eleanor's duties lasted another ten minutes.

"That Mr Anderson, didn't he lose his wife last year?" Mrs Mayfield asked, as they came to an end.

"Yes, that's right," Eleanor replied.

"I thought so. So how do you know him?"

"He helped Tom and me with our singing."

"That's it! I knew there was something else," Mrs Mayfield exclaimed.

"Something else?" Eleanor asked.

"Yes, as well as working in the church office. He seems a very nice man."

"Yes, he is," Eleanor agreed, hoping that she sounded neutral.

"Well, thank you again, Eleanor."

As she rode her bicycle home, she hoped that she had not sounded too enthusiastic about David being a nice man. She also wondered if she had been too forward with her earlier remark about being invited. It wasn't as if she had a good reason, apart from wanting to go. Too late now, she thought, but was she being silly in wanting to go. If nothing else, she wanted to know more about what James had said to David. The problem was, she did like being with him. No, it was more. She liked him. But was it similar to the way that some of her friends had had a so called crush on one of her young male teachers? No, David was not a young male. And she did not have a crush. They were friends. And it wasn't as if there could be a future for them, she a schoolgirl and David, a family man, well, a widowed family man. Once he got past his grieving, then he would want to meet a lady from his own age group. And she would be off to university – and maybe meet a man with whom she might then have a future. But, meanwhile, she could enjoy his friendship again. Another thought then flashed through her mind. Was it her mother, and what exactly did the pastor say to David?

David noticed that he was tense during and after his

lunch. It was one of his standard meals – spaghetti Bolognese. He had not attempted to follow up on the meal he had cooked for Daniel and Stephanie. After washing up, he phoned Jill for his weekly chat. She commented that he had phoned early, for which he apologised. His reason was that he didn't want the call interrupted by the arrival of Eleanor. In the end, there was a very large time interval before she arrived. David tried to find things to do, but he could not relax, and ended up wasting his time. Although she had been to his house several times, it had almost always been for a reason; the first time in order to meet him to go to the cemetery, then being part of the youth group, and of course to practise their singing. This time there was no reason. He tried to read a book. He checked several times that his house was tidy. Then he began to feel panicky, as if he was on his first date. Finally, he wondered, no he hoped, that it was all a misunderstanding, and that she wasn't actually going to arrive. He looked at his clock – five past four. No, she wasn't going to come, and he heaved a sigh of relief.

Ding-dong. David jumped at the sound, and then went to the door.
"Hello, David," Eleanor said breathlessly.
"Hello, Eleanor," David replied.
"I've put my bike round the back," she added.
"Oh, good. Come in."
For a moment they stood in the hallway, facing each other and not knowing what to say. David broke the silence first.
"Is that your tea?" he asked, indicating her polythene bag.
"Yes."
"Right, do you want to take it into the kitchen?"
"Yes, okay," Eleanor said, walking through.
"Drink or juice?" David added, following her.

Eleanor turned and smiled. "I thought juice was a drink."

"Sorry, you know what I mean."

"I know." She smiled again. "No, I'm fine."

They moved into David's lounge, and sat looking at each other. Another silence.

"Well," David finally said. "So how are you?"

"I'm all right. And you?"

"The same."

Another silence.

"So, what shall we do?" David asked.

"Well, I was listening to your music, remember?"

"Of course," David said, jumping up. "Right, come on, the loft beckons."

The stiffness that had existed between them disappeared as they browsed among David's albums. Finally, with Eleanor carrying three long playing records, they returned to his lounge. David put her first record onto his turntable, and then instead of leaving Eleanor alone to listen, he stayed with her. Although they sat in silence, it was not an embarrassed silence. Eleanor held the album jacket, and read the information on the reverse. David, sitting across from her just watched her. At one stage she looked up, saw him looking at her, and smiled at him.

"I'm glad you came, Eleanor," he said quietly.

"Thank you for inviting me," she answered.

"Does your mum know you're here?" David said.

Eleanor shook her head.

"What about your friends?" David asked.

"They're not expecting me – I didn't go last time. I've not been going to the after church meetings either."

"But why not?"

Eleanor shrugged. "I just haven't felt like it."

"But you're staying on tonight, aren't you. It's Romania,

isn't it?"

She nodded. "Yes. I've got to say a few words."

"Well, I'll be there, cheering you on."

"James won't approve of that," she said, smiling at him.

"Okay, perhaps I won't actually cheer out loud."

They went back to their listening, stopped for tea, and then cycled together for most of the way to church.

"Okay, you go on, Eleanor," David said. "I'll give you five minutes."

"So is this goodbye?" she asked, but with a smile.

"I think it had better be," David answered. "Until next week, then."

David watched her ride away, and by the time he arrived, Eleanor was with her friends. There was a special after church fellowship in order to hear reports from the Romania team. As expected, there was no opportunity for a proper talk, and he went home with mixed feelings. Although they had already agreed that they would not spend any more time with each other that evening, they had agreed to meet after the evening service the following week. Part of David was happy that they had spent time together, but he was sad that it had to be in secret. He also felt guilty that it meant deceiving Eleanor's parents.

By midweek, he was missing Eleanor. It was his non-school day, so he drove and parked near to her school entrance, and then he stood near to the gates. There were a few other people, parents, he guessed, also by the gates, so he did not feel out of place. Soon after the end of school, the girls began pouring out. Some were met, others set off walking or riding their bicycles, while others walked to the bus stop. It was over five minutes before he saw Eleanor. She was with two other girls, one being Lizzie. Lizzie saw him first. She immediately nudged Eleanor, and pointed to David. Eleanor's face showed surprise, and then concern. She broke away from the other two, and walked to him.

"David, is there a problem?"

"No, I just wanted to see you," he replied.

"Oh."

"Sorry, I've embarrassed you," he said.

"No you haven't." She turned and beckoned to the other two girls who had stopped, and were waiting. "How did you get here," she then said to David.

"By car," he replied, and then turning to Lizzie, he said, "Hello, Lizzie."

"Hello."

A pause.

"Can I offer you all a lift," David said, looking at Lizzie and Jayne.

"Actually, we're okay, aren't we Jayne," Lizzie replied quickly.

"Sure?" David asked.

"Absolutely. Come on, Jayne," Lizzie said, and pulled Jayne away.

David waited until they were out of earshot. "Sorry, I didn't mean to break up your group."

"Are you? I could go back to them," Eleanor said.

"Do you want to," David asked.

"No, silly man. Come on, take me home." Then, to David's surprise, she tucked her hand through his arm.

"Eleanor?" David said, indicating her hand.

"Are you embarrassed now?" she said, with a grin.

David stopped. "No, Eleanor, I'm not. But aren't we supposed to be acting discreetly? What will Lizzie think?"

"She knows."

"She knows what?"

"She knows I spent Sunday afternoon with you. I told her," Eleanor said.

"Why?"

"She said I was different on Sunday – that I was not so miserable as I have been, so I told her why."

"Oh, Eleanor," David said, as they approached his car. "It's okay, she won't say anything. In fact she suggested that I invite you to join us on Saturday afternoon. We're going to the cinema. I said you probably wouldn't be interested because it's a rom-com."

"A rom-com," David said, once they were in the car. "Maybe I'll pass, but thank Lizzie for suggesting it. So, how was school?" he added, to start a new conversation. Because Eleanor was taken home by car, they arrived early. She made David park two streets away, rather than outside her house, and they sat and chatted until it was time for her to go. As David then drove home, he thought about Lizzie's suggestion. Actually, he would have enjoyed a rom-com, as they were called. Never mind, he thought, not too long to Sunday.

Eleanor and David only spoke briefly on Sunday morning, just to confirm that instead of Eleanor going to the young people's fellowship, they would meet after the evening service. David left immediately after the service and Eleanor arrived five minutes later. After making drinks, they moved into the lounge.

"What did you really think about Lizzie's suggestion?" David said.

"I told her to find a better film next time," Eleanor said, laughing.

"It wasn't the film, Eleanor."

"Wasn't it?" she asked.

"Eleanor, when did you last see a film with a boy?"

"With a boy? Oh, a year ago, maybe."

"And no one since?"

"No. Why are you asking?" Eleanor asked

"Eleanor, you don't have a boyfriend. Why not? You're a very attractive girl."

"Hey, that's a bit personal, isn't it?"

"Too personal, even for friends?"

"Okay. Well, there's no point, is there?"

"No point in what?"

"In getting involved with a non-Christian boy. Do you understand?"

David hesitated. "Yes, I do. Sorry, I didn't mean to intrude."

"That's okay. Anyway, if it wasn't the film, what was it?"

"I don't know how to tell you."

"Was it because of Lizzie? She's over you."

"No, it's you, Eleanor. I like you – I like you a lot. Maybe too much. When you took my arm the other day, I felt very proud – you're an attractive young woman. Why do you think I asked you about school, once we were in the car? To bring me back to reality. I wanted to hug you outside your school gate. Sorry."

"So do you think we shouldn't hug? I hug my friends."

"If I said I wanted to give you a fatherly hug, I would be lying. Look, sitting here in different chairs and having a civilised conversation is one thing, but sitting with a very pretty young woman in a dark cinema is another thing."

"Why?" she said, looking straight at him.

"Come on, Eleanor."

"I asked you why," she repeated, in a low voice.

"Because I would want to hold your hand," David said forcibly. "Do you think that is appropriate?"

"Wanting or holding?" she asked.

"Eleanor, be serious."

"I am. Do you think it is wrong?"

"Eleanor, you're seventeen, and I am over forty."

"Then why am I here now?"

"Why are you?" David said.

"Because I like being with you, and I thought you like being with me."

"And what about the future, your future?"

Eleanor hesitated. "Who knows what the future holds?" she whispered.

"Meanwhile, should friends hug?" David asked.

"Friends should be able to show affection."

Chapter 21

An Invitation

As the summer term progressed, David and Eleanor managed to see each other at least two or three times a week, David met her from school one day each week, which sometimes increased to two. They did not hug by the school gate, but he did kiss her goodbye – an affectionate kiss on her cheek. And he did not deliver her to her house, just in case one of her parents was already home early from work. They managed to spend time together most Sundays, but only by varying the time. Whenever Eleanor arrived at David's, she was hugged and kissed, but again, it was an affectionate kiss on her cheek. They also met at the Jazz nights, but as before, David waited inside. David also agreed to try the cinema – accompanied by Lizzie and Jayne. Lizzie was all for David and Eleanor sitting in the back row, but David insisted that because they went as a group, they sat as a group. That didn't prevent David and Eleanor holding hands, but that was as far as it went. The next time they met, Eleanor told David that Lizzie found their relationship amusing.

"In what way?" David asked.

"Well, she asked me if you were a good kisser."

"What?" David exclaimed. "What ever made her ask that?"

"She regards you as my boyfriend," Eleanor said, "and in our circles, boyfriends and girlfriends kiss. Actually, kiss wasn't the word she used."

"But I'm old enough to be your father."

"Lizzie doesn't see that as a problem."

"So what did you say?"

"I said you kiss me when you meet me, and also when we say goodbye."

"Is that why she thought we should sit in the back row?"

Eleanor nodded. "Yes. Didn't you ever do that?"

"Yes, what about you?"

"Yes."

"Eleanor," David said, after a pause. "Are you happy the way things are – I mean, do you think we should sit in the back row?"

"David, I'm very happy the way things are. No, that's not true. I don't like deceiving my mum, but I know she would create a fuss if she knew. You should have heard her going on about some actor whose girlfriend was much younger."

As they approached half-term, David was anticipating spending more time with Eleanor. He knew that she had the opportunity to work, but the hours were flexible, so they spent over an hour in the park each lunchtime, eating their sandwiches together. On the Friday, instead of riding to work, she rode directly to David's house. They then drove out into the country, well away from where anyone would know or recognise them. They spent some time walking together, before having a ploughman's lunch in a country pub, and then driving back in the afternoon. Eleanor needed to be home before her mother. David needed to be home because he was expecting Daniel and Stephanie for the week-end. Stephanie and Daniel had sorted out their wedding day, and this visit was to confirm a few things. By this stage, David had told Jill something of his new relationship with Eleanor, and wondered if she might have told Daniel. With Jill he had stressed the friendship aspect of their relationship.

"And may I ask if there is anything physical?" Jill had asked at the time.

"Of course. I hug her when we meet. That's what people do nowadays!" David replied confidently.

"You don't hug Keith."

"Oh, perhaps I should then," David answered. "Do you think I should?"

"I think he's happy with the handshake, Dad."

Apparently, Stephanie and Daniel assumed that they were still singing, and so Stephanie had asked that Eleanor should join them on the Sunday. It meant that Eleanor had to tell her mother that she had been invited out for Sunday lunch.

"With Mr Anderson?"

"Yes, Mum. You met Stephanie and Daniel at Christmas."

"But that was a long time ago."

"Mum, they said they wanted to see me."

"Why?"

"I don't know."

"I don't see why you have to go to lunch."

"Mum, I'm sure they won't kidnap me," Eleanor said, trying to inject some humour.

"Don't be silly."

"Do you want me to tell Stephanie that my mother won't let me go?"

"Don't be silly, Eleanor."

"Right, I'll accept," Eleanor said.

"I'd still like to know why," her mother muttered.

The reason became clear once lunch was over. They were sitting in the lounge, with after dinner coffee.

"Eleanor," Stephanie said, "you know we're getting married this summer?"

"Yes, David told me. I'm pleased for you."

"Well. What we would like is for you to be a guest."

"At your wedding?"

"Ye-es," Stephanie said, with a smile.

"When is it?"

"Wednesday of the first week of the holiday. It was the only day we could get at short notice. All the Saturdays in July and August have been booked for months."

"The first week?" Eleanor said slowly. "I'm going to camp the first week. I'm a junior officer."

"Oh," Stephanie said.

"Hang on," David said. "Where is the camp?"

Eleanor told him, and then added, "Why?"

"I could collect you. You'd be allowed to go to a wedding, wouldn't you?"

"I'm sure you would," Daniel said. "We had someone who had to go to a funeral."

"But what would I wear?"

"Eleanor, come on, you've got lots of clothes," David said.

"You don't understand," Eleanor said. "Mum made a fuss about today!"

"But if you went from camp, Eleanor, she needn't know," Daniel said.

"Daniel!" Stephanie exclaimed.

"Her mum doesn't approve of Dad," Daniel said to Stephanie. "That's what Jill said."

"Stephanie," David said. "When we met you, Eleanor and I were singing together. Well, somebody, or people took exception, and words were said – to me."

"Who by?" Stephanie asked.

"By our pastor, on behalf of Mum," Eleanor said.

"We don't know that for certain. Anyway, there was no more singing. Then, one morning in the Easter holidays, I was woken up by a phone call. Eleanor had been with a group in Romania, and someone's car wouldn't start."

"My dad's car, actually!" Eleanor said, butting in.

"So I drove to Heathrow to collect Eleanor. On the way back we chatted and agreed that we still wanted to spend time together, even if we couldn't sing."

"But when David dropped me off at home, Mum was so rude to him. I was really angry."

"So now we see each other, but without Eleanor's mum knowing," David said.

"Did you know this?" Stephanie asked Daniel.

Daniel looked embarrassed. "I knew they still did things together, and that her mum didn't approve. Jill told me."

"Thanks for telling me!" Stephanie said to him.

"Don't be cross, Stephanie," Eleanor said. "I think Daniel finds it hard to understand."

"Do you?" David asked him.

Daniel waited a moment. "I do, Dad. Sorry."

"Is it my age?" Eleanor asked. "Would it be okay if I was your Dad's age?"

"What does it look like, Dad?" Daniel said, ignoring Eleanor's question.

"I know what it looks like. That's why I'm surprised that you have invited Eleanor as well."

"It was my idea, Dad. Are you, er, very close?" Stephanie said.

"I think we are. Look we're both aware that it's an unusual relationship, based on our ages, but we seem to click," David said, and shrugged.

"It's all right, I won't go," Eleanor said quietly. "Besides, I won't have anything to wear."

"Daniel, it's up to you," David said. "If it wasn't for the fact we're family, I wouldn't come without her."

"Really?" Daniel said.

"Sorry, Daniel."

"Right," Daniel said, turning to Eleanor. "Then please do come."

Eleanor looked at David.

"I would like you to go," David said.

"But what will I wear?" Eleanor wailed.

"Eleanor, stop worrying, just leave your clothes for me to bring," David said.

"But I need a new dress. How will I explain that to Mum?"

David stood up, and walked over to where she was sitting. "Eleanor, we'll talk about it later," he said. "Come on, time to go."

Daniel and Stephanie left after tea. Together with Eleanor, they had accompanied David to the cemetery after coffee. Then they had gone for a walk round the local park – Daniel and Stephanie holding hands, of course.

"Well, what do you think?" Stephanie asked, as they sat on the train later that day. "Will you be getting a step-mother younger than me?"

"I hope not!" Daniel said.

"The thing is, Danny, when I first met her, I assumed she was our age," Stephanie said. "And they're not all lovey-dovey. There was a chap near where I lived with a very young wife, and he couldn't keep his hands off her. It was embarrassing."

"And so would this be."

"There is something between them. Didn't you notice how Eleanor was comfortable going with us, I mean to the grave of his late wife?"

"And you think she's planning to take her place?" Daniel asked.

"Daniel! I'm sure she isn't! Don't say things like that."

They sat in silence. Finally, it was Daniel who spoke. "Stephie, the thing is, things like that do happen," he said quietly. "Lonely old man bewitched by sexy young female."

"Your dad is not that silly."

"I do hope not. Whatever made you ask Eleanor to our wedding?"

"Danny, we've been over that. I just felt that we got on so well at the New Year."

"But we haven't seen her since, Stephie."

"I think we may see more of her in the future. They're obviously very fond of each other – you can tell from how they look at each other."

"Well, with any luck, it will be over by then," Daniel said.

"Eleanor, are you sure about coming to the wedding with me?" David asked her, as they drove to the church together that evening.

"Apart from having no dress, yes, of course. What about you? Will you mind being seen with a teen-age totty?"

"Eleanor! That's not how I see you."

"So how do you see me?"

"As an attractive, intelligent, caring and mature young woman."

"Who also needs a dress," she said, and laughed. "Oh, David, you are so gallant."

"Not that gallant. I'm about to kick you out and make you walk the last bit, sorry."

The second half of the term continued in the same manner as the first half. David met Eleanor from school to drive her home. It was an opportunity to plan when they could see each other at the week end. Since that first time, David waited in his car, rather than meet her by the gate. There were two jazz nights, and two more visits to the cinema after work on a Saturday, with Lizzie and Jayne.

The two girls then suggested a trip to the swimming pool because the weather was so good. David liked swimming, and knew the outside pool well, but he felt unsure.

"Please come, David," Eleanor said, after she had told him about the plan. "I thought you liked swimming."

"I do," he admitted.

"What is it? Is it Lizzie, or Jayne? We go to the cinema with them." She paused, "and we sit close together in the dark," she added, with a grin.

"It's not the girls – I like them, I mean, they seem to accept us."

"But Lizzie still finds our relationship funny," Eleanor said. "So what is it?"

"I don't think you'll understand."

"Well I won't if you don't tell me."

"Okay, what will you wear?"

"David! You're not serious," Eleanor exclaimed.

"See, I said you wouldn't understand."

Eleanor touched his arm. "Then please help me," she said quietly.

Eleanor waited. "Eleanor, I'm a man and you're a woman," he said slowly.

"Yes, I do know that," she said, grinning.

"Eleanor, be serious," David said rather sharply.

"Sorry," she said, and tried to look sorry.

"Do you want me to continue?"

Eleanor nodded. "Yes please."

"Do you remember once asking me how I saw you?"

"Yes, you said I was caring. That was nice. Oh, and mature."

"There was more."

Eleanor shrugged. "You said I was attractive."

"Yes, that's quite a wide term. You can attract people by being vivacious and by your character. Girls can also be sexually attractive."

"Oh," Eleanor said.

"Eleanor," David said after a pause. "Let me tell you what first struck me about you. I remember your baptism because I thought you spoke from the heart. I noticed that when you sang with Tom, your face was radiant. But the big thing was that time you came and spoke to me on the bus – you recognised me as a person. Then, of course, you brought me that cup of tea, remember?"

Eleanor nodded. "Go on," she whispered.

"But I can't ignore that other aspect, sorry. I found it quite hard when I had to put sun-cream on your back last summer."

"Oh, David, I didn't realise."

"And it doesn't help that you're still a child – in a legal sense. If I let my thoughts wander, then am I a pervert?"

They sat quietly for a while. Then David spoke again. "Well?"

"No, of course you're not," Eleanor said quickly. "David, do you really think of me as a child?" she added.

"Of course I don't. But I am very aware of our age difference, and I did think James was right. The problem was that I missed you. Now I sometimes have sessions of guilt when I think you should be with a boy of your own age."

"Don't worry about that. I would rather be with you," she said.

"Until you do meet someone your own age, Eleanor."

"Well, that's not likely at the moment."

"But you might at university."

There was another pause. "David, I might not go to university," she said.

"Of course you will," David replied.

"Why should I?"

"Well," David began. "Because, because you ought to!"
Eleanor laughed. "That's not a good reason. Did your
daughter go?"

"No, but we wanted her to go."

"Then why didn't she?"

"She was going out with Keith, and didn't want to go
away," David said.

"Well, perhaps I might meet someone."

"I thought you said that's not likely."

"Ah," she said. "Anyway, are you coming? I've got to go
now, because Mum knows about it, and if I don't go
home smelling of chlorine, she'll ask why."

He did enjoy being with Eleanor and the girls at the pool;
however, it was a time of mixed feelings for David.
Eleanor was in a bikini, but apologised to David about it.
"The only one-piece I have is my school cossy, and the
girls would have asked why. I couldn't tell them that my
boyfriend is embarrassed by a bikini, could I?" she said,
with a twinkle in her eye.

The girls met a couple of boys they knew, which meant
that David and Eleanor were left on their own for a lot of
the time.

"I wonder what the boys think of me," he said to Eleanor.

"Does it bother you, David?"

"I feel for you," he said. "It's a good job there are only
two of them."

"Why?"

"Well, if there were three of them, they would have
expected you to join them."

"So?"

"Wouldn't you have felt obliged?"

"No."

At one stage, Eleanor took a bottle of sun-cream from her bag.

"David, if you are too embarrassed to do my back, I'll call Lizzie across," she said, after she had creamed her front, arms and legs.

"I'll close my eyes," David said.

"Okay," she said, handing him the bottle.

"I was joking, Eleanor. Turn around."

David did not find it easy – partly because he had to undo the strap, but more so because he felt an urge to kiss her bare back. It was obviously out of the question, but he finished off quickly and handed the bottle back.

"That wasn't too bad, was it?" she said brightly. David didn't answer; how could he tell her that he thought her back was beautiful, and that he had wanted to kiss it? "Oh, I'm sorry," she added. But inside, she felt a thrill. Did it mean he had feelings that were more than just affection?

They had their first disagreement just before the end of term. An opportunity had arisen for Eleanor to spend most of Sunday with David, and she suggested that she cooked their lunch. David had been given a shopping list of necessary items, and Eleanor arrived before morning church to start things off. Then they rode their bicycles to church, separating only for the final road. They both left early, but separately, to meet up and ride home together. Lunch was good, and after washing up (David did not have a dish washer) he suggested that they went out for a walk.

"Not a bike-ride?" Eleanor asked.

"No. Let's go far enough away that we won't be seen, and anyway, as much as I like cycling, the traffic makes it less sociable. Conversation keeps being interrupted by cars."

"Okay," she agreed.

"We could take a picnic and make a long afternoon of it," David suggested.

"Yes, I'd like that," she said.

They ended up twenty miles away. David had a haversack containing drink and sandwiches, and they set off.

Immediately, Eleanor reached for David's hand.

"Eleanor, the wedding," David said, as they left the car park.

"Yes?"

"You said you needed a new dress."

"Well, I just fancied a new dress. I do have a dress."

"Okay. So if it was one of your family, what would you have done?"

"Mum would probably buy me one," Eleanor said.

"Just a dress? I thought women did the whole outfit – bag, shoes, hat?"

"Well, sometimes. Mum might have included them, if I was lucky, but it's all irrelevant anyway, isn't it."

"I would like you to have a new outfit."

"So would I," Eleanor said sadly.

"So I'll buy it for you."

Eleanor stopped dead, pulling him round.

"Pardon?"

"I said that I'll buy it for you."

"You've decided have you?"

"Pardon?" David said.

"Have you or have you not decided to buy me an outfit for your son's wedding."

"No, I haven't decided."

"You said, and I quote, I'll buy it for you."

"Eleanor, what's got into you?" David said, surprised and baffled by her outburst.

"I just don't think you should decide."

"I haven't decided. I was offering."

"Then thank you, David, but I'll pass."

"What?" David exclaimed. "But you said you wanted a new dress."

"Yes, but it's not your problem. And anyway, what will I do with it afterwards?"

"I didn't think of that."

"Anyway, apart from that, I don't think you should buy me a dress. Come on."

They walked in silence for a while.

"Eleanor, if I was really your boyfriend, would it make a difference?" David asked.

"Lizzie says you are my boyfriend," Eleanor replied.

"So do boyfriends have rights?"

"Rights? What kind of rights?"

"The right to offer to buy her a new dress?"

"Okay, yes, you can offer. But the answer is still no."

"Would you like to tell me why," David asked quietly.

"I don't know. Maybe it feels like your trying to buy me."

"That's rubbish," he said.

"I said feels like. David, I don't want to get too close. I don't want to be too hurt when you wake up to the fact that I'm only a teenager."

"Maybe I worry about you waking up to the fact that I could be your father. Anyway, I'm not trying to buy you. If you don't want a new dress, then fair enough. But not a single word when we go to the wedding."

"At least I won't have to explain it away to Mum."

"You wouldn't have to. Your mum wouldn't see it. It would be my dress – maybe my next girlfriend will like it."

Eleanor stopped and pulled him round.

"What did you say?"

David laughed. "You heard."

"Are you serious?"

"No, you silly girl – well not about another girlfriend. But yes about the dress. I thought the idea was for me to bring it for you to change into when I collect you, right. Then I will take it back at the end of the day – your mother needn't know about it."

Eleanor suddenly threw her arms round him and kissed him, well, kissed his cheek. "You clever man," she said.

"So are we going shopping?" David asked.

"Yes please."

Chapter 22

The Wedding

Having agreed that David would buy her a dress for the wedding, the problem was when. Fortunately, both of their schools closed early on the last day, so Eleanor waited for David to pick her up from her school. Eleanor knew where she wanted to go, and David recognised the row of shops from his married days. Eleanor also had some idea of what she wanted, and found it in the second shop. She showed it to him, and he agreed it looked nice. But when she reappeared from the changing booth, he nearly gasped audibly.

"What do you think, David?"

"Eleanor, you look fantastic," he whispered.

"Not me, the dress," she said.

"Yes, that looks nice as well," he said. "Do you like it?" She nodded. "Yes, I do."

"Then we'll take it. Sorry, I mean shall we take it?"

Eleanor smiled at him. "Yes please," she said.

As Eleanor reappeared in her school clothes, and they waited for the dress to be packed, David turned to her, "Right, where do we go for the rest of the outfit?"

"The rest?" Eleanor said.

"Half-penneth of tar," David murmured.

"Pardon?" Eleanor said.

David grinned. "It's an old expression. Don't spoil the ship for just a small amount of tar." He turned to an assistant. "Excuse me, Miss, where do we find the accessories?"

Ten minutes later, they left with a dress and a handbag. Then it was straight to a shoe shop, where besides heeled

sandals, tights were included. Tights because they were
not part of her camp clothing, and so would be brought by
David along with her outfit. He then dropped her off one
street away from home. It was goodbye until Wednesday.

Wednesday was very special for David. It was also very
poignant. David felt his heart almost busting with pride
seeing Daniel waiting at the front with his best man,
hearing Daniel make his vows, and then seeing Daniel
standing with his new wife for the photographs. However,
his happiness was mixed with sadness. The sadness was
the absence of Daniel's mother as a witness of the
occasion, but he thought it was possibly worse for Daniel.
The day had begun very early for David, leaving home at
six for the ninety minute drive to Eleanor's camp. There
was then a three hour drive to Stephanie's home church.
Neither had had breakfast, but David had allowed time
for a breakfast stop.
"You're very quiet," he said to Eleanor, over the
breakfast table. "Tired?"
"No," she said. "I was thinking if I should have accepted
Stephie's invitation."
David had wondered about that too. Would the presence
of Eleanor serve to emphasise the absence of Jenny? But
he didn't want Eleanor to feel this. "Why?" he said.
"Weddings are family occasions. I'm not family. And
there is something we haven't talked about."
"Go on," David said.
"Won't your parents be there? Do they know about me?"
"No, not specifically."
"What do you mean by that?"
"Eleanor, we became friends through the singing, and I
told them that I was helping a young person. They
accepted that at face value. I didn't tell them about our
renewed friendship for one very good reason – they

would not have understood. Look, Daniel didn't did he?"

"Are you ashamed of me?"

"Eleanor! Of course I'm not. Look, I went out of my way to bring you. If I didn't want you with me, all I had to do was let you stay at the camp, let alone buy you the dress. The thing is, Stephanie invited you, and I'm glad she did. However, I do feel bad when I think of Jenny's parents. What are they going to think when they see the widower husband of their deceased daughter turn up with a young woman. Maybe Stephanie was rather naive to invite you," he said. "But it's too late now. I'll introduce you and say that she invited you, and I'm looking after you."

"That sounds odd, David. And what about your parents? What will they think?" Eleanor asked.

"I don't know."

"I do. What on earth is our son doing with a schoolgirl."

"Correction – doing with an attractive young woman. I'm not going to introduce you as a schoolgirl, and you certainly don't look like one at the moment."

"I think they are going to be shocked, sorry! On top of that, I feel that I'm replacing someone who should be there," she said.

"Replacing, but not displacing."

"What is the difference?" Eleanor said.

"Eleanor, you are a football team manager. You think your striker isn't trying, so you pull him off, and replace him. But actually, the second player has displaced the first player. Then your goalkeeper breaks his leg and is carried off. The man you then send on did not displace him, even though he replaces him."

"That still doesn't make me feel any better. Do you understand, David?"

David reached across the small table and held her hand. "Of course I understand. I want you to know that I am looking forward to being with you, but we must not do anything that draws attention to us."

"Like introducing me as your girlfriend?" Eleanor said with a smile.

"I'll try to remember," he replied, laughing.

"So what am I, officially?"

"Well, since it was Stephanie's idea, you are going as a friend of hers, I suppose. But I would like to say girlfriend, that is, my girlfriend."

"I would like that too," she whispered.

"Where will we change?" Eleanor asked when she knew that they were getting close. They were both in casual clothes, Eleanor in jeans and a sweatshirt, David in casual trousers, shirt, and sweatshirt. Eleanor's outfit was in the boot, together with his suit, shirt, tie and shoes.

"I did think about the breakfast place, but decided against it. Could we change in the car? Or I could pull off down a side road?"

"So long as you don't mind seeing me in my bra."

"Oh, sorry, so shall we wait until we get there?" David said.

Eleanor laughed. "David. Don't be silly. You've seen me in a bikini."

"That's not the same – a bra is underwear," he said seriously.

Eleanor laughed again. "In which case, just close your eyes. Look, there's a side road, turn down there, David." Just a couple of minutes drive down the road brought them to a field with an open gate. David reversed into the gateway, and just hoped that the farmer wasn't about to visit his field. By standing on the grass behind the car with the raised boot, they were screened to a degree as they changed. David turned away as Eleanor lifted her sweatshirt off, and then replaced it with the new dress, and at the same time, he changed into his suit trousers.

"Please can you zip me?" was the signal to turn back. Just when David thought they were ready, there was another delay, although David should have anticipated it. Out came her hair brush. Then her make-up bag. He waited patiently, resisting the temptation to say she didn't need it, but what he did say was that she looked even more amazing. He was rewarded with a smile, and then they were off again.

Despite the breakfast and stop to change, they still arrived early – even before Daniel – so they went for a walk. Without thinking, David reached for Eleanor's hand as they left the church car park.

"David," she said, lifting her hand up. "How friendly are we meant to be, I mean, today?"

"Oh, I forgot, sorry," he said, releasing her hand.

"But we're not there yet, are we?"

Without a word, he reached for her hand again, and they walked on.

"How far are we going?" Eleanor asked. They had reached the road, and they could see shops one way. There was a park the other way which they had passed a few minutes earlier.

"To the park?" David asked.

She nodded, and they walked to and then into the park. Neither had been talking.

"You're quiet," Eleanor said, as they followed a path in the deserted park.

"So are you."

"Are you missing Jenny?"

David stopped and pulled Eleanor round. "Do you think I should be?"

"That's not what I asked, David," she said in a low voice.

"I was thinking about her, sorry."

"That's okay, I would expect it," she said.

"Eleanor, what has happened has happened. I'm with you today. No, I was thinking about my kids missing their mum today."

"I was thinking that, too."

"Just my kids?"

Eleanor hesitated. "Okay, I was thinking that you are missing her too."

"Oh, Eleanor. I am glad that you are with me today." Without thinking, he pulled her into a hug. They stood for a long while, cheek to cheek until he felt her shaking slightly. He quickly released her, and looked at her.

"Sweetheart, don't cry," he said. His overwhelming urge was to kiss her properly and tell her he loved her, but he knew he ought not to. Instead, he reached for his handkerchief. "Won't your mascara run?"

Eleanor laughed. "That shows just how much you've noticed me. I'm not wearing mascara – I thought I might cry. Girls do cry at weddings."

"I did notice you," David protested. "I think you look beautiful anyway. Anyway, why do girls cry?"

"It's mourning yet another sister who has been sold into domestic slavery."

"What?" David gasped, stepping back. This was a side of Eleanor he had never seen.

"Oh, David," she cried, laughing at him. "I was joking! Your face."

They continued their walk, but now talking, mainly about things in the park, and then back to the church. They were talking about the building itself, still hand in had, when they suddenly realised that Daniel and his best man were now there, as well as other arriving guests. David released her hand quickly, but he knew they had been seen.

"I think they saw us," David said quietly.

"Sorry," Eleanor replied.

"But we'll now act as though they didn't, okay."

Daniel spoke first as they approached him. "Dad! Where have you been? I recognised your car. Both grandparents are waiting inside."

"We arrived too early, so we've been exploring. So, the big day has come," David said, embracing his son.

"Right, introduce me," he added, indicating the best man, "Before we go in."

"Oh yes, right. Dad, this is Barry. Barry, this is my dad and," he hesitated, "this is Eleanor."

"Yes, Stephie invited me. You can call me Elly." She turned to David. "David, I'd like to pop to the loo." Then she turned to Barry. "Barry, you couldn't show me, could you?" she asked sweetly.

"Well, yes, okay," Barry replied.

Daniel waited until they were alone. "Dad, were you holding hands?" he asked.

"Yes, but it won't happen again," David replied. "Sorry."

"I don't understand. Are you, er, an item as the saying is?" Daniel asked.

"I suppose we are, in a way."

"You suppose? What does that mean?"

"We like being together, okay. We occasionally hug, and sometimes we hold hands. Nothing more. Goodness, Daniel, how many girls' hands have you held."

"They were girls my own age, Dad," Daniel replied.

"Daniel, we didn't mean to embarrass you. I'm sorry,"

"Is that all you can say, Dad?"

"Yes, for the moment. Look, we're friends."

"Just friends?"

"Just friends, but special friends. Oh look, here comes Jill and Keith. Don't say anything, well not today."

"Not today?"

"That's what I said." He turned away and walked towards Jill.

David put his arms out to hug and kiss Jill, and then shook Keith's hand. After exchanging greetings with David, and then with Daniel, including comments on their journey, Jill took David's arm and led him away. Barry had returned and was talking to Keith and Daniel.

"Dad, are you on you own?" Jill asked confidentially.

"No," David replied carefully. "Why?"

"Keith thought he spotted you – holding hands with a woman. Walking out of a park? We missed the church and had to turn round by which time we found you here. But no woman."

David shrugged. "It was probably me."

"Who was the woman then, and where is she now?" Jill asked, and looking around. Then she spotted Eleanor walking across towards them. "Oh!" she gasped. "So Keith was right!"

David turned to see Eleanor coming across. "Well, Eleanor, did you find it? You remember my daughter, Jill, don't you?"

"Yes," Eleanor replied brightly. "Hello, Jill."

Jill was still recovering from her surprise, so David answered for her. "Eleanor, Keith and Jill passed us on the road and Keith saw us," he paused, "holding hands."

"Oh," said Eleanor.

"Jill," David began, "Eleanor is officially here as a friend of Stephanie, and I brought her. We didn't want to cause any embarrassment, but I didn't bank on you seeing us in the road. We'd just been for a walk because we were early."

"Daniel and Barry saw us too," Eleanor said. "Barry just asked me if I was your girlfriend"

"Oh. What did you say?"

"I said yes." She shrugged. "Sorry."

David put his arm round Eleanor's shoulder. "I guess we've just come out of the closet. Sorry to shock you, Jill."

Jill smiled, and kissed Eleanor's cheek. "Maybe I'm not that shocked, Dad. It might shock Keith though."

"I'm afraid it's shocked Daniel. Even upset him," David said. "Eleanor didn't want to come in case that happened."

"Why, Eleanor?"

"Because your mother should be here on a day like this," Eleanor said.

Jill looked at her, and then hugged her. "I'm glad you're here. I've got Keith, Daniel's got Stephie, and Dad has got you. Don't worry about Daniel." Then she turned back to David. "Dad, I assume Mum's parent's have been invited, and what about Grandma and Grandad Anderson."

"Daniel said they're already inside, why?" David answered.

"Do they know about Eleanor?"

"We were talking about that on the way here," Eleanor said. "Neither know about me, that is as a special friend of your Dad. And we don't think today is the best day to tell them. I'm officially here as Stephie's friend."

"Then no more holding hands," Jill said, with a smile. She suddenly grinned. "But I bet Barry isn't so happy. I think Daniel had told him about you. Come on, let's go in." She grinned again. "So what side are you sitting on – a friend of the bride or a friend of the groom?"

"She's sitting with me," David said firmly, "but I had better introduce her to both sets of grandparents first."

"Wait, Dad, let me introduce Eleanor. I can say that Stephie invited her, but that we are looking after her. Then I'll go back for Keith."

As far as other people were concerned, Eleanor might have been Daniel and Jill's sister. Eleanor did not expect to be called for the photographs, but when it was Stephanie and Daniel, together with Jill, Keith and David, then Stephanie insisted.

"Could Eleanor join us?" Jill had whispered to Daniel. Stephanie overheard, and looked at Jill, with a questioning look. Jill nodded.

"Eleanor," Stephanie called. "Come and join us." Eleanor shook her head, so Stephanie walked forward. "Please, Elly." Eleanor complied, but she refused when it was the happy pair and parents. However, when they finally moved on to the reception, although she did not take part in the welcome line up, she found that she was placed on the top table.

"Did you expect to sit on your own," Stephanie answered, when Eleanor questioned her about it.

"But I'm not family," Eleanor said quietly.

"Yet?" Stephanie replied quietly, and raising her eyebrows.

"Don't be silly. We're just friends."

"I've noticed the way you look at each other, Elly. I'm not daft. You're potty about each other."

"Stephie, I'm seventeen."

"I believe the legal age is sixteen," Stephanie said. Eleanor stared at her.

"I meant for marriage," Stephanie added quickly. "I wasn't suggesting, you know."

"There is nothing going on like that," Eleanor said firmly. "And as for marriage, come on, be serious. Daniel would be horrified."

"It's got nothing to do with Daniel. Would you say no?"

"Stephie, change the subject, please," Eleanor said. "It's not going to happen! Now what about this seating?"

"I put you on this table deliberately. My bridesmaid is

married, and wants to sit with her husband. Barry doesn't have a partner, so I put you with him, in place of Beth. It just happens that you will also be next to David. All right?"

Apart from the incident with the photographs, and the discussion with Stephanie about the seating plan, Eleanor enjoyed the wedding. She knew they couldn't stay for the evening celebration, so when David suggested that it was time to go, she went with him to say goodbye to the newly-weds. As Eleanor and Stephanie hugged, Eleanor thanked her for the invitation.

"And thank you for coming, Elly," Stephanie replied. "I hope you'll be able to come and visit us with David soon."

Eleanor stood back, and looked at Stephanie. "Shouldn't you check with your husband, Stephie?" she asked.

"But if he did agree?"

"And my mother?"

"What about when you are eighteen?"

"We'll see."

She stood back to let David embrace and say goodbye to Stephanie, and looked at Daniel. He had been with David, and she wondered how much he had heard of her conversation with Stephanie. He looked at her, and held out his hand. "Thank you for coming, Eleanor," he said. "Please don't hurt Dad."

"Daniel," Eleanor whispered, "I would never do that."

It was a long drive back, with plenty of time to talk. They talked mainly about the wedding of course, but Eleanor did not tell David about her chats with Stephanie.

"I'm really glad you came, Eleanor. It made the day even more special. Are you glad you went?"

"Yes, yes I am."

"So it wasn't as bad as you thought?"

"No, but I think we upset Daniel. He asked me not to hurt you," she said.

"What made him say that?"

"Perhaps he thinks that I'll get fed-up with you before you get fed-up with me,"

"How long did your previous boyfriends last," David asked.

Eleanor thought. "The longest was about a year. I was seven at the time and I can't remember much anyway, it's what Mum told me,"

"Eleanor! Be serious."

"Okay, not long – a couple of months. Maybe three months."

"Why did they end?" he asked.

"David!"

"Sorry."

"They usually ended up getting heavy. Possessive. Too physical. Even unpleasant suggestions. I felt I was being asked out for the wrong reasons. Apart from when I was seven, I first went out with a boy when I was thirteen. We went to the pictures. Then he walked me home. He didn't touch me at all. I was so disappointed. I wondered what was wrong with me, and I cried myself to sleep! That was it. But the next boy was different. Wow. We kissed all the way through the film – I particularly wanted to see it – and he put his arm round me going home."

"How long did it last?"

"Two weeks. I couldn't see him because we went to a wedding, but I heard that he had been with another girl. The rat. So I gave up boys for a while. I knew a nice boy when I was fourteen, and we used to sit in the park holding hands. I think he was shy so I taught him to kiss."

"Eleanor!"

"But he was a fast learner, and soon wanted more than

kisses. After a couple or so more boys like him, I lost interest. Most seem to have one-track minds – two if you count football."

"It seems you don't keep boyfriends very long."

"That's because I'm particular."

"How long do you think I will last – three months, six months," David asked, laughing.

"Well, I go away in a year."

"I wonder if we'll last that long."

"Just so long as my mum doesn't find out," Eleanor said.

"Then we'll have to be extra careful."

"If she could see us now, she'd have a fit. Especially with me wearing a dress that you bought."

"Eleanor, you looked really pretty today. I think you were the prettiest girl there," David said, glancing at her.

Eleanor laughed. "See, typical male. I've heard that line so may times."

"That's not why I said it," he said quietly

"Sorry, David, I know. I'm glad you like it. I just wish I could keep it."

"Maybe you can. Listen, what would it cost in a charity shop?"

Eleanor snorted. "Huh, a lot less than you paid."

"Suppose I gave it to a charity shop with the proviso that only you can buy it. Would you be interested? If I made a donation, I could tell them to reduce the price."

"David! You can't do that."

"We've got nothing to lose. What day do you go away next week?"

"Wednesday."

"So let's try it on Monday."

"It won't work."

"It won't if you don't try. I'd like you to be able to keep the dress, don't you want to?"

"You know I do. It's special because you bought it,

David."
"Well?"
"All right."

They made a brief stop for coffee and the call of nature. Then it was non-stop to Eleanor's camp, so that Eleanor arrived wearing her outfit. This was because the girls in her tent wanted to see her outfit. It meant that David had to wait for her to change, before setting off home by himself, carrying her outfit. Because they planned to meet on Monday, they did not meet on the Sunday.

Monday went better than Eleanor expected. She met up with Lizzie, and then with David. David took the wedding outfit into a charity shop and asked what price they would put on the dress if he donated it and then went out and told the girls. They were happy, so David went back in and negotiated the deal. He handed it over, and then Eleanor bought it. After a while, Lizzie went home, leaving David and Eleanor alone. They had coffee together before going home separately. He knew he would not see Eleanor for over two weeks, and was not looking forward to the time apart. His mind wandered as he wondered how he would feel if they were still friends in a year's time and Eleanor was about to go to university. Maybe by then their friendship would have waned, he thought.

Chapter 23

Absence Makes The Heart ...

Eleanor's parents had booked a ten-night holiday in
Scotland. The advantage was that postcards posted in
Scotland arrived within two days, especially when
enclosed in an envelope, and with a first class stamp. The
first card arrived on the Friday. "Lousy journey. Nice
hotel. Missing you already! xx Eleanor." There was
another card on Saturday, with a similar message. It was a
brief comment about the hotel, but more about missing
him and with three kisses. The daily cards continued on
Monday, each one telling David that she was missing
him, but now adding that she was looking forward to
seeing him. Each day had one extra kiss. At the same
time, David felt he was missing her more and more.
Saturday came, and David had a card saying that she
couldn't wait until Sunday. He assumed that this was just
a phrase, so when the doorbell rang on Saturday evening,
he didn't rush to the door. He was just about to say he
didn't want to buy anything when he realised it was
Eleanor. For a moment, he just stared, then she was in his
arms and kissing. But it wasn't a kiss on the cheek, it was
a full mouth kiss. Suddenly David realised what he was
doing, and he released Eleanor.
"Sorry, Eleanor, I'm sorry!" he gasped.
"Are you?"
"Yes, no, oh, Eleanor. What are you doing here,
anyway?"
"It was another horrendous journey, so I said I needed to
get out and get some fresh air. And see my boyfriend,"
she added, with a grin.
"You didn't!"

"How do you know?" she grinned. "Anyway, did you get my cards? It was really hard not letting Mum know."
"It must have cost you a fortune in stamps, but it was a good idea using envelopes."
"I thought you would want me to be discreet and not tell your postman that someone was missing you," she said.
"Not for that, I meant to get them here on time. Mind you, at the moment you can tell the world that you missed me."
"Did you miss me?" she asked.
"I did. I was looking forward to tomorrow."
"I wish we could sit together at church, David."
"So do I. How long can you stay tonight?"
"I ought to be going. I said it was a ride to clear the cobwebs – do you want to ride some of the way back?"
They stopped one street away, and kissed goodbye. A brief affectionate kiss, but this time lips to lips.
"See you tomorrow," they both said.

Over the next two weeks, they continued their clandestine meetings. Some days they met at lunchtime and ate their sandwiches together. Because Eleanor could vary her hours, she was able to leave early on both Fridays, and they went back to the river to check on the swans, and then on to the tea-shop. It was the second of the two visits to the tea-shop that brought things to a head. They were about to leave when suddenly Eleanor froze.
"David, that's my neighbour," she whispered.
"Where?"
"To your right and slightly behind you – don't look. Oh, bother, they've recognised me." She waved and smiled. "Oh no, they're coming over."
"Act normally," David whispered.

As Eleanor waited, she felt her heart beating faster, but she tried to stay calm. "Eleanor," the lady said, obviously expecting to be introduced.

"Hello, Mrs Thompson, Mr Thompson" Eleanor said, smiling at them. "David, this is Mr and Mrs Thompson. They live next door." Then she looked up again. "Meet my friend David. We've been to look at a family of swans."

"Oh, where?"

"On the river," Eleanor said. "Do you often come here," she then asked.

"Yes, don't we," Mrs Thompson said, turning to her husband. He nodded. "And you?" she added.

"Not as much as I'd like to." Eleanor looked pointedly at her watch, and then at David. David took the hint, and stood up.

"Please excuse us," he said to the Thompsons. "Eleanor, I'll go and settle up. Meet you by our bikes." He turned to the Thompsons again. "Nice to meet you," he said, and went to settle up inside rather than wait for the waitress to bring him the bill. When he came out, Eleanor was waiting by their bicycles.

"I wonder if they'll tell Mum?" Eleanor said.

"Why should they?" David asked. "Anyway, does it matter? You won't have to feel guilty if she knows."

"I think I would rather feel guilty," Eleanor replied. "I see trouble ahead."

"Stop worrying. Come on, we need to get moving."

Eleanor was right, there was trouble ahead, but it did not blow up until the next day. After working as usual on Saturday morning, Eleanor went home for lunch, and then said she was going out again.

"Going anywhere special?"

"Probably not," Eleanor replied. After all, although she

thought that David's house was special, he did not.

"Any idea what time you'll be back, dear?"

"No, but I won't be late."

"Got your phone?"

"Yes, Mum."

"Going on your bike?"

"No, not in this dress." She was in the new dress, but without the handbag, and sandals. Her mum had accepted the apparent second-hand bargain with little comment. But Eleanor didn't think she would accept second hand foot-ware, so the sandals were at David's, along with the handbag.

"Are you meeting a boy?" her mother asked.

"What? I mean, pardon?" Eleanor said, surprised by the direct question.

"Are you meeting a boy?" her mother asked again.

"No, I am not meeting a boy. But suppose I was?"

"If he was a nice boy, I would be pleased. It's a pity that boy you sang with had to go to university."

"Who, Tom?"

"Yes, that's his name, Tom."

"Well, he did," Eleanor said. She did not add that Tom already had a girlfriend.

"How is he? Do you see him?"

"Yes, I'll see him tomorrow, Mum. At church."

"And you haven't thought of singing together while he's home?"

Actually, it had been suggested by David, but she had said no.

"Mum, we haven't sung together for a year now. Would he want to?" Eleanor said. "Anyway, shall I tell him you asked after him?"

And with that, Eleanor turned to go.

Once out of sight of the house, she phoned David to tell

him she was on her way. Her phone was a pay-as-you-go phone, so it was a brief call. Then she deleted the record of the call, in case her mother tried to find out who she phoned. Her parents had provided the phone, and paid for the cost of using it. The phone was basically for use as a method of communicating with home, and not for chatting with friends. Even excessive text messaging was frowned upon.

"Darling, use the phone – you know calls are free."

"But not to mobiles, Mum."

She had thought of buying a second mobile phone herself, but didn't want to run the risk of being caught out by her parents. And since David didn't own a mobile phone anyway, it wasn't worth the risk.

David drove to meet her.

"Hello gorgeous," he said, after he had kissed her cheek.

"David!" she exclaimed. "Typical male – man looks on the outward appearance."

"Is that a problem, Eleanor?" David asked. "You know that's not the main reason I like being with you. Anyway," he grinned, "you do look rather nice in that dress. I am so glad you let me buy it."

"Mum couldn't get over how cheap it was."

"Yes, it was, wasn't it," David said, with a straight face.

"David! You bribed her, didn't you?"

"I donated it on condition that she sold it below its value. And I made up the difference."

"How much?"

"That's between me and the lady," David said. "Now, what shall we do? I've brought your sandals."

Eleanor thought for a moment. "I don't know."

"We talked about going to Bourton."

"I know. It's just that Mum has just grilled me, and she's

bound to ask where I've been."

"You could tell her," David said quietly.

"Be serious."

"I am. Are you ashamed of me?"

"David," she cried. "How could you say that?"

"Sorry," he said quietly.

"You don't understand. I'm an only child and they have always been very possessive."

"Do you mean protective?"

"They would say that," Eleanor said.

"What about the boyfriends you told me about?" David asked.

"She only knew about two of them. The first one, the one I cried over, and the last one. I came home upset and she asked me why. When I told her what the boy had suggested, she went bananas and was all for seeing his parents. That would have made it worse for me, so I wouldn't tell her. I don't know what she would do about you."

"We won't know unless we tell her."

"Well, not yet."

"Eleanor, if she is going to ask anyway, does it matter what we do?" David said.

"Okay, let's go to Bourton."

Eleanor's neighbours were in their back garden, and they saw Eleanor's mother in hers.

"Hello, Sheila, nice day."

"Hello Betty, John. Yes, gorgeous."

"Saw your Elly yesterday. With a gentleman friend."

Sheila blinked. A gentleman friend? "Oh, yes? Where did you see them?" She hoped she sounded casual.

"There's a little tea shop," Betty replied. "I don't know where exactly, I leave that to John. They were about to leave."

"Did you speak to her?"

"Oh yes, she introduced him to us," Betty said. "David, I think."

"Oh."

"But then they had to leave."

"What was he like, this, er, gentleman?" Sheila Jenkins asked, still trying to sound disinterested. It had to be the same David.

"Just a man – he seemed quite nice though."

"Ah, good."

"Do you know him?"

"Probably a friend from church."

Sheila Jenkins made some more small talk with her neighbour, and then went indoors to see her husband.

Eleanor enjoyed her afternoon with David at Bourton. They walked hand in hand by the river, and visited the tourist attractions. The main thing was that Eleanor was distracted from her concerns. After buying some sandwiches and drink, they then drove out into the countryside for a picnic. They had driven away from the road, and were sitting overlooking a valley.

"David, what am I going to do about Mum and Dad?" Eleanor said after a while.

"How old are you?" David said.

"You know how old," Eleanor said.

"You're seventeen – old enough to choose your own friends. My goodness, you'll be leaving home in a year's time. What will you do then?"

"What will I do? What about us?"

David sat in silence. It was so quiet and peaceful. He knew what he wanted – he wanted to keep Eleanor all for himself. For ever. A totally selfish thought and he felt ashamed.

"Eleanor," he said slowly. "When the time comes for you to move on, a new life, and maybe a new man, I hope we can still be friends. You are very special, and this is a very special time. I think I will always remember sitting here with you."

"Are you saying goodbye?"

"No, I hope there will never be a goodbye. I want to be friends forever. I want to be invited to your wedding and I want to be around when you have children."

Eleanor didn't reply, and they sat in silence, wrapped in their own thoughts. David was thinking that he was a liar. Yes, he did want to be friends for ever, but he didn't want to be invited to her wedding. Unless it was … He swallowed and put the thought out of his head, and sighed. If only he hadn't fallen in love with her. Eleanor had her own ideas about marriage and children, and it was obvious that they didn't match with David's. She was also thinking about that kiss, the kiss on the doorstep. It hadn't been a fatherly kiss. She sighed and slipped her hand into his. He turned, and mistook her quietness. "Eleanor, I'm sure your mother won't ask where you've been. Now stop worrying."

"I think we should go, David. Do you mind?"

David dropped Eleanor off as usual one street away, and watched her walk away. Something had come back to him on the way home. It was a remark that Eleanor had made months ago. Something about not being involved with a boy if there was no point, or was it no future? They had no future, so why were they involved? How had it happened? More to the point, what should they, or was it he, do about it. It was all very well to say they could just be friends – more and more he wanted to hold her properly. And kiss her properly. If they had to separate, wouldn't it be better to do it sooner, rather than in a year's time?

Eleanor's concerns were different. She didn't like deceiving her parents, but she didn't want to stop seeing David. But what she really dreaded was if they found out and told her not to see him. She believed that children should honour they parents, and should obey them. But for how long? Was she bound to obey her parents for ever? Even as an adult? Would she ever be free to make her own decisions, if by doing so, it went against their wishes? Still thinking about these problems, she walked up her path and let herself in. Her parents were sitting in the lounge, with no television. That struck her as odd, but it did not sound warning bells.

"Hello, Eleanor," her dad said gravely.

"Where have you been?" her mother added, before she could reply to her father.

"To Bourton."

"Who with?" This from her father.

"A friend."

"Which friend?" her mother asked.

"A friend from church."

"Which friend?" her mother asked again.

"It was David, David Anderson, the man I sang with. Okay?" she burst out.

There was silence for several moments. Then both her parents stood up. "Right, let's go and sort this out," her mother said.

"What do you mean?" Eleanor asked.

"Where is this Mr Anderson now?"

"At home, I suppose."

"Good. We'll see him there," her mother said.

"You can't do that. Anyway, you don't know where he lives."

"I said, we. We're all going."

"I won't go."

"Eleanor, either you take us, or we'll go to your pastor and ask where he lives!"

David was pottering in his front garden when their car drew up on his drive. For a moment he stared, then he went forward as her parents got out.

"Hello," David said.

They did not return his greeting, but instead asked if they could go inside. Then they asked Eleanor to come. He saw that Eleanor was crying, and hesitated.

"Shall we?" her mother said, indicating his door. "I think what we have say is best not said outside."

David opened his door, and stepped back. "The lounge is that way," he said, pointing. "Eleanor, can you put the kettle on?"

"We won't be staying long," Sheila Jenkins said. "You needn't bother."

"Please sit down," David said.

"It's all right, as I said, we won't be staying long."

David was annoyed. "Look, you asked to come in. Where I come from, it's common courtesy to ask one's guests to sit, and equally courteous for them to accept a seat. It's also considered courteous to offer a drink, but of course, I can't make you accept that. So, please will you sit down? Otherwise I won't meet you."

"We can say what we have come to say without sitting down."

Now David was really annoyed. "How dare you ask to come into my house, and then tell me what to do? Are you going to sit or not? Otherwise, please leave!"

David had been standing in the doorway. Now he took one step back into his entrance hall. Mr Jenkins backed down first, and sat on the settee. Eleanor sat next to him, so David then entered and sat in one of the two arm chairs. Sheila had to sit. Then David looked at Mr Jenkins.

"So how can I help you?" David said, making an effort to sound pleasant.

"You've been seeing Eleanor?" Mrs Jenkins said.

"Yes," David said.

"Well, it's got to stop."

"May I ask why?"

"For goodness sake man, isn't it obvious? It's obscene. It's obvious what you're after!"

"Dad!" Eleanor exclaimed. "It's not like that?"

"Isn't it? You obviously know your way around the house. Do you know the bedrooms too?"

"Dad!" she said again, shocked by her father's comment.

"Was that necessary?" David asked quietly.

"Well," her mother said. "Are you saying you're not intimate?"

"Of course we're not?" David said.

"You're not?" Sheila Jenkins echoed. David wasn't sure if it was relief or disbelief.

"We're not married," David said.

"You're not suggesting marriage, are you?" her father said, incredulously. "You're mad."

"But I would say yes," Eleanor said.

"Don't be stupid!" her mother almost spat out. Then she turned to David. "Do you really think you should put such thoughts into a young girl's head? You should be ashamed."

"I didn't suggest it. But I have thought about it."

"Have you?" Eleanor said, looking at David.

Eleanor's mother stood up. "This is getting silly. We didn't come here to talk about marriage. We came to say that we don't want you seeing our daughter. And our daughter will not be seeing you. Len," she added, looking at her husband, who then stood up. "Come along, Eleanor!"

Chapter 24

Decision Time

David did not sleep well that night and in the end, he was up and out riding his bicycle at five-thirty the next morning. It was a long ride, with the same thoughts and questions going round and round in his head. Marriage. Between him and Eleanor? Seventeen year-old Eleanor, and him. The thought of not seeing her at all really gnawed at his heart. But marriage? Yes, he had thought about it, but not seriously. He had no doubt that whoever did marry her would be a lucky man. Why shouldn't it be him? He had fallen in love with her, but that didn't mean it was right, or even appropriate. Had Eleanor's parents merely brought forward the inevitable? Should he feel relieved that the decision had been made for him? But on the other hand, there was a feeling of emptiness. He needed Eleanor. And that was selfish. But now he had lost her. Suddenly there was a chink of light. She would soon be eighteen, well, in November. Then her parents couldn't stop her from seeing him. And they would have to make a decision – whether to continue to see each other with a view to marriage, and if so, with what time-scale?

Eleanor also slept badly. On the one hand, there was the trauma her parents had caused. But there was also the revelation that David had thought about marriage. However, the factor that preyed on her mind was for how long she should obey her parents. In a moment of uncontrolled anger on the way home, she had told her parents they could not stop her from seeing David.

"While you are under our roof, you will do as we say," they had said.

"Even when I am eighteen?"

"That's got nothing to do with it."

At the time, she had been so surprised that she had not answered. But age was not the issue, it was obedience itself. Apart from the command to honour one's parent, there was the edict from Paul the apostle for children to obey their parents. When was a child no longer a child? Or was one a child for ever? When she got home, she went to her room, and remained there for the rest of the evening. But no tears. She was too angry to cry. And she had to think. The only person she knew who could help was her pastor, James. She would ask to see James.

David went to the morning service hoping and expecting to see and talk with Eleanor. He arrived early, locked his bicycle and waited outside for Eleanor. After the previous evening, he wasn't sure if she would be there, so when it was time to start, and she still had not arrived, he went inside, but feeling disappointed. He could hear the first hymn being sung, so after a visit to the cloakroom, he had a word with a steward in case he had missed her.

"Do you know if Eleanor Jenkins is here this morning? I was hoping to speak to her," he said casually.

"Yes, Mr Anderson. Near the front on the left. She was late as well. There are still a couple of seats next to her."

"Thank you very much," David said, and followed the steward's directions. It was not until he had slipped into the empty place next to Eleanor that he realised that her mother was on the other side. She had decided to accompany her daughter that morning to make sure that Eleanor did not speak to David. Eleanor's eyes opened wide when she saw who it was, and she mouthed the word hello. Then her mother noticed David. For a moment she just stared; then she moved. She began to push past Eleanor.

"Come along, Eleanor, it's too hot here," she whispered. "I need to sit somewhere else." She pushed past David, and then turned to wait for Eleanor. "Eleanor," she repeated.

Eleanor pretended not to hear, and moved sideways into the space vacated by her mother. When her mother realised that Eleanor would not move, she pushed back past David, and into Eleanor's vacated place. They remained in those positions until the last hymn. Suddenly Eleanor pushed past her mother, and David. It caught them both by surprise, but then her mother tried to follow. David deliberately swayed forward to block her mother. He could not maintain the position; however, it enabled Eleanor to gain a head start for where ever she was going. By the time her mother reached the door, Eleanor had disappeared. One of the stewards left his place just inside the door and followed Mrs Jenkins.

"Are you all right?" she asked.

"I don't know. I seem to have lost my daughter."

"Is she Eleanor?" the steward asked.

"Yes. Eleanor Jenkins."

"Perhaps she's in the toilet?"

"Oh, of course." Sheila Jenkins felt foolish, and smiled at the steward. "Thank you," she said and walked into the toilet, and checked the cubicles. All free. No Eleanor. By the time she came out, the steward had gone back in, so she then went out to the car park. No Eleanor. Then the road. No Eleanor. Feeling angry, she went back in to the foyer. The hymn had finished, and the pastor was saying the benediction which meant she could not go back inside again. She decided to wait for David, assuming that he knew where she was. David saw her waiting and guessed she was waiting for him.

"Mr Anderson, where's Eleanor?" she demanded.

"I beg you pardon," David answered. "Why should I know that?"

"Just tell me where she is!"

"Mrs Jenkins," David said pleasantly, "why don't you come and have a cup of coffee. I'm sure she'll turn up."

"Do you know where she is?"

"Of course I don't. Now calm down and have a cup of coffee. I take it that you have checked the toilets?"

"Of course I have!"

"Would you like me to look for her?"

"Oh. Yes. Would you mind?" Sheila Jenkins said, trying hard to sound gracious.

"Then you go into the lounge, and if I can find her, I'll know where you are."

Feeling uneasy, David watched her walk away. Was Eleanor running away? This wasn't like Eleanor at all. She had come with her mother, so she had no bicycle which meant she couldn't go far – assuming she had gone. He set off briskly to check the minor rooms, but they still had children. The office? No. The pre-meeting prayer room? No. What about the balcony? He rushed to the centre of the worship area and looked up. There she was, but with Lucy, James' wife. At least she was safe. He went back to the lounge to find Sheila Jenkins.

"I've found her," David said.

"Where? Outside?"

"No, but she's talking to the Pastor's wife."

"Right, show me," Sheila Jenkins said impatiently.

David looked at her. "Your daughter is seventeen, Mrs Jenkins, I would say that she is old enough to have a private conversation, wouldn't you?"

Sheila Jenkins flustered for a moment. "Well, yes, I suppose so," she said.

"But not with me?" David asked quietly.

"That's different."

David's initial reaction was to tell her that her answer was silly, but he managed to hold his tongue.

"Please tell me why?" he said.

"Because you're over twice her age," she replied, triumphantly.

"Yes, I do see your point," David said.

"Then you'll keep away?"

"Only if Eleanor wants that."

"She doesn't know what she wants. She's only a girl."

"If I said I would keep away until she's old enough to make up her own mind, what would you say?"

"What do you mean?"

"Until she's eighteen, Mrs Jenkins," David said.

"Not while she's still at home."

David could not think of an answer to this. Then he saw Eleanor and Lucy coming.

"Ah, Here comes Eleanor now," he said.

"Hello, Mum. Hello, David," Eleanor said.

"Where have you been?" Sheila Jenkins demanded.

"She's been talking to me, Mrs Jenkins," Lucy replied.

"Mum, this is Mrs Butler, the Pastor's wife," Eleanor said. "I rushed off to find her."

"Well, I've been waiting for you," Sheila Jenkins said.

"Sorry, we held you up, Mrs Jenkins. I've invited Eleanor to tea, is that all right?" Lucy said.

"To tea? Today?" Sheila Jenkins said.

"Yes, Mrs Jenkins. Would you like me to pick Eleanor up?"

"No, no, of course not. Or is it far?"

"No, Mum, I can bike there," Eleanor said. "Right, Mrs Butler, I'll see you later, thank you."

Sheila Jenkins handed her cup to David, and led Eleanor away.

"I hope she doesn't change her mind," Lucy said, as they departed.

"What was that about?" David asked.

"Can't you guess?" Lucy asked, smiling at David.

"Us?" David said.

"Yes."

"What did Eleanor tell you?"

"Not a lot. You've been seeing each other secretly. Her parents found out, and have banned her from seeing you."

"And I don't suppose you approve," David said.

"Why don't you come to tea as well, David?" Lucy said, smiling at him. "In fact, come early."

David arrived at three o'clock, as instructed, and was shown into their lounge. They waited until they all had a cup of tea before they began.

"Right, David, let's hear your side."

"My side?"

"Yes, start at the beginning and tell us how your association started. When did you first become interested in Eleanor, or better still, when did you first notice her."

"Jenny and I both noticed her at her baptism. You know they speak, or give a testimony, well, with most young people, they tend to use the stock phrases. Eleanor didn't. I'm not saying that the other people's testimony is less worth while, but Eleanor's was remarkably mature. Then, of course, we both heard her singing – and even then, there was something about the way she sang. Her face showed the emotion of what she sang. That was all. There was no personal interest at all. I suppose the next time was one day when I saw her on a bus – and this was after you had seen me about working in the church – she was with friends, but then she came and talked to me. I was quite surprised – I mean, how many teenagers talk to adults? Oh, there was another incident. One morning, one of the old ladies asked me where Jenny was, and I'm afraid I didn't cope. I went up to the balcony and had a little cry. Eleanor had overheard the lady, and she just brought me a cup of tea – very quietly, no fuss. Then Tom and Eleanor asked me to help with their singing, and it just took off."

"Did you do other things, beside singing?" Lucy asked.

"Well, yes. One day I accidentally met her and Lizzie in town, and they told me about a regular jazz evening, so I went with them. More than once. Oh, and I took her to see some swans – we had to cycle. But it was all just as friends – mind you, I think it helped me more than she realised."

"Didn't you ever question your motives," James asked.

"Motives? No, I wasn't aware that I had any. We just seemed to get on well."

"And you never questioned it?"

"I knew it was unusual. But I didn't think it was wrong."

"Were you upset when James spoke to you last Christmas?" Lucy asked.

"Of course I was. But I did understand. I think Eleanor was less understanding, especially as she thought it was her own mother who caused it."

Lucy and James looked at each other.

"I saw you two sitting in a tea shop, David," Lucy said.

"Oh," David laughed. "That was when I had taken her to see the swans. She was getting burnt by the sun, and I had to cream her back. I wasn't comfortable at all."

"But then your, er, friendship restarted?" James asked.

"Did you know that Mark phoned me up in the night to help collect people from Heathrow? I brought Eleanor back, and when I thought she was fast asleep, I muttered that I had missed her. She wasn't asleep, so we talked it over, and agreed that if we were discreet we would see each other. That's it. And I became more and more fond of her."

"How fond, David?" Lucy asked.

"What do you mean?"

"Love?" she said.

"Yes, okay, I've fallen in love again. And with a seventeen year old. I know it's inappropriate. Is this why I'm here? To be told to back-off again?"

"No. Unless you're not serious about her."

"That's just it. I am very serious about her. If I was nineteen, I would ask her to marry me, or if she was, say thirty even. But seventeen. Come on, be serious."

"Is it obvious that she's seventeen?"

"Who to? To me?"

"All right, to you."

"No, I don't think about it. I'm usually totally unaware of it. Except I know it. I took her to a wedding – my son's wedding – and I don't think anybody realised just how young she was. But if she was twenty, twenty five, people would still disapprove, wouldn't they. Can marriages survive with such an age difference? Would it be fair on her? And me being a widower?"

James and Lucy exchanged looks again. "My first wife was killed in a road accident a year after our wedding. I was thirty, and I had no intention of marrying again. Ten years later I met Lucy, and she changed my mind." James said.

"And," David asked.

"He is fifteen years older than me," Lucy said.

"But only fifteen," James said.

"It was an issue – for our families, not for us. David, I've been a pastor for thirty years. I've married lots of people, sometimes when it was against my better judgement.

Sadly, a number of those marriages have not lasted, but it was never an age issue. Other factors, but as far as I'm aware, not age. Before marrying Lucy, I researched age difference in relationships. Age is not a significant factor in marriage break-up. Something I read about was whether such relationships are accepted and also the question of what counts as a significant difference. Apparently, that it has varied over time. It varies over cultures, different legal systems, and different ethical systems." James paused. "I didn't mean to talk about weddings. I, er we, just wanted to know your side of the relationship before Eleanor arrives. Talking of which, I think she is here."

Lucy brought Eleanor in. She had not seen David's bicycle outside and so was surprised to see him in the room. David stood up, walked across, and kissed her cheek. "Hello, Eleanor," he said. They sat down together on the settee, and instinctively, Eleanor slipped her hand into David's.

"We invited David, because he is the problem," Lucy said.

"David's not the problem. My parents are the problem," Eleanor said quietly.

"So explain the problem, Eleanor," James said.

"Mum and Dad have forbidden me to have anything to do with David. Oh!" She pulled her hand away from his. "That's why Mum took me this morning, to make sure I didn't speak to David. She wanted me to promise I wouldn't, but I wouldn't do that."

"But Eleanor will be eighteen soon," David said.

"Pastor, how long should children have to obey their parents?" Eleanor asked, ignoring David's comment.

"With respect to this issue in particular?" James asked.

"Yes, of course," Eleanor said.

"I think it depends on how serious you are – whether you really want to marry. And if so, when. May I ask something personal? When did it become physical?"
"David calls it being affectionate, we don't kiss properly," Eleanor said.
"Would you like to?" Lucy asked her.
Eleanor nodded, so James turned to David. "And you?" he said.
"Of course I would. I'm not made of wood – oh, sorry."

"Eleanor, how long have you felt like that about David," Lucy asked, after a pause.
"Do I have to tell you?"
"No, but it would help if we all knew where we stand," Lucy said.
"I think it was when you took me to see the swans, a year ago, but I knew it was me being silly, I mean, it was not long after … you know," Eleanor said, hesitating to mention David's bereavement.
"Was it just you feeling sorry for him?" Lucy asked.
"I did feel for him. We talked about swans and grief, but the main thing was, I just felt comfortable with David." She stopped and giggled, and looked at David. "Except when you did my back, with sun-cream. You were embarrassed, but … "
"Yes?" Lucy said.
"I liked it. Sorry."
"Don't apologise, Eleanor. I remember the first time James touched me," Lucy said.
"Do you?" James said.
"When did you feel you weren't being silly?" Lucy asked.
"Not until," she paused, and looked at David, "you said that you had missed me. You know, on the way back

from Heathrow. After the Romania trip," she added for the benefit of James and Lucy.

"Yes, James has told us," James said.

"Oh?" Eleanor said.

"We wanted to hear how he felt about you?" Lucy said.

"Oh," Eleanor said again.

"And I think we can safely assume that your feelings are mutual, and are more than just affectionate," James said.

Eleanor turned to David. "Is that true, David," she said quietly. "You've never said."

"I think it's because he loves you and wants the best for you, Eleanor," Lucy said.

"Sorry?" Eleanor said. "I don't understand."

"Your future, Eleanor. You're seventeen, and have your whole life ahead of you," David said. "Of course I want you for myself, but that makes me feel bad."

"Like being a cradle-snatcher? Or what people might say?"

"No, Eleanor, I felt so happy when you came to the wedding with me."

"I'm not sure that Daniel felt the same way," Eleanor said.

"Something else to talk about," James said.

"But we're not allowed to talk," Eleanor said bitterly.

"Don't worry about that for the moment. If necessary, I'll go and see your parents, Eleanor. No, first of all, let's go though the issues. Let's be formal, and list them."

James went to his study and returned with a clip board.

"Is that necessary," David asked.

James laughed. "I've done counselling, and yes, I find it does help. Sometimes people say things, but withdraw them if they see they are written down. It helps me if nobody else."

"Think of it as a shopping list," Lucy said.

"A shopping list, Mrs Butler?" Eleanor exclaimed.

"Yes, to remind him where he is, mentally speaking. And, Eleanor, please call me Lucy."

"And me, James," James added. "Right, so if you were a young couple coming to me about marriage, what would be the first thing on my mind?"

He waited.

"I don't know," Eleanor said.

James looked at David. "Faith, are they both Christians?" David said.

"I won't marry non-Christians, or even if only one is," James said.

"And, boy, has that caused some upset," Lucy said quietly.

"So that's the first hurdle passed," James said. "Right, number two?"

This time neither had an answer.

"Age – first, age of consent, and then age generally."

"Have you ever married anyone under eighteen?" Eleanor asked.

"Yes. But she was pregnant."

"Pregnant?" Eleanor said. "But … "

"It happens, Lucy. Have you never gossiped, lost your temper, told a lie, been unkind?" Lucy asked.

"Yes, but," Eleanor said.

"Or felt, er, passionate about David? You said you liked him creaming your back, and then you complained that he hasn't kissed you properly."

"He did once," Eleanor said.

"And?"

"I didn't want him to stop. But,"

James raised his hand. "That's my next point. Sex."

Eleanor looked at him, surprised.

"What is the purpose of marriage, Eleanor?"

Now Eleanor was embarrassed. "Children?" she whispered.

"The Apostle Paul said it is better to marry than to burn. And he was talking about females. But, you are right, it is also God's way of propagating the species. I have had one couple, an older couple, who insisted that they had no interest in sex, but wanted to live together in a right and decent manner, as they put it. I don't discuss sex, as no doubt you'll be pleased to hear," he said, smiling at Eleanor, "but the church does run pre-marriage courses and sex is one of the topics. Mind you, with pre-married couples, we often skip that, unless specifically requested, but it's something that should be discussed by you both. That and contraception. I mean, will you both want children?"

Neither replied.

"Eleanor," Lucy said quietly, "have you ever thought about having a family?"

Eleanor shrugged. "Or course I have," she said.

"With David?"

Eleanor nodded.

"Oh, Eleanor, I didn't realise," David said. He reached for and took her hand.

"David?" Lucy asked quietly.

"I never let my thoughts run away," he said.

"Never?" James said. "She's a very attractive girl!"

"Okay, I tried to stop them running away," David said. "I never thought that anything romantic would come from our friendship. My main concern was to avoid giving Eleanor the impression that," he stopped, and smiled at Eleanor, "that she might have my children!"

"And now?" James said. "Or is it too soon to say? You must talk about it. I wouldn't marry you until you do."

They sat for a moment.

"Next?" said David.

"Money. We have another session with someone who talks about money. Coping. Budgeting. Spending. Saving. Sharing. You may want to skip that, David, but you must talk about it."

"Next," David said.

"Careers – now that can be a real problem later in marriage. Which leads me into the role of husbands and wives. Another very contentious area. That moves onto families in general. Bringing up children, if relevant. And in-laws. Their role, and how to deal with them."

"And step-children?" Eleanor asked

James thought for a moment. "Yes, that could be arranged, we have a family with step-children."

"Who are older than the mother?" Eleanor said.

"Ah. But coming back to children. Not all couples can have children. Would that be an issue. Oh, and back to the age thing, I personally have no problem with your age difference, I was telling David earlier, I've looked into it. But as I said to Lucy, because men tend to die before women, an older man will die that much earlier, leaving a younger widow."

"I've already thought of that," Eleanor said quietly.

"And so have I," David said. "It's not a nice thing. Could I do that to you Eleanor? Would you be better off marrying a younger man and growing old together?"

"David, not everyone grows old," James said quietly. "I lost my first wife at thirty!"

They sat in silence for a while.

"I'll go and put the kettle on," Lucy said, getting up. She looked at James. "The children have been very quiet, I'll go and check on them."

"So, a lot to talk about. When shall I see you next?" James said.

"We have a problem, Pastor. I have been told not to talk to David."

"Not to talk, or not to meet? I'm sure they wouldn't expect you to be discourteous if you end up in the same room through no fault of your own," James said, with a grin.

"Can we stay here and talk, James?" David asked.

"Sure. We might even ask you to child-mind so that Lucy can come out tonight."

"But what about my parents, Pastor? I know the Bible tells children to obey their parents."

"All right, let's look at the principles. If your parents told you to steal, would you?" James asked

"No, but they wouldn't anyway," Eleanor said.

"Principles, Eleanor, I said if, and if you did, the law would not protect you."

"All right, then what if they forbade me to marry, anybody?"

"Principles again, Eleanor. It is an even higher principle for a man to leave his parents and take a wife. The same principle must apply to the woman."

"Am I a woman or am I a girl."

"That's the problem, Eleanor. In ancient Jewish custom, you would be a woman. Here in Britain, you are a minor. You are also living at home under your parent's protection, as it were."

"They said it was so long as I was under their roof – in other words, being eighteen doesn't come into it," she said.

"Eleanor, I think it all depends on your final decision. If you and David decide that you do not have a future together, then there is no problem. In fact, it would be

315

silly to keep seeing each other. But if, on the other hand you decide you want to marry, then you could be regarded as being betrothed, to use an old fashioned term. I think morally, you would then be free to disregard their injunction."

"But I would still be under their roof. They have taken my phone away, so I can't even phone David. They might even kick me out!"

"James," David said, "speaking hypothetically. If we became betrothed, to use your term, would you marry us?"

"Of course I would."

"When?"

"Whenever you said. Of course, Eleanor would need parental consent until, was it November? But won't Eleanor be at school for another year?"

"And living under my parent's so called protection!" Eleanor said. "You know what most people would do! I don't suppose you would allow that?" she said, looking at David. "Even with separate rooms?"

"I don't think it would be right, Eleanor," David said.

"Unless you were married, still speaking hypothetically," James added. "Which I am not suggesting. What I would do is see your parents, though, Eleanor."

"But supposing they did throw me out?"

"Eleanor, you're getting ahead. I don't think they would. At the moment you are still just friends. Now, what say you that we take a break for tea."

"Sorry, but I can't ignore it," Eleanor said.

"Then I am sure that I could find somewhere where you could lodge meanwhile."

"And I would pay," David added.

James' and Lucy's children were still low primary age, and did not see anything odd in their being joined by a

couple with such an age disparity. One of them did ask,
innocently, if David was Eleanor's father. She accepted
the reply that they were just friends. In fact, the subject
was not mentioned at all and it was a normal family tea
time, reminding David of his own family tea times those
years ago. And they were pleasant memories. After tea,
they had family time until it was time for James and Lucy
to leave.

"David and Eleanor are looking after you tonight, and I
will ask how you behaved," Lucy said. "Bedtime is seven
thirty, you both know that," she added.

James handed his clipboard and notes to David. "In case
you need it. I'm afraid you won't get much privacy or
time to talk, but at least you are together."

"And it would be rude not to talk," Eleanor said, and
laughed.

They spent an hour with the twins, partly playing with
them, and sometimes just talking. At one stage, they were
both curled up next to Eleanor as she told them a story,
and then again, just before bedtime, when she read them
their Bible story. This was another side of Eleanor that
David hadn't seen, and it just endeared her to him even
more. Despite Lucy's instructions, it was seven-forty
before they came down from seeing the children into bed.
David sat on the settee, and Eleanor snuggled up close.
David kissed her on the cheek. She turned her head, and
they kissed, briefly on the lips. Then again. But then
passionately. And it wasn't a brief kiss. Suddenly David
pulled away, and stood up.

"No, Eleanor, no. We must talk," he said, sitting in a
chair and facing her.

"What else is there to talk about?" she asked. "I don't
have any money, and I don't know anything about sex. I

think I'll leave that to my husband," she said, with a twinkle in her eye.

"Eleanor, if we become engaged, we will go to those sessions. Who knows, maybe I might learn a thing or two." He grinned. "Okay?"

David picked up the clipboard. "Okay. In-laws," he read. "We know there would be a problem with my parents, but what about yours?"

David grinned. "My mum would have a shock. She was surprised to see you at the wedding, but officially you were there to pair up with his best man, and as Stephanie's friend. But she would love you – everybody does."

"Don't be silly. No, it's your children that scare me. They would be my step-children."

"I think Stephanie had an inkling that I was fond of you, and my daughter, Jill. Look, when you have problems with your husband, you would have two married women to turn to for help."

"They might take your side," Eleanor said.

"Don't you believe it. My daughter can be very independent at times."

David picked up the clipboard again. "Okay. Husbands and wives," he read.

"I've heard James preaching about that, and the role of parents. I don't have a problem there. But what about children, David. Could you face having children at your age?" Eleanor asked.

David put the clipboard down. "Eleanor, if we stay together, then we must never raise the issue of age. If I take you, Eleanor Jenkins, to have and to hold, then I am knowingly taking a seventeen year old to have and to hold. And the same applies to you. Whether or not we have children is irrelevant of age."

"So, if we were married, would you like children?"

"If you had asked me that a year ago, well, apart from not expecting to marry,"

"At all?" Eleanor said, interrupting David.

"Yes, well not in what was the foreseeable future. Not even you, pet," David said, using a term of endearment for the first time, and smiling at her.

"I do love it when you smile at me," Eleanor said, interrupting again.

"Eleanor! What was I saying?"

"You were saying that you knew I was the girl for you right from the start," she said, laughing at him.

David sighed. "Eleanor, what's got into you?"

"Sorry. You were saying about children."

"Yes, a second family would have been out of the question."

"And now?"

"If, and I say if. We are still talking. If you were my wife, then, yes, I would like you to be a mother. That's if it was possible, of course."

"And that's where age comes in, David. I know that men can still father babies up into their sixties, although I did read that fertility does start to decrease in middle age. So, it's not for me, it's for the kids. I can choose to marry an old man – hey, don't throw that at me, it's not our house! As I was saying, I can choose an older man, but the kids can't. We've got a girl at school, and her dad looks like he could be her grandad."

"Perhaps he is."

"He's not. She was teased about it by a couple of nasty girls. So, possible future husband, since I am not your wife, I don't have to submit. If you want to marry me, then you do it as soon as possible, and we will try for a family!"

"Eleanor!" David gasped.

"Take me and make me pregnant!" she said.
This time he was too shocked to reply.

"Sorry, David," she said after a few moments. "I've
shocked you, haven't I?"
"Well, yes."
"I'm sorry, but if you had seen this girl crying, and heard
what she said about her parents, you'd understand. Look,
we had sex lessons at school, and they discussed
conception. It can often take well over a year to conceive.
Two years is not unknown. Do you want to be older than
you need to be at our children's sports day and prize-
giving?"
"And you are not thinking of yourself?"
"No, as you said, I accept you for what you are. A man
old enough to be my father. Dearest David. Remember
how I tucked my hand through your arm when you met
me outside school?"
"Yes, I did wonder about it,"
"Well, I got teased – about my sugar daddy, and was I
that hard up that I would pick up anybody?"
"I'm sorry."
"Don't be. It didn't bother me at all."

David pondered for a moment. "Eleanor, when you say as
soon as possible, how soon? Next summer? What about
university?"
"David, I'm not waiting four years!"
"Do you expect me to mess up your schooling as well?"
"David, I love you, I want to live with you, I want to have
your children. It's a no-brainer, as they say from my point
of view. I can study again when the children are older. I
thought you wanted to marry me!"
"I do, Eleanor. But I feel so selfish. It would destroy your
education as well as your life, that's extra hard."

"Are you saying that it's too hard for you?" she whispered.

"But what do you want?"

"I think you know what I want," she said.

Just then, they heard the front door. They hadn't heard the car.

"Hello, you two. Children okay?" Lucy said, entering the room.

"They were perfect," Eleanor said, as David stood up.

"Please sit down, David," Lucy said, as James followed her in.

"Oh, did you disturb them, dear," he said to his wife.

"No, we've been talking. About things," David said.

"And I think David had just come to a decision when you walked in," Eleanor said.

Three pairs of eyes focused on David. He understood what Eleanor was saying. It either meant marriage in the near future – or no marriage at all. In which case they would have to cool everything and go their separate ways. For ever.

"I think that we should," he paused and looked up. "We should …"

The end

What did David suggest and what
was Eleanor's answer? To find out
the consequences of his decision,
look for the sequel to this story –
Eleanor's Answer.

Printed in Great Britain
by Amazon.co.uk, Ltd.,
Marston Gate.